# Praise for Award
## C. Hope Clark

# The Novels of C. Hope Clark

## The Carolina Slade Mysteries

Lowcountry Bribe

Tidewater Murder

Palmetto Poison

Newberry Sin

Salkehatchie Secret

## The Edisto Island Mysteries

Murder on Edisto

Edisto Jinx

Echoes of Edisto

Edisto Stranger

Dying on Edisto

Edisto Tidings

# Salkehatchie Secret

A Carolina Slade Mystery - Book Five

by

# C. Hope Clark

Bell Bridge Books

Bell Bridge Books
PO BOX 300921
Memphis, TN 38130
Print ISBN: 978-1-61194-987-2

Bell Bridge Books is an Imprint of BelleBooks, Inc.

We at BelleBooks enjoy hearing from readers.
Visit our websites
BelleBooks.com
BellBridgeBooks.com
ImaJinnBooks.com

10 9 8 7 6 5 4 3 2 1

Cover design: Debra Dixon
Interior design: Hank Smith
Photo/Art credits:
Art Credits - Scene (manipulated) © Carmen Hauser | Dreamstime.com

:Lssw:01:

# Chapter 1

*Slade*

TALL AND LEAN, the woman slid into the leather seat directly across from me and to the right of Wayne. She moved as if taught how to glide her young, pretty self from birth, as if her mother were a ballerina and the genes carried down.

"This is an awfully nice place for dinner, Agent Largo," she said, smiling sweetly at the waiter filling her glass with water, then craning her head to take in Saluda's decor. "I hope this isn't just for me."

I was hoping the same thing, but then scolded myself. This girl was Wayne's newly assigned partner, though frankly, on the street I'd have pegged her as more of a college intern from the University of South Carolina.

But Wayne was thrilled to have a partner, any partner. He'd operated solo for three years until he could prove the Carolinas merited two agents instead of just him. His last partner had turned in his badge after being injured on a case Wayne led.

"Actually," Wayne said, "I'm killing two birds with one stone." He shook loose the sculpted napkin standing at attention on his plate, rested it in his lap, and smiled. "Celebrating the introduction of my new partner to my regular partner." He dipped his chin toward me. "Carolina Slade, meet Jasmine Bright. Jasmine? Meet Slade."

Long, delicate fingers reached out to shake my hand, skin almost the color of Saluda's well-known mahogany bar. I couldn't help but measure our ages, me being old enough to be her mama if I'd been knocked up in high school.

My best smile intact, I shook her hand. "Nice to meet you."

"Nice to meet you, too, Ms. Slade." Lowcountry vowels molded her words—so, from my neck of the South Carolina woods. "Mr. Largo told me about some of y'all's cases," she said. "Made me wonder why you aren't in this job instead of me."

"I didn't get involved young enough, so I do the next best thing which is turn over rocks and stumble on cases. Then my agency passes off our criminal agriculture cases to you guys," I said. "To those with arrest authority. But you'll grasp that soon enough."

"Yes, ma'am."

Ma'am? Jesus, someone hand me my cane.

I looked to Wayne for any sign he'd told her of my conflict with the badge versus badgeless world I lived in with him, but only read a blank slate in his expression.

"Believe me, I'd be there every step of the way if they let me," I said, not eager to explain my job as Special Projects Representative . . . a catch-all title that allowed me to troubleshoot problems with USDA's clients and employees. The position came with a less helpful plastic badge in a leather case I rarely pulled out of my purse. Especially since my plastic badge was viewed as less to those carrying real badges.

To think this girl has more authority than I do.

"No matter what she says, Slade does all right racking up cases from her slot with Agriculture," Wayne said. "Has solved more cases than half my peers." Then a raised brow. "Riskier ones than the majority of them."

Was that bragging or chastisement? I decided to own the former. "We've chased down our share of bad guys," I said. "But I envy you, Jasmine. The federal law enforcement hiring cut off is thirty-seven years old, which is about the time I started, unfortunately." I lifted my water glass. "But kudos to you for getting it right from the get-go." We toasted. "And here's to you ridding the agricultural world of all its nefarious scum."

I was just hoping she stayed long enough to make any difference at all. Wayne's last partner had been five years older than Jasmine, male, and with a linebacker's body. However, once Eddie resigned after being injured by the murdering farmer we were after, headquarters held the accident against Wayne. Nothing official, but they'd sure dragged their feet about assigning another partner. I embraced the idea of a partner for Wayne. I'd hated that he was the one-man show for the Office of Inspector General.

Jasmine, however, was an incredibly different package than I'd envisioned. Looked like she'd be more of a newbie babysitting job. I worried about her. I worried more for Wayne. This girl was supposed to carry a weapon and cover his back?

I needed a real drink. It was Tuesday afternoon around four thirty, and judging by the half-empty dining room, a tad early for the dinner crowd at Saluda's Restaurant in Five Points. I debated on whether I had to drink wine suggested by the second glass at my place setting, when I much preferred a bourbon. Saving me from a decision, Jasmine unexpectedly launched into a gushing display of appreciation, almost embarrassing in its level of enthusiasm.

Made me grateful for the thin crowd.

"To think I get to start with St. Clair Simmons." She leaned over the table and lowered her voice, shifting into some sort of co-ed dialect. "*The* St. Clair Simmons. I've heard of him since I was a kid."

Like that was so terribly long ago. The way she spoke under her breath made this paunchy, rude, redneck Colleton County farmer sound like public enemy number one.

Wayne chuckled, and I gave him a quick look like he'd lost his mind.

"What's so great about St. Clair Simmons?" I said. "He's a row crop farmer near Walterboro. I passed you guys a simple conversion case that honestly, I thought you'd thumb your nose at . . . Agent Largo."

Wayne shrugged, maintaining a grin as he returned my look.

I'd met this farmer, and the only person who considered St. Clair Simmons a badass was St. Clair. A guy who had political views that approached those of a Libertarian but fell far short of being fanatical based upon his willingness to accept federal loans. He considered himself a pillar of a rural community between two rivers that might have five hundred people living there. He'd be a big fish in a small pond with half the little fish not caring what he and his farm did down that long dirt road. Yes, he was lord of Mini-Hawk as he dubbed his enterprise in the Salkehatchie community, but that was about it.

I turned back to Jasmine, who was gushing again. "He's wicked," she said, scrunching her shoulders to match her nose. "Taking him down would impress a lot of people in the Lowcountry, don't you think?"

Wicked? Were we discussing the same guy?

But she wasn't done yet. "I'm honored Agent Largo chose this one, so I can look good to my family." The young agent took a swig of her water as if it were whiskey. "Tickles me to pieces this is my first case. Don't you wish you were in on this one, Ms. Slade? Does it not give you chills?"

*Her* case, huh? And no, it didn't. "Um, it's just Slade. Wayne and I don't always get to work together, but seriously, I'm excited for you and wish you luck." I held up my glass in a toast.

Wayne beamed, proud as a new papa.

The waiter read the end of the toast as timing to take our orders.

Our meals arrived quickly, the aromas heady with seasonings and butter, the pork chops continuing to sizzle on the plate. Most of the food was sourced from local farmers, a practice popular in the capital city . . . most from farms I recognized, a couple farmers whom I'd butted heads with.

We enjoyed our meals between telling war stories. Jasmine soaked up the tales, saying several times, "I want to talk more about that one later, Mr. Largo." And each time he'd had to correct her. "It's just Wayne."

"This was really nice," she said, laying her napkin on the table. "Let me help with the bill."

"No, ma'am," he said. "My treat, but it's downhill from here."

Jasmine hesitated. "Pardon?"

"It's barbecue or hot dogs on the run from whatever joint we pass when we're running in the field," he said. "Or PBJ in a paper bag."

"Not to worry." Her laugh was cuter than I cared to admit. "I know every hole-in-the-wall diner in that county. We don't go hungry." She put aside her napkin. "Thanks for the evening, but I must get on the road. See you in the morning, Mr., um, Wayne. At the Colleton County ag office, right? I've been thinking about that. Would it be best the agriculture folks not know we're down there? If so, we can meet at my momma's since that's where I'm staying tonight anyway. Don't want St. Clair Simmons catching wind we're on his trail."

"No, we don't," he said. "Don't tell anyone why you're there and don't attempt anything on your own, you hear? I'd almost rather we went together in the morning, so we could talk strategy. It's not a difficult case, and we don't have much time to waste on it, but regardless, we don't show our hand until we have to. Don't even tell your mother."

She gave a pout. "You can trust me better than that, Wayne."

The girl still had some growing up to do, in my opinion.

"I get it. No talking about the case. But the truth is I just want to sleep in my old bed," she said. "Maybe see old friends. Chat with Momma. What are the odds my first case is at home?"

With a mock sigh of concession, Wayne grinned. "Your momma's it is. Text me the address and be careful on the road."

She bobbed her head, so eager, so happy. "Will do. If you get lost, call. Around eight tomorrow morning?"

Wayne glimpsed at me, and I caught the vaguest glint of . . . something. "Make it ten, if you don't mind," he replied. "Like you said, nobody knows we're coming."

We parted with the proper formalities, then Wayne and I settled into our real selves. "She's . . . sweet," I said.

"She's green. They want me to train her." He motioned to the waiter and ordered a Wild Turkey, neat. "It's after five now, and we're off duty. You want one?"

"Bulleit with a splash," I said, preferring my own label. "Is her being green . . . safe?"

"We're all virgins in the beginning," he said. "Give her a chance."

"Not talking about her safety." And I wasn't. My concern was more about the cowboy seated across the table from me. "If things get dicey, can she hold her own, but more importantly, will she have your back?"

He didn't move for a long few seconds, and I sensed the words in his head were being scrambled and carefully reformed into a response he felt I wouldn't balk at. I understood my lawman.

"Some would say you were a liability in terms of my safety," he said.

That subtext was clear. I'd been a novice times ten and lacked a lot of trained-agent skills.

"But look how you've fared," he added, bringing it around. "Look at the cases we've solved."

I shook my head. "That's different. We don't often solve cases side by side. I root them out, and you jump in when they turn nasty. Jasmine, however, will be the one alongside you during the danger."

He reached over with both hands, one covering mine. "Like you haven't handled your share of nasty. Just not like I would, and often not like I like, but you manage in your own way, Butterbean."

"I *rock* my cases," I added with a coy toss of my chin.

His hand remained over mine. *Hmm* . . . wasn't he being particularly loving?

"And most of our investigations are anything but daring," he said, "like they'll be with Jasmine. It'll be a while before I introduce her to anything challenging. Why do you think we're taking on St. Clair?"

His subsequent chuckling warmed me, and when he patted my hand, hope blossomed into possibilities for the evening after our drinks, leading me to wonder how much time we had. I could take off tomorrow morning. He, however, had to meet Jasmine a hundred miles south.

Gazing at him, I lifted my glass with my free hand and took a slow pull on the bourbon, the first taste always the best. His hand kept hold of my other, peculiar but pleasant. The lawman had a romantic side he let loose every now and then. "This case," I said. "It's still just a simple conversion, right? He sold crops and pocketed the money?"

"Yes."

Was he even listening to me? "You wouldn't be suspecting him for anything else, would you?" Nothing would irritate me more than to hand him a simple case that wasn't . . . that I hadn't sensed as more complex first.

What usually got converters caught was what they did with the money, which Wayne constantly pounded into my head. *Follow the money. Follow the money.* Problem was he had access to subpoenas and legal tools I didn't, so he often took up where I left off, and even then he caught maybe half the cases.

On top of it all, the US Attorney rarely bothered to prosecute them. Agriculture often restructured the debt, took more collateral, and continued doing business with someone who'd most likely do it again. I hated those cases.

Wayne could have this one, as far as I was concerned, especially since this would probably be a textbook teaching exercise.

He leaned back in his chair, hand sliding off mine to cup his Wild Turkey. Resting on the tablecloth, however, was a box. A maroon velvet box. A familiar box. And he waited, watching, a slow smile creeping up in the corners.

A sudden vacuum sucked air, sound, complete life out of the room, leaving only my heartbeat. I looked at him, then around me . . . other diners studying us with expectation . . . wait staff stationary.

I thoroughly forgot about St. Clair Simmons, other than realizing that Wayne had used meeting Jasmine as a distraction so I'd never see him coming.

"Um." I started to lean in then didn't, as though that box would scald me. "Um, what is that?"

Wayne sank the remnants of his whiskey, eased out of his chair around the table, and went to one knee.

My mouth agape, I closed it, licking my lips once, the anxiety in my chest screaming for me to breathe.

We'd done this before. On my lake porch. The box had sat on my dresser unopened for eight months, the lawman giving me ample time to adjust to the concept of matrimony. To this day I couldn't tell you the size stone or color band, afraid to look.

Then after an investigation that peppered my belly with buckshot, we fell out, did a time-out for a few weeks, then he returned with a plan. He claimed rights to a future do-over and took the box, therefore removing the pressure between us over that stupid simple question I could not bring myself to answer.

And here we were again.

*Holy shit.* I wasn't so sure I was anywhere closer to being able to answer than before.

But would I ever?

"Slade?"

With hitches, I tried to take in a breath. I seemed to have forgotten how.

He inhaled slowly, waving his hand through the air, demonstrating. "Like this, Butterbean," he said softly. He inhaled again.

I managed to do it right this time.

He continued. "Should I ask you or not?"

My eyes widened.

"You don't have to dive off a cliff here," he said. "If it's no, I'll wait a while longer." He let that sink in. "If it's yes, I'll be the happiest man on earth. Should I ask or not?"

Flash forward to him in my house. Picking up kids. Joking with my live-in sister. Grilling out. He already did a lot of that, but he always went home. I always hated seeing him leave. Likewise hated slipping off to his apartment for booty calls, knowing full well my sister and the kids read the full meaning of *working late with Wayne on a case.*

I had no excuse to say no. Why was I even seeking one?

"Can I peek at the ring first?"

He did a legitimate double-take, and someone behind me did a snort-laugh. "If that makes you happy, open her up," he said, remaining on his knee, now leaning his forearm across it to wait.

With trepidation, I eased the hinge open. White gold. One diamond bracketed by two on each side. Not showy, almost heirloom in nature, making me cringe that he might've given me his grandmother's ring or something. I hated flashy, and this was anything but, and the fact that he made that connection threw an instant block of tears in my throat.

I must've hung up a second too long, because he felt the need to break the silence. "Should I ask you or not?"

"Yes," I whispered, the words coming from outside my body somewhere.

The glow on that bearded face melted me, the ring tumbling to insignificance. "Will you marry me, Carolina Slade?"

A gasp sounded to my right, the room in suspended animation.

"Yes, Lawman, I will."

Applause and cheers erupted as Wayne rose to his feet and swept me to mine.

And not twenty minutes later, in a whirlwind of departure, driving with hands clasped, we swept into his apartment to consummate the pledge. Several hours later, we lay sated and spent in his bed, the intensity of his emotions driving Lawman to a degree I hadn't minded one damn bit.

Bed askew, I reached to the floor to retrieve a pillow then retreated beneath sheets that had come completely undone from the mattress. The clock on the nightstand read five in the morning. "Are those candles next to the clock?" I asked, then spotted more on his dresser, the window ledge.

He chuckled low from somewhere inside. "There's wine in the fridge, too. And these dumb chocolate strawberry things. A playlist. Guess your *yes* blew those plans right out of my head."

"Well, I'm famished. Let's not let them go to waste," I said, flipping back the covers, letting him watch me leave naked. Upon finding those preparations and more, I set us up a second celebration at his kitchen table.

God bless him. Look at this stuff. A baby cheesecake. White chocolate pretzels. I wondered why the hell I'd waited to accept his offer. I just hoped broad daylight didn't give me jitters. Hand me the hardest case and I was fine. Personal relationships, however, were rough for me. Nobody had to tell me I was set in some of my ways.

"Wayne?" I beckoned, working awkwardly with the wine cork, almost giggling at wine for breakfast. Oh no, we weren't about to go to work after finding all of this. Jasmine could just visit with her mom an extra day. "You coming?"

When he didn't reply, I feared he'd fallen asleep, and I wasn't about to let that happen. I returned to the bedroom.

But Wayne wasn't sleeping. Seated on the edge of the bed, he held phone to his ear, notepad on the nightstand, his brow knotted. "No, ma'am, haven't seen her. She left around six, after dinner." More listening, serious concern etched in the lines of his mouth. "Of course, ma'am. Let me go by her place, the office, and then I'll head down there. I'll phone the local sheriff. You sit tight. Afraid it'll take me a couple hours, but I'll head that direction." More listening, a mild wince in his eyes. "Yes, ma'am," he repeated, then hung up.

The agent had replaced the fiancé just that quickly.

I was afraid to ask. "What?"

He lifted the phone. "Jasmine's mother said she never arrived." He thought of something, then his fingers danced on the screen. He pinched the results wider, studying closer. "You familiar with this area?"

Moving to his side, I took the phone and moved the map coordinates around. "That's Old Coon Road about fifteen to twenty miles outside of Walterboro city limits. Why?"

"That's where Jasmine's phone is pinging."

Ice water coursed down my spine. "You mean right now? At five in the morning?"

The fact we stood there naked, on what should be one of the best nights of our lives, mattered nil. A federal agent was missing, and the people finder app on Wayne's phone placed her in St. Clair Simmons's neighborhood.

"Get dressed."

He didn't have to speak twice.

And I wondered what the hell Jasmine had grasped about St. Clair Simmons that maybe we didn't.

# Chapter 2

*Slade*

OUR SHOWERS brief, fifteen minutes after the mother's frantic call, I snared my purse and Wayne his weapon as we bolted out of his apartment. He wasn't talking, and I didn't try to make him. He was thinking, running options, considering odds. Jasmine hadn't answered six of his calls. Having already notified the Colleton County Sheriff's Office, he ran antsy and eager to head south and join them in the search for his rookie.

Regardless of the fact that St. Clair Simmons was supposed to be an easy, routine first case, if something had happened to Jasmine—Wayne's judgment would be in question, not unlike when we met on the bribery case that almost cost both of us our jobs. He hadn't done anything wrong then and hadn't erred this time, but he would question himself . . . because others would. His silence for the twenty minutes to my house carried so much weight.

He turned onto the road to my lake house, and headlights from a contractor's pick-up highlighted the creases around Wayne's eyes. His cold, stoic reaction and the idea that an agent could go missing like this started a low-key, steady drip of concern through me, and suddenly I didn't want to see him head down there alone.

But I wasn't about to tell him that. Not with that concentration.

Selfishly, I wanted Jasmine's naivete to be the cause of her disappearance, not the fact she was law enforcement, because that made Wayne less of a target. When law enforcement fell on the job, the brotherhood ramped up their game, and woe be the culprit on their radar.

Above all if it was your own partner.

I prayed she had scooted home for some romancing of her own, maybe a high school beau. Maybe her mother didn't check her texts or voice mail when Jasmine had chosen nooky over a home-cooked dinner.

But a tryst didn't explain her phone pinging on Old Coon Road.

"Drive careful," I said, resting my hand on his arm for assurance.

But he only allowed a light kiss from me and barely let me step back before leaving. His lights strobed through the trees until they rounded the bend, headed toward Old Lexington Road. Once he hit interstate, he'd crank his speed to something I cared not to think about, lights flashing, and he'd be twenty miles gone before I could drop into bed.

Not ready to disturb the sleep of my sister Ally Jo by coming in early, I sat on the front step, listening to ducks awakening in the cove and the occasional creature snapping a twig in an early morning hunt. Dew smelled fresh on the dying grass, and light teased the dark sky. I fingered the foreign object on my hand, its diamond catching hints of light in the early morning.

Wayne hadn't even discussed the option of me going, and under other circumstances, I might've been pissed at the robotic oversight, but if Jasmine's life was in peril, he didn't need the age-old debate with me on where my duties stopped and his took charge. And neither of us needed to face the fact we'd been happy and gotten engaged on the night Jasmine disappeared. I shouldn't feel guilty. I did. I texted Wayne a reminder to keep me apprised, as if that would make me feel helpful. It didn't.

My mind turned to other avenues of thought that might be of assistance if I could puzzle anything out.

Fact: St. Clair Simmons was a farmer on our rolls, and a case I offered to the US Department of Agriculture's Office of Inspector General, Wayne's employer, with the quasi expectation of it being declined. They didn't have to take everything and often passed on the smaller fry cases regardless of the illegal aspects. St. Clair Simmons sort of rode the fence of importance, which is probably why Wayne chose it as a learning tool for Jasmine.

Fact: Names meant a lot in the Lowcountry. Identity was rooted in family. His name was St. Clair Simmons. Not St. Clair and not Simmons, both Lowcountry families that his mother probably had needed to appease. The former name too family-specific for just anyone and the latter too common to know which of a zillion Simmons you meant. So they'd cultivated all three names. Like John Paul Jones, a name said in one roll of the tongue. The farmer often commanded full use of his identity, and that was St. Clair Simmons.

Fact: He was an arrogant ass, correctly pegged by Jasmine. In each of my two meetings he'd dismissed me with a scowl as though he'd eaten something rancid. When he fell behind in his debt, suspected of pocketing his crop income instead of paying his loan, I felt no hesitation at the chance to blacken his name. All three of them.

Fact: He wasn't a huge farmer. Nothing remarkable in that. We suspected ol' St. Clair had disposed of crops last year without paying for loans used to plant them, but such situations could be difficult to prove. Those who bought the mortgaged crops never fessed up, and hired hands didn't talk for fear of losing a job. Farmers often reported crop failure, and if someone from USDA hadn't seen the crop, well, the politics favored the farmer. And here it was November, after yet another crop, and he was unable to cover his debt. Some rumors about marijuana, the illegal sort, not the medicinal, floated around agricultural gossip mills, but if he was making any decent amount of money at it, you'd think he'd pay and avoid suspicion.

Fact: I'd never felt physically threatened by the man and never heard anyone else having that concern either. Therefore, I doubted the man had a hand in whatever happened to Jasmine.

Still, something didn't feel right, but I could be fretting prematurely. I hadn't spoken to St. Clair Simmons in ages, and Jasmine might have wrecked her car, had a flat tire on a deserted road, or partied too hard with an old boyfriend, nothing to do with farming. Maybe someone coincidentally lived on Old Coon Road.

The porch light came on. "What are you doing out here?" Ally Jo spoke in a hard whisper, a cotton robe held tight around her with both hands. "Aren't you freezing?"

"It's fifty degrees, Ally."

"That's cold to me." She sat beside me on the step. "What happened? You ought to be tucked in snug next to your cowboy."

The morning cold easily penetrated the dress slacks I'd worn to Saluda's. "He had to go out. I'm sitting here wondering if I should've gone with him since it's one of my agency's customers, but it happened incredibly fast. There I was opening the wine after . . . never mind." Gripping the lapels of my equally dressy jacket not designed to ward off the temps, I tried to cocoon myself up tighter.

"Wait . . . oh Holy God and all the saints and angels," she said, inhaling enough night air for both of us. "Hold out that left hand and tell me that wasn't there before last night."

I flattened my hand and displayed it. Felt weird. The move also made the engagement real.

Ally's controlled squeal still had enough energy behind it to rebound off the oak and pine woods surrounding my three acres. "He did it. He finally did it!"

Who couldn't crack a grin at her? She was the comic in this family, and amidst depression and ill luck she frequently found the positive one-liner to fracture anyone's guard. She'd been wanting Wayne in our midst since the day she laid eyes on him, and had helped orchestrate the first proposal. Since then she'd never missed a chance to club me over the head with my stubbornness and lack of acceptance.

"You had no idea?" I asked.

"None! Gracious, even more crazy is I can't believe you truly said yes." She hugged up against me. "When you telling Mom and Dad?"

"Not until Wayne gets past this," I said.

"Past what?"

"His new partner's missing," I said. "Poor taste until we learn more about her, okay?"

Ally blinked in staccato, part from slow uptake and part from interrupted sleep. "He has a partner? And it's a she?"

The cool dawn air began penetrating my clothes, and I scooched closer to her. "He used introducing her to entice me to the restaurant last night. So we'd meet. Got the call about her missing an hour ago."

"Wow, what a way to ruin your engagement, huh."

Leave it to Ally to state the obvious and say the unsaid.

She hugged me once more. "I'm still happy for you. And you still need to be happy, okay?"

"I know," I replied.

She leaned into me and sniffed, then pinched me on the back of my arm. "Bet you haven't had a minute's sleep, have you?" Giggling ensued. "My thoughts of that man naked . . . damn."

"Crossing lines, Ally. Crossing lines." I climbed the steps and went inside, weariness owning me. Which made me wonder how exhausted Wayne would be before the day was over. Of course, the news he received would dictate a lot of that.

For now I honored Wayne's request to be home. Later, I'd phone and check on him, maybe decide whether anyone down there needed my attention first hand. My passing St. Clair Simmons to Wayne gave me a sinking feeling I'd started this ball rolling, but no doubt there'd be enough law enforcement without me getting involved.

THE PHONE CALLS started not long after my eyes closed . . . which I didn't quite grasp until Ally banged on my door. "Don't you need to take those calls?" she hollered even as another came through. "How are you sleeping through that?"

I groped over my nightstand and answered my cell. My hello came out full of sand until I cleared my throat. "Hello?" I managed the second time, about the same time last night's events tumbled into my consciousness.

"Thank God," said the female voice on the other end. "I had to make sure the missing agent wasn't you."

Sitting up, I doubted a second whether I recognized the voice. "Callie?"

"Deputy Raysor woke me saying he got word an agriculture agent was unaccounted for in his county. First person I thought of was you. What's going on?"

During what was supposed to have been a romantic getaway on the coast with Wayne, Edisto Beach Police Chief Callie Morgan had scooped us up into a murder investigation last August, sending us undercover as a couple visiting a bed and breakfast. After a rough start, we'd formed a comrade-in-arms friendship. We'd learned some of her secrets, and she'd teased out a few of ours. We'd sworn to stay in touch, but it had been three months since that experience, and this was our first reconnect.

"Excuse me but I didn't get to bed until almost five. Worrying," I said. "Raysor's the Colleton County deputy on loan to Edisto, right? The big, round guy?"

She gave a humorous *humph* at the description. "He phoned me the second he heard, thinking, like I did, that it might involve you."

I was touched. Then I instantly grew concerned I'd heard nothing from Wayne. What time was it? "Can I put you on hold a second?"

"Sure."

Shortly after nine. Flipping through screens, I hunted for updates in terms of voice mail, texts, hell, even instant messenger. As hard as I'd slept, I could've missed his. Nothing.

I went back to Callie. "Wayne should be down there. What have *you* heard?"

"They found a car. Phone and purse inside. No sign of her yet. You know her?" she asked.

"Just met her." A sad urgency took hold of me. "She's Wayne's brand new partner. Didn't even have the wrapper off her yet. She went down there to spend the night with her mother. She and Wayne were supposed to meet up this morning and start interviewing her first target."

Some silence. "His partner? Damn. Give me your personal description of her. I'd rather hear details from someone who's laid eyes on her."

The evening at Saluda's rushed back. The girl's grace, enthusiasm, the sort of energy that made you remember feeling young. "She's about five foot eight, a hundred and twenty pounds. Dark-skinned black with hair cropped tight. Pretty. A necklace with some sort of geometric design, gold. No ring. Unmarried."

The last sort of slipped out and mattered nil.

I sensed Callie taking notes. "What was she wearing? Age?"

Jasmine's dark slacks and handsome tunic popped to mind, the thick scarf she wore coming in, then again going out. I regurgitated the personal details I knew about the young agent. "But Callie, this is what worries me. She was just out of college and the Federal Law Enforcement Training Center. I doubt she was more than twenty-three or four. She was over the moon excited about her first case being she's from the area."

"Would she investigate on her own?" Callie asked.

I wanted to say no way, but how the heck would I know? I'd just met her, and she was as green as they came. I remembered the pout. "I don't know, but no matter what, she's young and inexperienced. Worries Wayne, too."

"So why didn't you come down with him?"

He didn't ask, for one, but I didn't want to highlight this adversarial thing we did with him taking over and leaving me behind, though Callie must certainly be aware. Technically it was him doing his job and me doing mine, but it often turned into a hierarchy of sorts. More my problem than his. I wished to God I'd learned to love investigations before I'd hit the feds' cut-off age.

Maybe she'd forgotten my parameters. "Callie, I'm not a real agent."

"I know."

"So what makes you think I ought to be involved? This sounds like pure LEO stuff."

She gave a sigh, and I waited.

"Because he might need you," she said softly. "In case this search goes sour."

Playing with the stitching on my bedspread, a choke filled my throat. I'd spent almost three years trying to prove I was valuable to Wayne, only most people considered that logic flawed because of me being civilian. And I'd been too stubborn to say maybe he could emotionally use me for fear it made him appear weak . . . or me too feminine.

To think it took a woman in law enforcement, one with a painful history at that, to understand.

When I didn't speak up, she did. "Come on down and stick with me. Ride piggy back on *my* badge. Even better, pack a bag and spend the night at my place. I'll keep you from crossing lines, Slade."

Her unexpected generosity made it through that tough shell I cultivated and touched my heart.

"The beach might do you good," she continued. "Of course I'll extend the invitation to Wayne as well. What do you think?"

Wiping the moisture on my cheek, I covered the phone to clear my voice. "Jesus, Callie, how can I refuse that? Let me clear my schedule with my boss, and I'll hit the road. Where shall I meet you?"

"At the Colleton sheriff's office," she said. "We'll ride in my cruiser, so we'll have no problems."

Ally came in with a cup of coffee and halted at my emotional state. Fearful, she stood with mug in both hands, awaiting my signal.

I had a support system in my family and a couple of particular co-workers, but nobody to the degree they understood my deep hunger to assist in righting wrongs. The calling might have come a couple years too late to don a uniform or tote that shield, but fate had given me this custom chance with Agriculture that took me as close to the blue line as I could get. "Tell you what," I said. "Meet me at the Agriculture office in Walterboro. Would rather leave my car there. They know me."

"The Agriculture office it is. Text me when you're getting close."

With renewed vigor, I rose from the edge of the bed. "You are awesome, Callie Jean Morgan. See you in two hours."

My sister returned, apprehension in her soft, barefoot padding to my bedside. "They find Wayne's partner?"

"No." I grabbed clothes from drawers, the closet, surprised at how eager I was to get going on three hours' sleep. "But do you mind me being gone for a couple days? Anything pressing with the kids? The schools?" Then I tacked on, "You?"

"Nothing that beats the crap on your plate, Sis." She handed me my coffee during my pass by. "Wayne letting you team with him for a change? Maybe it's the ring thing."

After a sip I bolted into the bath and cranked up the shower. "Wayne doesn't know," I said. "And I believe I've found a partner of my own."

# Chapter 3

## *Callie*

AT THE EDISTO Beach Police Department, Callie hung up and looked across her desk at Don Raysor, the Colleton deputy who'd brought her the news. The backup cop had been shared between the county and Edisto Beach for the last ten years, and though he wore the county uniform, he was recognized more as Edisto's property.

"Mind managing the beach while I help hunt for that Ag agent? I can put Thomas on standby," she said. Today only she and Raysor were on duty, but early November was one of the slowest months of the beach's tourist calendar. "I sort of feel a connection here, Don. Slade says hi, by the way." She left off Slade's *big, round guy* description.

He sat molded in his corner chair, having just reported for duty. "Sure thing, Doll. Damn glad it wasn't her." The middle-aged, barrel-chested man easily fell back on the nickname he'd given her when they first met, butted heads, and did their best to demean each other. The criticism had become an endearment.

"You and me both," Callie said. "But the missing agent is a baby, Don. And Wayne Largo's new partner."

He gave a painful scowl. "How young?"

"Right out of college. Twenty-three."

"Damn," he said, making the word two long syllables. "After the way they helped Edisto this summer, guess the least we can do is help them. Go ahead, take off." He rose and headed toward the door. After getting his marching orders from Marie, their lone admin type, Raysor would take the reins and patrol the three-mile stretch of sand along with the two square miles of beach houses, expecting no more than a traffic ticket before the day was through.

Slade wouldn't arrive in Walterboro for two hours, she'd said. Callie'd reach the county seat in an hour, tops. "Don?"

He poked his head around the door again. "Yup. Whatcha need?"

"Had a thought. Maybe you know this girl, Jasmine Bright. Slade said she had family in the county."

Leaning on the frame, he barely shrugged. "Heard of the family but not her. Not many Brights in the county. Maybe ten at best."

Though amused at ten being a lightweight family tree when she could count her living family on one hand, Callie recognized what Raysor meant. The Brights weren't fifth generation Colletonians with quality gossip and notorious characters, and if anyone could collect intel in this region it would be Deputy Don Raysor. His family numbered in the dozens, and if you got into the second-cousin-once-removed category, the census probably logged a hundred.

"Off the top of your head, you recall any of them getting into any trouble?" she asked.

Gazing at the ceiling, he did a mental tally. "A Bright in his thirties got caught stealing cars a couple years ago. He's doing time, wait . . ." He retracted his finger. "No, he might be out by now."

"Nothing about the girl?"

He shook his head. Watching his boss for a moment, he added, "Hope she's safe, Doll. For her sake and your friends' sake."

Callie rose from her desk, checked her phone for messages, and finding none, grabbed her coat with POLICE across the back and the Edisto Beach PD insignia on the sleeves. "I'm just glad it's not quite holiday time."

"Humph," he agreed and let her by.

Outside she appreciated the lined coat. While it wasn't icy, the temps had dipped into the upper forties that night. Cold hung in the morning air to remind people and animals that this was a taste of the month to come. If Jasmine had spent her night in the cold, Callie prayed she had some sort of warm cover . . . assuming she wasn't dead. But her prior fifteen years of detective experience for Boston PD leaned her in the latter direction.

She cranked her cruiser and headed off the beach onto the big island, then thirty minutes later hit the mainland and stepped up her speed toward Walterboro. Regardless the news, good or bad, she hoped it came through before Slade arrived.

Frankly, the offer for Slade to partner with Callie was more a professional courtesy toward Wayne than Slade. Last August, in the week she'd come to know this couple, she recognized Slade's propensity to make decisions and moves based upon her gut laced with a wealthy overabundance of knee-jerk judgment. The woman couldn't help herself, and her behavior both enhanced and clashed with her guy friend, Largo, the real federal agent.

But regardless of Slade's deep-seeded need to assist, now was not the time for her to interfere, so to temper that enthusiasm, Callie jumped in front of the problem. She liked the Ag agent a lot, and Slade seemed to respect her in return. This could work out as a help to Largo and a way to channel Slade's impulses.

Plus Raysor was right in that they owed Slade as a result of the Indigo Plantation case, but Callie wasn't a bit guilty about putting a leash on her friend by inviting her to work together. This was best for all parties concerned, and if Slade couldn't see it, that much better.

# Chapter 4

## *Slade*

"NOT YOUR TURF, Slade," Monroe said. "Stay home."

I'd rung my new boss rather than go into the office, to avoid any sort of directive to return to my desk and deal with the tangible work strewn across it. If the conversation didn't go well, however, I would play the sick card. He'd recognize the ploy, realize how badly I wanted this, and meet me in the middle somehow.

One of my best buddies and a peer for years, Monroe Prevatte had actually participated deeply in one case, wrenching his knee going for help when I'd gotten stuck on a farmer's shed roof down on St. Helena Island, monitoring a modern-day slavery operation. He said it then and he reiterated it now, "You poke your nose where it doesn't belong. You're better off not getting involved."

Monroe cared more than he should about me, but kudos to him for locking up those feelings since he assumed the director role. No more personal remarks about him stepping in Wayne's shoes if the cowboy ever left me. No more blindsided kisses in the parking garage. To be honest, him being my boss had sort of neutered him. I much preferred life when we could throw barbs at each other.

"What's going on with that peach theft in Edgefield?" he asked.

No way he'd ever one-up me on my work, and he should know better than to try. Just because he'd been promoted to State Director of our agricultural agency, steeping him in politics and infusing him with clout, didn't mean he could out-think me. He could order me, but I'd get even on some future issue. Our friendship went too far back, our knowledge of each other's buttons too keen.

"The guy in Edgefield filed a police report, Monroe. Someone stripped a third of his trees. They think it's a hired hand who sold the fruit across the line in Georgia. Let him file insurance, file charges. Case closed. I need to head to Colleton."

"What about . . ." he started, grappling for the name of any other case.

"Please don't." I was serious this time. Callie opened a door for me without burdening Wayne, an opportunity I could not pass. Wayne needed support.

"You're already on the road, aren't you?" he said.

The town of St. George went by in a blur on my left off Interstate 95. "Maybe."

The old friend in him came back to life. "How long will you be out of pocket?"

"Till they find her, I guess. Hopefully just today."

Silence except for tire noise on the highway. "Tell Wayne I hope it turns out all right," he said.

"I will. Thanks."

"Slade?" he said louder, afraid he'd lost the connection.

"Still here," I said.

"None of your dare-devil crap down there. If that woman was murdered, this is absolutely out of your comfort zone. You hear me?" His nervousness came through loud and clear. "I swear I'll fire you if you insert yourself where you don't belong and get hurt."

"Sure you will, Monroe."

"I mean it." His voice rose on the end. "And I'd have Wayne helping me."

"I'll be careful," I said. "Gotta go." I hung up as I had many times before, feeling lucky to have a friend who could find a way to care about me and still not fire me.

The road sign said eleven miles to Walterboro, and I still wasn't sure what the hell I expected to be doing down here. Other than a burning urge to help and to be near Wayne, was there a logical reason?

St. Clair Simmons, of course, but Wayne had pushed that case to the side for the time being. So if I wasn't trained enough to hunt for Jasmine, who said I couldn't do what I was paid to do . . . investigate agriculture issues. With Wayne occupied, nobody could judge me for trying to solve the farm case again myself. Besides, I had a cop escort for a day or two, maybe longer since I was staying at her place. My bag held three days of clothes, and nothing said I couldn't wear something twice.

I'd arm-chair investigated St. Clair Simmons, relying on the Colleton County staff in Walterboro to do the leg work, computer work, and paperwork, and not that they weren't qualified to do what was asked of them, but the fact I hadn't been hands-on left a speck of regret in me. I'd been pulled into a case in the upstate at the same time I had St. Clair Simmons, and I'd been unable to put my own boots on the ground in Colleton, my own face into that of the suspected culprit.

Plus, the county fell into manager Savannah Conroy's three-county territory of Beaufort, Colleton, and Jasper, her headquarters in Beaufort where her reputation as a community mover and ag supporter was legendary. Savvy was my best girlfriend, a phenomenal Agriculture manager, and energy on speed. A do-gooder who'd go to the mat for anyone she believed in, to include me. When I'd been in the field, overseeing the Charleston County office before a bribery case promoted me into Columbia, we'd been best buds and a formidable tag team.

With half a state between us now, we rarely saw each other. To be completely honest, I'd not investigated St. Clair Simmons myself because the turf was hers.

As I turned off the interstate into the town limits of Walterboro, it hit me I probably should tell her I was in one of her offices. I rang her up not two miles from my destination.

"Hey, girl," I said.

The strong voice came through, ever confident. "Hey, yourself, stranger. What you been up to? How's that man? If you tell me you broke up, I'm coming up there to whip your ass."

Wayne and I had saved her job once upon a time, and when Wayne had deemed the case purely law enforcement and excused my participation, he'd taken damn good care of her. Savvy didn't forget her friends.

"Well, I'm about to pull into the parking lot of your Walterboro office. Need to take another peek at St. Clair Simmons, if you don't mind."

She got quiet and I spotted exactly what she was doing . . . processsing that I'd ventured into her kingdom without advanced notice.

"Thought you passed it to Wayne's OIG people," she said.

"I passed it to Wayne, specifically, and he'd planned to jump on it with a new partner."

"Oh?"

"Smooth your hackles, Savvy. His partner went missing early this morning, in the county. That's not for public dissemination, by the way. The Colleton Sheriff's Office is helping him hunt for her, so that's taken precedence. I'm rechecking St. Clair Simmons in Wayne's stead while sticking close to Wayne."

"Need my help?" she asked, temper instantly cooling.

"Not yet. Will let you know if I do."

"We're talking St. Clair Simmons, Slade," she said, saucy. "I'm quite familiar with that son of a bitch."

"And that's why I don't want you in on it. Need fresher eyes and a less adversarial presence."

"What?" she said, her disbelief sarcastically clear. "You don't like him either."

"But he's only met me twice. He sees you at least once a year unless you haven't done your job. And he gets under your skin way easier than mine."

"Honey, please."

As I pulled into the parking lot off Robertson Boulevard, I spotted Callie in her patrol car at the far end.

"Well, I'm here, so let me get busy," I said.

"Hmmm. You better update me. And don't be surprised if my staff isn't happy about the drop in."

"Don't be surprised if they learn to get over it, either," I said, attempting humor on a day that was anything but humorous. "But I'll keep you apprised, okay?"

"Yes, ma'am."

I eased my F-150 pickup next to the patrol car. A bit warmer this close to the coast, the humidity bolder. Callie motioned for me to get in, but I motioned instead toward the office as I walked around to the driver's door. "I need to run inside first," I said. "I'll explain after. Coming in or waiting out here?"

After exiting and locking up her car, she reached arms out. I accepted the hug, my arms more engulfing her tiny self than the other way around, squeezing her close like old friends whose history gave them a union that didn't merit words. I sensed this woman didn't give out hugs that freely, and I considered myself lucky.

"You okay?" she asked, drawing back, studying me.

"Yeah. I didn't really know the new partner. Neither did Wayne, but he's wound up awful tight."

"Understandable." Then Callie smiled. "When did that happen?" she said, eyes catching the ring.

"Last night," I said. "A few hours later we got the word about Jasmine."

Enough said except for her patting me on the shoulder. She wasn't a person of many words, let few people into her world, and I counted myself honored to have her in my circle. Following me inside, she stood behind a few steps, respecting the jurisdiction.

The entire office of four people froze.

A clean-cut, khaki-wearing man in his early thirties came forward.

Connor Boone, Savvy's assistant in charge of the local office. "Ms. Slade, we had no idea you were coming."

Not a word about the officer that came with me.

"Sorry, last minute decision, Connor. Just got off the phone with Ms. Conroy, so she's aware. Think you could pull up everything you have on St. Clair Simmons? Everyone you've talked to about him, his crop, his payments. Online, on paper, personal notes, spreadsheets."

Still no movement from the staff until Connor asked, "Thought we sent you everything. Are we in trouble?"

I peeked back at Callie who raised a brow. "You mean because of the uniform? No, she's a friend helping me on something else."

"No, ma'am," he replied. "It's just nobody sees *you* unless . . ."

"Nobody's in trouble," I said. "I'm just fresh eyes on what you've already done."

"Um," he continued. "When do you need this information?"

If I were Connor, I'd be asking why I hadn't come down armed with the file already sent up the line, but he didn't seem mentally armed enough to ask. "Today, if possible. For now, copy me his basic file. Better yet, just give it to me. Notify me when the rest is put together." I set a few of my cards on the counter, which seemed to catapult them into action, one soon handing me a manila folder. "I'll be in touch if I don't hear from you first," I said, "and I'll get out of your hair."

Connor approached instead of saying goodbye. "I can take you out there. Sort of feel responsible since he's my farmer."

But I waved him off. "No need. Appreciate the offer, though." Then to everyone else, "Thanks, y'all."

We left, heading toward her vehicle. "What was that about?" she asked.

"Tell you in the car. This guy," I held up the folder, "might be connected to Jasmine and Wayne."

"I see."

The comment sounded full of meaning. "What does that mean, *I see?*"

"I see how your focus commands a room and gets you want you want."

I scoffed. "Don't you think it was more that your uniform rattled them?"

She shook her head. "They barely glanced at me, but they almost wet themselves when you walked in. What sort of reputation do you have with Agriculture?"

Her remark gave me pause, and I entered her vehicle, rerunning my conversation with that staff. "Do you ever second-guess your behavior?" I asked.

"I'm a cop, Slade. That comes with an extra helping of certainty sometimes. But you get more from people by working with them than running over them," Callie said. "You didn't give those folks a chance to even breathe. You want respect, not fear. The latter is reserved for the most critical situations . . . situations you probably should never have to address. Those circumstances are reserved for the trained to diffuse or cope with in the most efficient manner . . . tools and training you haven't yet been given for your toolbelt."

She pulled onto US Highway 17A, then County Road 63, assured in where she was going. "It's something to think about as you catch more cases. You talk to Wayne yet?" she asked.

"I was about to ask you the same thing." It had been a while since I'd traveled Colleton County, and I fought to regain my bearings. Or rather that's what I told myself staring out the window in lieu of thinking about my behavior and attitude with Savvy's people.

Damn how Callie'd knocked me off my game. And there she sat, driving nonchalantly as if she'd spoken of nothing more than juggling who sat where for Thanksgiving.

"No, I didn't call Wayne," she said. "I figured he was too busy to chat. Deputy Raysor called me about them finding the girl's car. Figured I'd just show up."

"With me," I threw in. Sounded like something I'd do.

She turned and gazed long, almost making me worry about her keeping the car on the road. "Will your presence be a problem for him?" she asked.

I couldn't really answer that. "Wayne and Jasmine were about to embark on an investigation I handed off to them a month back. A local farmer you may know. St. Clair Simmons."

She shook her head. "But keep in mind my knowledge of people is mostly confined to Edisto Island. Go on." She slowed, and I hesitated before speaking, noting the road we were entering. About a mile down, Old Coon Road turned off of this one, if I was right.

"Anyway," I began, opening the file to refresh my memory. "The guy has pocketed money instead of paying his government debts. The type of behavior that's hard to take to court, with the dollars typically too low for the US Attorney to choose prosecution. Wayne wanted to train Jasmine with it. That's the problem."

Another peek over, quicker this time. "Not hearing the issue."

"Jasmine is *from* Colleton County," I said. "You put the idea in my head when we spoke this morning and you asked if she'd go it alone. In hindsight, I think she may have driven down early, taking advantage of him wanting to be with me, to do some preliminary snooping of her own."

We turned onto Old Coon Road, a distance I guessed to be about twenty miles from town. "And how'd you reach that conclusion?" Callie asked.

Jasmine's behavior at Saluda's vividly returned to mind. Jasmine exhilarated. Her asking with a sense of espionage that they be more clandestine in their arrival.

"She bragged about showing off to her family," I said. "That they'd respect her going after St. Clair, a name they'd know."

Staring hard forward, Callie let loose a soft grunt of sorts, making me take notice of what might be ahead, the subject clearly changed.

I counted five cars total. Two marked, one Wayne's, an unmarked that could be Jasmine's, and an SUV with K-9 on the sides and back. One officer guarding the unmarked. Had they seriously not found her yet?

Wait . . . or had they?

Callie pulled to within ten feet behind the K-9 vehicle. "They already brought the dogs."

"They're quicker, right?" I said, pulse quickening. "Isn't that a good thing?"

"Not usually." She threw the car into park and got out, her body controlled, a new stiffness in her manner.

I followed, but before Callie could say two words to the Colleton deputy, a hound bayed in the distance.

As Callie addressed the deputy standing guard, I took note of where we were per the file in my hand. St. Clair owned most of this acreage. Jasmine's car wasn't on the road, but instead pulled in on a doub-le-rutted turnoff, nosed against a chain between posts, a sign dangling about access limited to a deer hunting club. With Jasmine having disappeared in the night, nobody would've easily seen her car tucked in like that. No traffic and too dark.

Which meant she traveled on foot, which led me to question why leave her phone in the car. Which then escalated to maybe she was dragged out. Studying the ground, peering in the car, I saw no sign of struggle. No sign of blood.

Callie spoke with the standing deputy, and I headed over to ask a few questions of my own when his radio went off. I walked faster to hear.

"Heard the dogs, Sarge. Come again?" he asked.

"Reception's rough," came back the voice. "I said, call the coroner."

# Chapter 5

## *Callie*

WHILE THE DEPUTY buzzed the Colleton coroner, Callie moved back to Slade, studying her, not sure how her investigator friend handled the idea of a corpse, much less one in her world. Slade wasn't washed-out pale at the news by any means, but she had a frozen appearance, maybe like the news hadn't taken hold enough to shift her gears yet.

She waited for Callie to approach her instead of the other way around. "Did you catch that?" Callie asked, calm yet watching closely.

"Um, I think so," she replied.

Just to be on the safe side, Callie moved Slade so that her butt rested on the hood of her cruiser. It was midday, the Lowcountry air damp, the occasional whip of a breeze bringing with it the scent of rotting November foliage in the acres of forest around them.

"Want to leave?"

Slade stared into the woods. "No. I want to be here when Wayne comes out. Kind of thought I would be helping to look, you know?"

Callie recognized someone using their words to work through feelings. "Yeah," she replied, not telling Slade that she probably wouldn't have let her get that involved, but Slade needed a sounding board, not a reality check.

"I just had dinner with her last night." After a few seconds of remembering, she stared at Callie. "She was so damn young."

Callie waited for tears, not quite sure how to read her friend at a time like this.

"So vibrant. So . . . alive." But Slade only sighed deep. "What now? I guess the coroner comes and will spend some time at the site."

"If it's murder—"

"How the hell could it *not* be murder? She was twenty-three years old!"

Callie understood. The bodies she'd witnessed numbered in the dozens between her Boston past and Edisto present, amazingly a more than expected number on Edisto, a fact kept rather quiet due to the tourism.

But death was never truly fair. Everyone died too young, too pain-fully, too soon, too ironically, too horribly, too fill-in-the-blank wrong.

God . . . especially if you knew them. Too many birthdays blind-sided her these days . . . birthdays for people no longer around to cele-brate. She'd lost a husband, baby, father, lover, and officer in the course of four years, and if she thought too hard about them some nights, she drank until she didn't. She kept those nights to herself with so many Edisto eyes on her.

"Slade—"

"Good gracious, where's her mother?" Slade asked, coming up off the hood.

"At home, I hope," Callie said. "This is the last place she needs to be. You didn't know her, did you?"

"The mother? No. Was just thinking . . . not really sure what I was thinking." She slumped back on the cruiser's hood.

Then for fifteen minutes they waited, Callie seated beside Slade. A pair of squirrels gave them a show running up and down two pin oaks to their left.

"Waiting sucks," Slade said.

"It's not like time matters now," Callie replied, reading texts from Raysor and Marie as to the status of the beach. She put her phone aside. "Waiting is a huge part of law enforcement, Miss Ag Agent. I'm sensing that's not your talent of choice."

Slade sighed. "You sound like Wayne."

The deputy wandered over. "Chief Morgan?"

Callie shifted attention. "What is it?"

"I told Agent Largo when you first got here that you and Ms. Slade were on scene. He just now radioed, asking that you come in. He wants to hang tight until the coroner's people arrive, but said he'd like to see you."

"Me, too?" Slade asked, pushing to stand.

"Only the chief," he said. "You can hang with me."

"I'm honored," she replied, plopping back down on the car.

"Tell him I'll be right there, only I'll need someone to show me the way," Callie said.

The deputy pointed, and they instinctively looked as if a path would appear, but instead of a clear direction, Wayne stepped out of the trees.

Both women rose, stepping forward.

"Just the chief," Wayne said, unknowingly echoing the deputy. "Sorry, Slade. You understand why."

Callie hopped across a shallow ditch on the side of the road. Wayne offered his hand, and as a courtesy to Slade, she ignored it and made her own way into the thicket of pines, oaks, sweetgums, and hickory, glancing back once to see Slade beside the deputy, the feeling of being left out damn clear. Wayne told her to avoid some leafless poison ivy snaking up a tree.

Out of sight of the road, however, Callie stopped the agent with a hand on his arm. "Wayne, I'm so sorry about the loss of your partner."

"Stupid damn loss," he said, his facial features drawn tight. "Keep thinking I should've told her to wait. Or I should've gone when she did instead of having dinner with Slade."

She shook her head. "Can't do that, Wayne. That case didn't merit a dark-of-night call. And don't let this completely ruin your proposal."

He snorted with a bitter laugh. "Tell me that doesn't merit a do-over. Let's go. Watch your step there."

The sound of another vehicle on the road didn't stop them, but the radio from the deputy did. "Coroner's here, Agent Largo."

"I'll be right there," Wayne replied and turned around, telling her over his shoulder he'd be right back.

Wasn't long before the coroner and an assistant came high-stepping through the undergrowth. Callie marveled at how three times she'd had to deal with the Colleton County Coroner's Office only to land the same assistant coroner. Tall and droll Richard Smith.

He hesitated when he saw her, too. "Great."

"Lovely meeting you again, Richard," she said, then turned to follow Wayne's lead, knowing full well this assistant coroner said few words, and fewer than normal to her after she'd asked him to deviate from procedure on the last body, and taken evidence from the one before.

But this wasn't her case. She was here for support, not to run things, or worse, stir up trouble in someone else's business.

The trek took about fifteen minutes, the light dimmer the farther they went, the dew-soaked leaves noiseless underfoot. The first sign they'd reached the site of the crime scene was tape in a wide, almost rectangular shape that encompassed a wooden storage shed the size of a large bath, devoid of paint and electricity, with a slight lean to the south. Greenbrier and ivy thrived up its sides, finding the weak spots to enter. Deputies from the three other cars on the road stood scattered around on watch, quiet, one on his cell. At the sight of Wayne and the other arrivals, the phone disappeared.

The wood on the shed appeared shabby, very kick-downable, older than any of the live bodies standing around. The door hung ajar, intact on thick, eight-inch hinges with aged anchor bolts, constructed of planks same as the structure, with cross planks holding them firm.

About thirty feet behind the shed lay the remnants of a foundation. A residence from decades ago from the looks of the trees grown up where rooms used to be.

But on the ground, roughly six feet from the open shed door, lay Jasmine Bright huddled in a fetal position. Or whom Callie had to assume was Jasmine. Other than with clothing, anyone would struggle to recognize the virgin agent, but the geometric design on the necklace resembled Slade's description.

Jasmine's hair held dirt, dead plant life from the ground, her clothes in disarray, limp, wet, and filthy like she'd wallowed on the forest floor. But worse . . . welts from dozens, if not hundreds, of insect stings covered every inch of visible skin, bloating her cheeks, eyes puffed to slits, throat thick, straining her collar. Hands appeared three times their normal size, as if pumped with fluid. Her tongue thick enough to force her to stretch her mouth wide, as wide as she could, in an attempt to get air down a throat too blocked from the swelling. Her brow knitted incredibly tight, permanently depicting her final pain.

"Was she allergic?" Callie asked Wayne.

He exhaled hard, flummoxed. "Not that I'm aware of, but not sure I would know unless she felt the need to tell me."

"She might not have been," the coroner said, coming out of the shed. "These are hornet stings, not bees. They're more aggressive, and unlike bees, they sting repetitively with venom each time. Once one is threatened, meaning she stepped on it or swatted it, they put out a distress to the entire nest." He motioned back at the old structure. "Found a rather large nest in there."

"Reason we're standing outside, Doc," spouted one of the deputies, prompting a laugh clipped short by Wayne's stare.

The coroner gave a disgusted glare of his own. "She might not have been allergic to one sting, but given the hundreds on her, the high dose of venom could've prompted shock and cardiac arrest." His eyebrows met in the middle in thought. "Would've taken no more than ten minutes or so."

Callie analyzed the body's position in relation to the shed. "What the hell was she even doing here? Where exactly are we? I'm not buying that she walked all the way out here on her own, went in that shed, found hornets, and died."

"Not sure she made it into the shed, but I agree with you," Wayne said, studying the girl's Timberlane hiking boots tucked up against her butt.

Callie dug for dots to connect. "Slade told me y'all had concerns about a farmer out here. Where's he in relation to where we are now?"

"Not exactly sure." Wayne looked up at the deputies. "Anyone have any idea how far St. Clair Simmons lives from here?"

"Yes, sir," said the closest uniform. He gestured at what Callie guessed was almost due west. "His compound's not a half mile farther down the road. Just look for the ten-foot chain link fence with concertina wire across the top. His house is a few miles back in the other direction."

Wayne dipped his chin at the man, hands rising to his waist. "Come again?"

An older deputy came over. "Don't make it sound worse than it is, Johnson." Then to Wayne added, "He's a wannabe tough guy. Considers himself some sort of a half-assed militia type, but he's no threat. My brother comes over here and hunts. St. Clair maybe thumps his chest too much for my taste, but I hear his place has some mighty big bucks."

Wayne walked a few yards off, as though studying his phone. Callie followed.

"Any chance you can hang with Slade?" he asked low. "Just follow my lead when I talk with her, okay?"

"Sure," she said.

The deputy could be right that St. Clair Simmons was a blowhard pretending to be something he wasn't, but Callie had already decided to stick with Slade before Wayne spoke. Jasmine might've died from pure accident. More like a strong possibility. But as long as Slade was down here, Callie would help her finish up her case on this particular farmer. Wayne might have his hands too full to choreograph Slade's investigative tactics, and she wasn't comfortable with Slade going this one alone. Not with a questionable death in the mix.

If Wayne was concerned, Callie was, too.

Shouldn't take too long to do whatever it was Slade did anyway. How difficult could investigating a farm be? But however long it took, she'd shadow her. Wayne and Slade both would feel loyal enough to Jasmine to finish what the girl barely started, which meant Callie would, too.

# Chapter 6

## *Slade*

THE CORONER and his guy disappeared with Wayne into the woods. Everyone seemed to have access to Jasmine except me. Me and this deputy half my age who was way more interested in his phone. I could've hitched a wrecker to the car he guarded before he noticed. My stomach growled. Almost one in the afternoon. Lunch apparently wasn't on our agenda, and I wished I'd grabbed more than one of the kid's yogurt sticks when I ran out the door this morning.

Nothing was as important, however, as what was going on in the woods.

Movement in the trees turned both our heads. The canine handler appeared, a Malinois at his side on a leash. The younger deputy met him halfway, eager for details.

"Think you could watch this car for me? And watch that woman over there? I really want to see that crime scene."

"Not sure I can wait that long," said the other, opening the back of his SUV, the dog weightlessly taking the leap, turning around and sitting, eye on his handler.

"So is she murdered?" asked the younger man.

"I doubt it." The handler rested his backside on the edge of the open SUV. "Stung to death by bees. They'd have found her without Travis and me. Eventually."

"But it's the same girl that went missing?"

The dog handler nodded.

"Y'all know her?" I asked, having slid in their orbit to partake in the chat.

"Did you?" asked the dog handler.

"I did," I said, which surprised them both. "But she's from your county. Last name Bright?"

The young one's expression remained unchanged, meaning he didn't know squat, but the more senior man's micro expression said he was more unwilling to say.

"So you did know her," I said.

"Heard of the family," he said. "Met the mother when she bailed out the uncle. That girl in there," he tilted his head toward the woods, "must be the one who left for college."

Which told me he was familiar.

"What do they have to do with this farmer down the road I keep hearing about?" I asked.

"Which farmer?" he asked, testing my knowledge as much as I tested his.

I gestured up and down the road then behind me. "The one who owns this acreage."

He crossed his arms, tired of the game. "Lady, who the heck are you?"

Rarely did I flash my plastic badge at real badges. They were more prone to dismiss me, but these guys were locals and had probably never even heard of Wayne's agency, much less mine, so I gambled on their ignorance and pulled it out. "I work with the agents in there. The dead one and the live one. I do more audit investigative work, passing my findings on to them. Had dinner with both last night in Columbia, as a matter of fact."

Then the younger one asked the obvious. "Then why wouldn't they let you go with them to the scene? And why did you arrive with the Edisto Beach police?"

The older man mashed his mouth once, and in a turn to me seemed interested in how I'd respond.

"I was working on another situation. Chief Morgan is a friend and offered to accompany me to make introductions," I said in half lies.

I waited for another prodding question, but the sound of traffic coming made us turn. Not because we were in the road, but because the black Ram pickup slowed the closer it came. Soon it pulled alongside us, a driver plus another man in the passenger seat.

"Nobody called about coming on my property," said the driver.

Fiftyish, in a Mossy Oaks camo shirt rolled up three-quarter sleeves, the driver sat in his seat reared back and overly comfortable in his expectations of others being accountable to him. The passenger was also white, slim and similar in age, and from the way he agreed under his breath to himself, the yes-man to the driver.

"We didn't have to call you," replied the dog handler, "but for your information, we had a missing person report and found the car in this area, Mr. Simmons."

*Well, look at who decided to cross my path.* "Mr. St. Clair Simmons, I presume?" He'd grayed, spread, aged. Not sure I'd have recognized him on the street.

He couldn't honor me with full attention, just a split-second, cursory look intended to put me in my place.

Then he raised a lazy finger toward a vehicle, communication more directed toward the dog handler. "Well, you must've found her from the coroner's car there."

Neither deputy answered. Besides, the guy hadn't really asked a question.

But he'd said *her*, not him . . . not them.

"Maybe I ought to just park and wait," he said. "See who and what comes out."

But when the deputies didn't reply, he chuckled. "I'll leave you to it, then."

"Mr. Simmons." I stepped to the truck. "My name is Carolina Slade with the Department of Agriculture. I'd appreciate meeting with you sometime today. Any chance of that?"

"State or federal?"

"Sir?"

"Which agriculture are you? State or federal?"

"Federal. Drove down from Columbia."

His look remained blank.

Guess he didn't remember me. It had been three or four years. Maybe the Columbia reference threw him. I'd worked out of Charleston before.

"So why are you here?" he asked.

"To see you, as a matter of fact," I said. "Can we meet this afternoon?"

"Got errands in town."

"Just tell me when, and I'll be there." *I'm not going away, dude.*

"I might be back around two," he said. "Three maybe. Depends on things."

I smiled. "Sounds good. I promise not to be too much of a bother." Then on second thought added, "Unless you'd like to talk some now."

"Gotta go, Ms. Slade," he said, then drove on.

Turning to the deputies, I expected somewhat of a thanks for ridding them of the man, but instead they focused on the spot in the woods that would soon develop a beaten path with the comings and goings.

Wayne appeared first. Callie second. No coroner. They came to me.

"Wayne," I started, ready to explain my appearance at his crime scene.

He shook his head. "I don't have a problem with you being down here, Slade." He smiled. "Truth is, you're a sight for sore eyes."

"Is she . . ."

He heaved a deep sigh. "Yes, she is. Can't tell if it's accident or murder, and while we're leaning to the former, I still don't want to make any assumptions."

Regardless of those in attendance, I went to him with a hug. "Sorry, Cowboy."

He squeezed me back, saying in a soft, yet firm voice, "I want you to take a microscope to Simmons's operation for me."

Releasing him, I gazed up. "In the office?"

"In the office, on the ground, in his presence . . . all of it."

Blown away by the overt acceptance into an investigation, I was speechless, looking at Callie for any hint of guidance. She was no easier to read than Wayne.

"Be such an irritant," he continued, "that you occupy his attention. Totally distract the guy until we know better about Jasmine."

"Okay," I said. "How long?"

"Until I tell you otherwise. Don't, however, ask him about anything not related to agriculture. Focus on other funding sources, crop proceeds, last year's books. Get receipts for sales. Check out serial numbers on new equipment. Become his worst bureaucratic nightmare."

"I already told him I'd see him in a couple hours," I said. "He came by. Wasn't that impressed by me, though. He didn't remember me."

"Even better." A hand on my shoulder, he stooped to my level. "Don't worry about impressions other than making him believe he's in your crosshairs. I've seen you do it before. I'll brief Monroe in Columbia in case Simmons complains."

In our wealth of investigations, I'd never felt released with such a free rein. In other situations, I sometimes interfered with his plan, though usually I remained on target with a few sidetracks and zig zags . . . my instincts sending me in the right general direction. We'd butted heads. Yet today, Wayne asked me to be proactive and be almost fierce with it.

Which in light of him losing a partner, made him asking me to assist even stranger. He was a protective sort more of the time. Now, however, even with a ring on my hand, he wanted me on board when I would have expected the complete opposite.

But I wasn't asking why; I was more than happy to delve into this farmer who'd somehow attracted Jasmine to her death.

"What's up," I asked Callie once we returned to her cruiser. I'd hugged Wayne goodbye and updated her on my impression of Simmons. We had a hour or so to head back to his place, assuming he would keep his word about the general promise he'd made as to when.

Callie and I pondered swinging through a drive-in for burgers, but remembering Olde House Café in Walterboro, I suggested we hit their buffet and sit in a booth to talk things through. Half their dishes beat my mother's cooking; plus, I needed a firm grasp of how deeply she wanted to be involved.

I'd seen how committed the chief could be, but my case wasn't her case, and farmers weren't in her wheelhouse.

They gave us ten percent off our meal upon seeing her uniform, and we carried plates loaded with pulled pork, mac and cheese, hash, and green beans to a table back in the corner. The air was thick with home cooking. While I avoided the bread and dessert, my plate held enough food to carry me through dinner, or at least limit me to a granola bar snack. Out of courtesy, I let Callie eat half her plate before opening the conversation most important to me.

"You don't have to haul me around," I said. "Talking to farmers comes second nature to me, and the tasks Wayne gave me are routine work." Except for the prompt to be irritating. "Probably boring to someone like you."

She kept eating. When I stopped and took a few bites of my own, she replied. "I owe you for helping me. Use me," she said. "How many times have you had a police escort doing whatever this is you are doing?"

"Never," I said. "Sort of a dilemma trying to figure out how to work you into the equation."

"I can roll with whatever," she said and checked her watch. She aimed her fork at my plate. "Eat and let's get going. How do you go about this?"

"Make him account for his assets from sold crops to equipment. It's not rocket science."

"Not hearing any strong-arm work there," she said.

I laughed. "Nope, but they can fuss at the inconvenience."

"Well," and she wiped her mouth, laying the napkin on the table. "I'll follow your lead. Maybe my presence will streamline his cooperation."

"Maybe," I said. "But we just don't want to streamline the process too much."

Wayne had plans of his own, and while my assignment was needed, and I was more than willing to be a distraction for Simmons, I couldn't help wondering why, for what end?

"Did Wayne ask you to babysit me?" I asked.

"Do you need babysitting?" she countered, having started to stand . . . now resting her butt back in the booth.

"Wayne might think so." I held up a finger. "First, he might worry about my safety."

"Wait," she said. "Is Simmons a serious threat?"

I shrugged. "Not that I'm aware of, but I don't always predict what runs through Wayne's head. You might be simply taking care of his fiancée." I put the last word in air quotes.

Callie leaned on the table. "Keep counting."

"Oh, yeah. Second, he might be keeping me distracted, and your task is to keep me on *my* task in case there is mission creep. I'm sort of known for that."

Her expression held too much humor and not nearly enough denial.

"I'm right, aren't I?" I said. "He put you on my tail."

"Slade," she started, then seemed to rethink. "If you had ever been in the military, and law enforcement is quasi-military in its structure, you'd realize that each team member has their assignment. Each is important for the overall mission. Each may not hold the details of the other tasks, but they do their duty knowing the important thing is that each performs well for the good of the bigger picture. Ever think Wayne considers you team member with a specific job to do? A partner in this and not an adversary?"

The reference to running against the grain with Wayne didn't set well. "I've never been an adversary to him."

"Well, if you don't think of yourself as a partner, and you're not an adversary, what are you?" she asked.

The question stymied me.

"Quit thinking too hard, Slade. Let's do what we've been assigned and do it well."

Damn. She could shut me down in half the time Wayne could. And that trifling lesson of hers still didn't shut down the part of me that wondered what Wayne might be up to. Doing my job without asking about the bigger picture was completely unnatural.

# Chapter 7

## *Slade*

THE FILE IN MY hands indicated a home on another county road four miles west, but houses weren't necessarily the headquarters for farmers. I wasn't asking Simmons for direction, giving the man a reason to take off elsewhere. But we found no mailbox, no signage, and drove past two different dirt roads twice. We decided to take the one most traveled, which led us past the entrance to the woods that led to the crime scene.

Though the sun shined sharp in a clear autumn sky, the light dimmed as we finally found the right way in. The woods were less wild on either side, filled with planted pines, money in the bank for the landowner about five years downstream when he could sell the pines for lumber. Fifty yards on, we reached a rustic, homemade, welded iron gate with vertical bars, anchored to eight-foot tall chain link on either side that disappeared into the trees. Coils of wire around the top of the chain link. The entire containment appeared a couple years old from its finish and the honeysuckle, jessamine, and greenbrier vines having taken residence enough to hide sections.

Four signs. No trespassing. Violators will be shot. Property protected by cameras and dogs. Then this one: Is there life after death? Trespass here and find out.

Callie took in the setting, apparently measuring the risk. "I thought the deputy was joking about concertina wire. Were you expecting this level of security?"

The place suddenly held a creepiness factor. "Nope," I said. "Nothing in the file, either."

Callie rolled to the gate, eye-level with a squawk box, slid down her window, and pushed the button. When nobody answered, she pushed again.

Noting cameras on fence posts, angled to take in both driver and passenger side of any vehicle, I smiled at the one on my side while listening for barking dogs. But weren't the most vicious the quietest?

Maybe the dogs were a hollow threat, like security signs on houses without security systems.

"Yeah?" came a male voice, tinny sounding, the system far from top-of-the-line.

Callie leaned out. "Carolina Slade with the United States Department of Agriculture has an appointment with St. Clair Simmons."

A hum sounded, then a clink. The gate slid to the left, parallel to the fence.

"Proceed forward," came the demand. "Someone will direct you where to park."

She turned to me. "You sure you want to go in here?"

"Got GPS on my phone. I'm sure it's on your car," I said, the whole time texting Wayne, saying where I was, emphasizing I had Callie with me. "And there, now Wayne knows. So roll on, Chief. Let's do this."

Slowly over a thinly-graveled rutted road, we covered about two hundred yards, the less sunlight the deeper we entered. A six-point buck bounded across our path, and I was glad to see Callie understood to brake and watch for others. As expected, two whitetails bolted to keep up with the buck, a fawn in their wake, his spots gone. Once they left our sight, Callie continued driving.

At a bend in the road, a wiry guy in camo, full beard, and boonie hat blocked the road, AR-15 slung over his shoulder. Mid-twenties, maybe, a bit snappy in his movements. Without a word, he motioned with his left hand in stiff pinafore fashion to take a right. As we turned, I caught the name Godfrey above his breast pocket.

Another two hundred yards in, a minor parking area opened to us, with cement curbs lined up on two sides for ten vehicles. Seeing no place else to go, we parked. At the end of the lot, a field spread out, the rye growth over a foot high, offering clear vantage to whomever was in the double-wide on the other side.

I turned back around to Callie. "Are we supposed to get out or will someone meet us?"

"Um, we're being greeted," she said, motioning toward the wind-shield.

Two rottweilers, stretched out in a run, seemed laser-focused on our location.

"I believe we sit tight," she said and punched her locks as if the dogs would try the handles.

Sure enough, the dogs were the welcoming committee. Upon reaching the vehicle, they descended on the driver's door, trained to realize there was always someone on that side. Callie wasn't overtly frightened, but she showed a serious appreciation for our safety.

When they couldn't rouse a reaction from her, they scrambled around to my side.

"Is this their way of chasing us off?" Callie said. "Because it might be working. No way I'm stepping out with that waiting for me."

The dogs alternated my side, then her side, barking, leaping, fat pink tongues slobbering to coat our windows. Callie gripped her key in the ignition.

"No, wait." I inched my window down a bit.

She hugged her door. "What are you doing?"

The dogs were thrilled at the sign of movement and scrambled to my door. "Watch this," I said, lowering the window a few more inches to stick my right elbow out.

One dog backed up but the other leaped toward me sniffing, stopped, then sniffed again. When his bobtail wagged, the other animal returned and did the same.

"I'm getting out," I said. "If they attack, shoot them, but I somehow don't expect you'll need to."

I eased the door open, putting a foot out. More sniffs. My leg, then the other foot. Then when their tails wouldn't quit wagging, I held out my hand which immediately sent them into shivers of joy and downward dog moves, their rears in the air awaiting more love. "Good puppies," I said, and chuckled. "Come on out. We're good."

She got out. "I'll be damned. How'd you know?"

"Besides their cute wagging nubs on their butts? The fact they were young and not snarling. No sign of animosity. They just happened to be big, black, loud, and a breed that most people fear. Come on." I steered us toward the double-wide. "And some son of a bitch got his jollies watching to see if we'd wet our pants."

We set off across the field, an observer returning inside, the two of us not happy at being set up for his entertainment. The pups danced and circled us along the way, and upon finding a stick, I threw it in hopes of getting them out from under our feet. By the time we reached the trailer, Callie had dared pat one on the head.

"Go on, puppies," I said, waving toward the field. "Go play."

Inside the metal door, a secretary of sorts sat behind an army surplus metal desk. "Ms. Slade, Mr. St. Clair Simmons awaits you down that way."

"May I?" I said, picking up a brochure and a flyer from her desk.

The secretary gave a crisp nod.

The folded brochure touted tactical classes, close-quarters battle training, long and short gun transitioning, and concealed weapon permit classes for state certification. The flyer spoke of a barbecue event in two weeks along with a turkey shoot, open to the public . . . to those interested in learning how to handle a weapon.

My brain instantly registered he'd have a firing range, which we hadn't seen. He'd need equipment to mow it, keep it neat. Covers for the shooters. My mind logged where his money would go instead of to Agriculture to pay his debt. Habit of the job.

We went along with what smacked of charade for our benefit and headed where the secretary directed, passing hung photographs of assorted men with feet apart, arms crossed to pump up chests and shoulders. Men aiming at targets. Trainers aiding trainees. Others flaunted wildlife kills . . . deer, one bear, a hell of a long gator in another. One large photo showed men lined in a row, squaring their jaws, proving their manhood in front of a line of ten coyote carcasses.

Apparently, the man had the land and took advantage of it to charge for hunting and teach classes. Fine. Though I wasn't buying the whole militia business, not after those dogs. When we reached the doorway, St. Clair Simmons stood at parade rest behind his desk, in full camo this time. His shoulder holster held the fanciest pistol I'd ever seen, like something out of a western. I wasn't sure whether to take him seriously or not, but since he was armed and I wasn't, I went along.

He held his stance as we entered. A ten-point white-tail mount hung behind him. A wild boar head in the left corner. A full turkey, wings spread beside it. Six various mounts made the room claustrophobic.

Simmons gestured to two chairs before his desk, but as I stepped forward, in my periphery I caught sight of a monster in the corner with his own slung AR-15. Six-foot-six if he was an inch. Three hundred pounds if he was an ounce. Age forty, maybe. Rusty hair, judging by the remnants left on his close-cropped head. The cloth tag over his breast pocket read Snipes.

He'd been in half the framed photos. Guess he was worth showing off.

I was way more at ease with the dogs.

"Y'all must think we're real threatening people," I said, tilting my head toward the extra guy, hoping my voice didn't ring too nervous.

"You must think the same of us," Simmons said. "Bringing along a uniform for protection."

I sat, seeing Callie had already made herself at home. "Edisto Beach Police Chief Callie Morgan. She was assisting me on another issue and knows the county better than I do. You're not my only task, Mr. Simmons. See . . . what I do is look at cases where there's been some difficulty in payment. USDA wants to help farmers, and that includes assisting them in financial management."

"You . . ." He indicated Callie. "I've heard of you and how you don't mind handling a firearm."

Callie had a history I'd hoped hadn't traveled to St. Clair's ears, but the news reporter she'd killed . . . who'd killed her boyfriend . . . had gifted her with quite the reputation. Simmons slightly jerked his head, making the immense armed man leave, giving me some relief. Guess he figured us harmless after all.

"You seem different since the last time we met, Ms. Slade."

Thirty degrees of fear ran through me, and I couldn't justify why. Had he really not recognized me earlier on the road, recalling me later, or had he known all along? "It's been a few years," I said.

The tensed air shifted to awkward, and in my head I ran through how to present my mission in a firm, no-nonsense manner . . . racing to sound big, bad, and in charge as Wayne instructed. I was the distraction for whatever Wayne was doing.

But Callie stepped up first. "Do y'all do reenactments here?"

Reenactments? Where did that come from?

Simmons hesitated before frowning. "What gives you that idea?"

She loosely motioned a hand at his holster. "Maybe the nickel-plated staghorn grip on that .45 caliber Colt 1911."

"I'm a collector," he said.

"Ah."

But she'd given me the seconds I needed to collect myself. "I hate to interrupt the fascinating talk about guns, but Mr. Simmons, because of your size debt and your delinquent payments, our state office selected your account for closer review. That means you get my eyes and ears in the field."

I snatched a breath. "First, I want to commend you for the lengths you've gone to in order to protect your assets. Dogs, fencing, armed guards. Your being armed. This is to protect your property, right?" I gave him a moment.

He didn't answer my question.

I scanned the room as if encompassing the entire world around us.

"Records show that you were unable to harvest this year as well as the year before, so no money there . . . unless your sales went into other interests? My department just isn't feeling loved receiving nothing, then I come here and see guards and assorted weaponry. What's the deal?"

"Are you making fun of my dogs, my men . . . my firearms?" he asked. "To some of us, this is a way of life, Ms. Slade. And enjoying weapons doesn't mean we pretend to be something we're not, Chief Morgan."

"You still haven't justified the switch from being a farmer to heading up a military compound." The guy was hard to push. To have him offensive made our job harder if not downright impossible. Then I remembered what Wayne told me . . . to keep St. Clair Simmons busy, occupied, up to his ears providing information to me in the name of Agriculture, and my job was not to reason why.

"In other words, I'm busy, ladies," he said. "Can we move this along?"

"Sure," I said. "Thanks again for taking the time. Now, about your late payments . . ."

He shrugged with no sign of sincerity. "I know I'm late, but I always come around. My payment will get to you long before you can take any sort of legal action. So what's the difference this time?"

"Maybe you will be able to get that payment in," I said. "But the economy's changed. Of course, there's always the political environment. We're now required to look harder, plus this is your second year in a row. Puts you under closer scrutiny, being a repeat offender and all. We, the government, are responsible for protecting the taxpayers' dollars."

He looked at me as one would expect, disgusted and sick of bureaucratic bullshit.

"So," I started. "Please provide your accounts receivable, accounts payable, receipts for crop sales, leases, contracts. Your bank statements, of course. Will let you know if I need to request copies of checks—or can you provide that, too?"

If the reddening of his ears was an indicator, his blood pressure was climbing, yet I continued. "I need to inspect any equipment valued over ten thousand dollars, and the paperwork on any capital purchases made this calendar year. Have to check their serial numbers against our records since they should be collateral for the unpaid money."

"Are you crazy?" His voice slid up and loud on the word *crazy*. "You realize how much time that will take?"

"We have time," I replied. "The rest of this week, as a matter of fact."

Took me a while to find my groove, but I had. This is what Wayne wanted.

A grumbling rose in Simmons's throat. "You don't know what you're asking."

I nodded, as though having heard what he said many times before. "Truthfully, yes, I do, sir. I have a checklist for this sort of thing that I've followed so many times it's etched in my brain."

He rose. "Sorry, but I just cannot comply."

"Oh," I said, glancing at Callie as if she would understand. "You're no longer interested in our assistance. You're paying your loans in full? That works even better, Mr. Simmons. Make the check payable—"

"What?" Now his forehead had a red blotch running across its deepest furrow. "Hell, no, I can't pay you off."

"So you'll cooperate?"

His breath came out as somewhat of a snort. "All right, yes."

"Wonderful. Of course this afternoon would be too much to ask for the paperwork. How about tomorrow? Meet here? Is this your farm headquarters or is this more a clubhouse sort of thing?"

He let the clubhouse remark go. "My residence," he said, not offering the address, but no matter. I had it.

But I kept pressing. "As for the equipment, any chance you can show that to us this afternoon?"

He smacked the desk, and I pretended not to notice, though Callie stiffened a bit. "Damn it, woman, it's scattered," he said, "and I ain't got the damn time to cart you around to see it."

"Hold on," I said. "There's a map in the file." I fumbled, acting both relentless to get my so-called tasks completed yet bimbo-clueless that he wanted me gone.

He stood. "Shit, I said I don't have the time. Merrick?" he hollered.

I halfway expected the guy who'd spooked us when we walked in, but instead a middle-aged, six-foot sort entered. Dressed in camo, of course, but unarmed . . . that we could see. The same man who'd been riding with Simmons when I was on the side of the road earlier today. His tag read Cox.

Simmons slung a wave at Callie and me. "Show them the equipment."

"Sir?" Total confusion in Merrick's eyes, eyes with an eerie pale brown color, voice two octaves lower than expected. "What equipment?"

"For the farm," he said, staring at Merrick like there wasn't any other kind.

Holding up my folder, I smiled. "Got a list, Merrick. Plus any recent purchases?" I gave a puzzled back and forth at the two men. "We promise to knock this out quickly. Just snap pictures and be on our way."

"Boss?" Merrick wasn't feeling the assignment. "This could take hours. Drop what I'd planned?"

"Apparently," Simmons said, jaws tight.

"Fantastic," I said as Callie and I stood. "We'll follow you in our car."

"Wait, that car?" Merrick noted the parking lot where her patrol car awaited.

"Is that a problem?" Callie asked.

"Um, no ma'am," Merrick replied. "I'll meet you at your vehicle, I guess."

After handshakes, we left, and with dogs bouncing around us again, we returned to the Edisto Beach cruiser.

"I keep dog biscuits in my truck for times just like this," I said.

"I'll keep that in mind," Callie said, unlocking our doors. "Listen, is what we're about to do as boring as it sounds?"

"Not unless you let it be." I dropped into my seat. "Some of them tell you their life story. Others gossip. A few lie to test your mettle. If we had my truck, I'd make him ride with me, but I doubt we'll get much out of a man stuck behind the cage in this thing, so two vehicles it is."

Callie smirked. "You'd be surprised how that cage makes a man talk. But we'll save that trick for another time, when whoever we have back there needs to be."

I laughed, then let it fade, wondering if what we were doing was in any way leading up to such a moment. Wondering if only Callie had been read into Wayne's plan.

# Chapter 8

## *Callie*

CALLIE RECOGNIZED what a tractor was, but that was her limit of agriculture expertise. Slade, however, rattled off names, makes, and models of assorted pieces, checking her list, snapping pics of serial numbers. They finished about the time they needed headlights, with Merrick draped over his truck hood with an incessant finger tapping, impatience filling his eyes.

No telling how many acres they'd covered, not that Callie could measure acres, but they'd bounced down enough silt roads to coat her patrol car in brown. In the morning she'd have to put a hose to it. The Edisto Beach chief couldn't police her town in something that appeared to have drag raced on a dirt track.

Slade finally released Merrick who left with no semblance of good-bye, and she rode with Callie to Edisto Beach, leaving her truck at the agriculture office in Walterboro. Wayne would arrive when he could in his SUV, both he and Slade having accepted overnight accommodations in Callie's guest room.

"I learned way more than I cared to about farm equipment today," Callie said, breaking a long silence. Slade hadn't been so talkative once they'd ended the day.

Slade understood how to work her clientele, though. In talking the talk about bush hogs, cultivators, disc harrows, and tractors, she'd gotten Merrick to open up a bit, but he never spoke against his boss. He worked the compound-slash-shooting range almost full-time for St. Clair. His loyalty for the man ran deep.

The name Mini-Hawk was made clear though. A gentleman's club of a different nature. Men who hunted together, shot together, traded firearms and the stories behind them, and dreamed of politics their way.

"What do you think about Mini-Hawk?" Slade asked, coming out of her deep thoughts. "You ever dealt with militia?"

Callie laughed. "Militia might be a strong description for that group, but I'd let Wayne check into their history. Y'all never heard of them?"

"I haven't," Slade said. "But that wouldn't be unusual. I'd like to know if the Community Development Manager ever has, though, being this is her territory."

"Know her?" Callie asked.

With a trifling grunt, Slade answered, "Oh, yeah. Been near and dear to me for a good number of years. Sharp with a wide-as-hell independent streak, though, so just because she knows something doesn't mean she'll pass it to me. She's more likely to tackle issues herself before requesting help."

Callie studied me over. "No wonder you're friends. Similar souls and all that." She could say more about such renegade behavior, but she was bringing this renegade home to be a guest under her roof.

As Callie returned her attention to the road, they approached the Presbyterian Church and its graveyard on their left . . . where Callie's own similar soul was laid to rest. Though she could now pass without a crushing reminder of his demise, she never escaped the tug at her heart.

She sensed Slade watching her. She'd visited the place and spoken in depth with Callie's neighbor about the whole Mike Seabrook story. She'd know what the graveyard meant. "You seem good," she said. "Seeing anyone?"

Shaking her head, Callie pushed on, a bit surprised at the slight embarrassment she felt on the topic of her stagnant social life.

"Not even a prospect?" Slade continued.

"You set the date?" Callie countered to the uncomfortable line of questioning.

Slade spread the fingers on her left hand, studying the ring. "No. It's complicated."

"Yeah, same here," Callie said. "Hey, look." She held a gaze on the rearview mirror. "Your fiancé is about to catch up to us."

Wayne followed them for the remaining five miles, crossing Scott's Creek to Edisto Beach, ultimately pulling onto the white shell and gravel drive outside *Chelsea Morning*, the chief's residence on Jungle Road. Motion sensors lit their way, and Callie slowly drove deep under her home on stilts, an architectural requirement for coastal South Carolina homes. Wayne eased behind her.

"Really appreciate you putting us up, Chief." Wayne retrieved a gym bag as the ladies met up. Then he breathed in with drama. "Never get tired of this salt air."

Callie smiled, appreciating full well what the coastal environment did in rejuvenating people, then took the two dozen steps to the porch and opened up, disarming the alarm . . . one of the few alarms on the entire two and half square miles of Edisto Beach. Few were aware of her security issues, but she had lengthy experience which warranted her reservations about humankind, in spite of the nirvana reputation of the beach.

"In there," Callie motioning to the front bedroom, already undoing her belt. "Let me get out of this uniform and we'll talk food."

Before long Wayne and Slade sat propped against the kitchen bar, Neil Diamond vinyls drifting in the background, and the chief boiling up a pot of shrimp while dumping salad from a bag into bowls. "Not much, but the shrimp came from right out there." Her hands busy, she motioned with a shoulder to the back of her place, toward the marsh.

"I'll get the drinks," Slade said, and filled glasses with water.

"I have bourbon," Callie said. "Over behind the glasses beside the refrigerator."

"We know, but we don't need it, and you don't need to watch us drink it," Slade replied.

Callie stopped mixing the greens. "Well, at least you didn't come right out and label me a drunk."

"Forgive her," Wayne said. "She means well. We both do. Water's fine."

In minimal time, they peeled shrimp, silence broken only by the sucking and soft ripping noises until they'd each had their fill.

"I'm done," Slade said, pushing her plate back. "We had a huge lunch."

Wayne scooped more of the crustaceans onto his plate, picking out the bay leaf and flicking it back in the colander. "Well, I missed mine, so bear with me."

"Can you talk and eat?" Slade asked.

Mouth full, he nodded.

She fished a tiny piece of shrimp peel off his beard.

Callie enjoyed their energy. For a change she welcomed being assistance instead of lead. While she loved being police chief, she welcomed the lighter duty, but mostly, she appreciated these two. They were legit about doing right, rabid about meting justice, and provided enough comic relief to remind her life could be fun chasing the bad guys.

But Wayne had lost a partner, curbing that fun. She got that.

She also couldn't obligate more than two or three days to assist them. "What'd you find out today?" she asked Wayne.

He wiped his mouth on a napkin already damp with shrimp boil.

"Preliminary cause of death is anaphylaxis, but they're doing an autopsy. Initially no sign of other injury. Not even a knot on the head."

Callie leaned an arm over the back of her bar stool. "Well, she fell on a moist forest floor of leaves, so I can see that."

"Yeah, but that means nobody conked her on the head, either," Slade said. "Figure out why she was on Old Coon Road? At night?"

"No," he said. "And I spoke with her mother, Magdalene Bright . . . Maggie."

Slade's eyes widened. "You had to deliver the death notice?"

"Only felt it proper," he said sadly. "I was responsible for Jasmine."

"Sorry," Callie said. "Been there. Never get used to those visits."

"But what did she say about Jasmine being out there like that?" Slade asked.

Instead of answering, Wayne took his plate to the kitchen, stacking it atop the ladies' plates on his way. He reached over from the sink, took their salad plates and ran water in them . . . like Slade hadn't asked the question.

Callie had been in his shoes, losing comrades and feeling useless in the whys and what-fors of wasted life, but the what-ifs were worse, and Wayne had to have beaten himself up about them the whole day long. She was surprised that at nine p.m. he wasn't spent from the emotional and physical exhaustion after a previous night of no sleep.

"Wayne?" Slade asked. "Did you interview her?"

"No, Slade, I did *not* interview her." His voice hardened. "I told her that her twenty-three-year-old daughter died in the woods alone. I couldn't ask her why Jasmine was out there because the mom was too busy crying, wailing, and asking *me* why Jasmine was out there." He leaned stiff arms on the sink, staring into the dishes a moment.

Slade wasn't talking so much now.

"Had to get her sister next door to come over and console her," he said, painfully dragging the words. But then he looked up. "Maggie had no idea her daughter was even coming home."

Everyone fell silent and motionless.

Callie'd been right guessing that Jasmine sleuthed on her own, green without a partner. Even if she died from hornets, she should've had someone with her. The woods, though. What led her to the woods?

"But Wayne, that makes no sense," Slade said with some angst. "She said she was going home, like it was planned and everything. I'm sorry, but nothing makes sense."

"I know it doesn't." Wayne refilled his water glass and came back around, wrapping Slade in a hug. "Sorry I snapped, Butterbean. Long day . . . after a long night."

Slade hugged him back hard.

"So," he continued, "tell me about y'all's day. You make Simmons account for everything? Excuse me, *St. Clair* Simmons. Does he really expect to be called that?"

"*Simmons* is putting his paperwork together tonight," Slade said. "I . . . we're meeting him at his house in the morning to see what he has. I dumped a lot on him and don't expect a complete accounting, but we'll see." She nudged Callie. "Our buddy got a taste of running down serial numbers."

That lightened things with the lawman.

They took turns describing the compound, the cameras, and camo overkill to Wayne, with Callie sounding way more serious than Slade who attempted to prompt laughter about the wannabe guard dogs.

But Wayne clouded over at the mention of semi-automatic weapons, at the name Mini-Hawk. "I'll locate my guy at ATF in the morning and a deputy US Marshal who works gangs and fugitive squads . . . see if I can pick their brains."

Callie agreed but tried to give a clearer assessment of the threat. "I saw nothing alarming. Not that I'm an expert, but these men were anything but threatening. They put on airs. No draped flags of any kind. I doubt many of them served."

"Well," Wayne said. "Militia, regardless the caliber, tends to draw those with criminal records. Maybe they're only acting, but they also might be trying to build a reputation to get accepted."

"Accepted by whom?" Slade scoffed. "Is there a brotherhood of these morons?"

"Yes," Wayne replied. "They go by Birds of Prey, and their headquarters is in Georgia, south of Macon. They deal in guns, mainly, but agriculture's involved. The disposing of crops, chattels, livestock—like we're looking at Simmons for—provides financing. Or at least that's what we suspect. That's why I want you to stick to the simple farming paperwork, Slade, okay? Not Mini-Hawk, not Jasmine, just agriculture-related issues. Pass what you see to me."

Slade's incredulous expression hung on her, and she started to speak once before stopping herself and starting again. "Those doofus guys are for real? Is that why you accepted the case?"

"No," he said with a tired, hangdog look. "I seriously thought it was a minor investigation for Jasmine to cut her teeth on. I should've checked it out better."

"No," Slade said. "She had to learn. You told her to wait for you."

"Yet she's still dead," he said.

The phonograph needle finished the last song on her *Moods* album, Callie's second favorite Neil Diamond record. It lifted and rested on its prop, the record player clicking off. The gentle lyrics of *Captain Sunshine* faded, leaving the air empty.

"You didn't know, Cowboy." Slade slid to his side, inserted her arm under his and around his back and made him take her against him.

"I'm not so sure I want you going back out there in the morning, Slade."

Callie walked over and closed the lid on her player and clicked off the living room lights. "I'll be with her, Wayne. Simmons wants us to see him as nothing but a redneck farmer who runs a two-bit hunting club. I'll go along so that Slade can do her paper gathering, or whatever it is she does, and not aggravate him. We'll bring you what we find, and you take it from there. Just what you want. What do you say?"

He looked from one woman to the other. "At his house this time, right? Not his compound?"

"Right," Slade said. "What can really happen sitting at his kitchen table going through receipts? You, on the other hand, would be the threat. What's your plan tomorrow?"

"Meeting the coroner. Talking with the sheriff again. Phoning ATF and the Marshall's Service. Handling a half dozen other cases in two states by phone to put out brush fires." He stopped at a thought. "I sort of expected to have a partner to share the load."

Slade reached up and laid a hand on his haggard, bearded face. In reply to her unspoken request, he leaned down and let her kiss him to ease some of the hurt.

Callie drifted quietly toward her bedroom. "See y'all in the morning. Seven work for you, Slade?"

"Fine with me," she said, leading Wayne to the guest room.

Callie waited until their door shut then armed the alarm. She had no idea that a militia of any shape or size existed that close to her backyard. Like Wayne, she also didn't care how immature Mini-Hawk appeared to be. Put a group of clowns with aspirations together with guns and you never knew what you would get. They might not become what they dreamed of being, but some bigger, more seasoned guy might take an interest. Maybe even one from Macon. And that's when trouble could happen.

Being local with enough gossip sources to whet her appetite, poor Jasmine had probably heard just enough to get curious. And accident or not, she'd set eyes on Mini-Hawk.

She could be wrong, but she owned a damn fine record of guessing right. She promised Wayne she'd help steer Slade and keep her safe. Whatever he told or didn't tell Slade was his doing.

# Chapter 9

*Slade*

I SLEPT LIKE THE dead for half the night, but Wayne wrestled with covers and woke me. Then my brain nudged me alert. By the time sun-beams came through the blind slats, reflecting off the white walls at dawn, I was more than ready to shower and get going.

When I returned from the bath clean and dressed, Wayne sat slumped on the edge of the bed. I sat beside him, hand on his back. "You good?"

"Dreams all damn night," he said, elbows on his knees, his focus on the seashell rug . . . when he didn't have his eyes closed. A total contrast to the perkiness of the room's nautical décor.

"I know. You kept taking the quilt," I said, massaging his shoulder. "Anything I can do?" I started to tell him to take the day off and catch up on sleep, but I'd be wasting my breath. He was on a case, and worse, one that robbed him of his partner.

"No." He stood, rolling his shoulders, twisting to stretch his neck. "Gotta get moving. You're still headed to Simmons's house, right?"

"Plans haven't changed since last night, Cowboy. You are rather out of it, aren't you?"

He kissed me on the top of my head in passing, as though more habit than emotion. "Just need a shower," he said, sighing with a mild moan hidden in it.

I was tired, but he seemed overly so. Mental anguish? Losing some-one close could drain a person, but he'd known Jasmine for, what, ten days?

Already dressed and cutting up bananas for cereal in the kitchen, Callie stood in civilian clothes. Sunlight filled the yellow kitchen brighter than my bedroom. "Good morning," she said.

"Can I help?" I asked.

"Nah, just have a seat at the bar." She slid the bowl, napkin, and glass of milk over to me.

I was a hot breakfast, high protein girl, but gladly accepted the generous gesture. "What's with the costume?"

She lifted her arms, studying herself, then got the joke. "The uniform seemed to bother people yesterday, and I'm *your* tag-along, not the other way around. Besides, we'll have the car, unless you want to go in your vehicle. A lot of people aren't fond of a patrol car in their drive."

Crunching on Cheerios, I weighed her suggestion. Not a bad thought lightening up on the intimidation factor. "Let's take my truck," I said. "I like that idea." But then I wondered . . . "Will you still be armed? Won't they dislike that, too?"

"Under the jacket in a holster. No problem." She peered toward the closed bedroom door. "Where's Wayne?"

With a scowl, I laid down my spoon. "He's really dragging this morning. While I'm not ready to run a race, we've had the same amount of shuteye. This has him torn up."

Callie came around and sat on the next stool with her own bowl. "He's bearing the burden a tad heavy, I imagine."

"I'm not trying to sound callous, but while Jasmine is a sad affair, he'd barely known her," I said.

"True, she'd been his partner for only a matter of days, but she was a partner nonetheless, Slade, and with him being senior, he feels the blame. Now he's driven," she said. "Been there."

She'd ceased eating, and I waited for the rest of her thought, but she seemed to file it away.

"How did you handle it?" I asked.

"Had no choice. Killed them."

At first I thought she was kidding. She kept scooping Cheerios while mine got soggy. "Killed?"

Just a nod from her, chewing cereal.

"Them?" I added.

"Two," she said. "Unavoidable and necessary both times. Makes for nights like Wayne's . . . or worse."

Couldn't help it. Pieces were coming together, not that the puzzle was that difficult. "That why you drink?"

"It's why I try not to drink," she said, then motioned with her spoon. "Need a fresh bowl?"

A subtle order my cereal was aging. "Um, no," I said. "I'm good."

Split second decisions made by law enforcement could be life-altering, no doubt. I'd been on scene when Wayne shot his ex-wife, a DEA agent gone bad, crippling her. He adjusted. Saw him shoot drug dealers, killing one, who'd captured both our sisters. Barely phased him.

He hadn't turned to the bottle like Callie; he internalized but always came out on the other side. I'd seen him pull the trigger both times, saving innocents from being shot, and watched him manage.

So if Wayne compartmentalized shooting people, why couldn't he do the same about Jasmine? Though not openly stated, she could be deemed foolish, her death self-imposed by immature curiosity.

This affected him differently.

Wayne appeared dressed, a bit more color in his cheeks, and welcomed the coffee and cereal. "Morning," he said to Callie, who replied in kind. When he caught me studying him, he winked and tried to act like nothing was wrong while Callie remained attentive to breakfast.

The pretense these two had obviously cooked up to keep me safe and productive was not as invisible as they thought. But my biggest worry was whether their keeping me on a tether would interfere with investigating.

If I spoke my mind right now, Wayne would say I read too much into things. Callie would change tactics. I should be flattered. Really should. My man wanted me safe, and my good friend took time from her job to serve as my bodyguard.

Being coddled, however, was as time-consuming to them as it was stifling to me, and so against my nature. Would Wayne put even more speed bumps in my investigative career once we lived under the same roof and shared the same name? If he was protective now, what level would he take it to then?

He wondered why I hesitated telling him everything. Truth was I shared my investigative thoughts with him only when I thought he could help or wouldn't be in my way.

What kind of wife would that make me for Wayne? Or even partner, for that matter.

I went back to studying my Cheerios. I didn't like these thoughts or what the answers might say about me. Not one little bit.

# Chapter 10

## *Slade*

CALLIE RODE SHOTGUN with me toward St. Clair's place. The chief was a good six inches shorter than I was, and her tiny form seemed even tinier in the wide passenger seat of my Ford F-150 Supercrew. Her feet barely touched the floor.

The farmhouse turned out to be five miles from the compound and fifteen miles from the Walterboro office where we'd exchanged her cruiser for my truck. The house was considered smack dab in the Salkehatchie area, but Mini-Hawk's address sat more on the edge. The house was close enough to the hunting club for daily convenience yet far enough for St. Clair Simmons to keep a divide between his worlds.

Although it was about eight twenty, the fog hadn't quite burned off. GPS took us to Whitetail Road off a state highway, but if the lone mailbox hadn't said Simmons, I wasn't sure we'd have found the house without trial and error and a couple extra miles of driving.

Three weeks from December, the grass clearly wasn't much to look at on the four-ish-acre area interrupted by three pecan trees, scattered loblollies, and a sheet metal-sided pole barn weathered and splattered two feet up with dried mud from the last rain. A chicken coop large enough for several dozen hens and a dormant vegetable garden left to rot except for one long line of rich green collards. In the back corner stood an empty, windowless cabin easily over a hundred years old that probably came with the land. Maybe had some historic value.

Nothing modern existed on the property. The bones of the main house had to date back to at least the thirties, but someone hung white Masonite-type siding over the exterior, giving it more of a seventies remodel vibe. One story, about three thousand square feet, and its brick porch sat four bricks taller than the ground—without railing. Prefab pillars from a building supply rose fifteen feet in a poorly executed attempt at an antebellum façade.

Decent enough if it was paid for, but it wasn't. St. Clair Simmons's real estate was mortgaged to the hilt. I hoped the acreage held enough value on its own, because the house held minimal attraction in a twenty-first century market.

A dull white Kia maybe five or six years old parked in the drive near the barn. The first sign Simmons wasn't home, unless he swapped cars with someone else. Surely no Mini-Hawk general would be seen driving a Kia. A woman of the right age to be Mrs. Simmons came out the front, plainly dressed in layers of worn clothes, an unwelcoming skepticism on her face as we exited our vehicle and approached.

"Hey," I said, reaching out a hand. "I'm Carolina Slade from Agriculture supposed to meet St. Clair Simmons?"

"He's not here." She spoke flat and waited to see how we'd take that news.

My dislike for this man was growing. "Did he tell you we were coming?"

"Yeah," she replied.

Wives often did the books, so I gambled we still had a chance to see records.

"Are you going to help us?"

"Might as well. Stayed up till midnight putting this crap together. Come on in." She turned and entered the house, the screen door banging behind her. She left the wooden door open, so we entered, stepping through a living room well-lived in and not dusted in a few weeks. Photos on the fireplace, hanging on dated magnolia-designed paper showed grown children, I presumed, with assorted grands, nieces and nephews. An old wedding picture gave me the impression she was the first, one and only Mrs. Simmons. St. Clair hadn't been a bad-looking boy.

I texted Wayne that St. Clair hadn't shown, but we'd analyze the records best we could and develop a laundry list of questions and follow-up to pester him with.

Ms. Simmons waited for us in the dated kitchen. No dishwasher and no icemaker in the refrigerator door. Linoleum with curled dirty edges under the bottoms of cabinets.

Maybe fifty, judging by the wedding photo and the looks of her hands, St. Clair's wife hadn't taken the energy to preserve whatever beauty she may have had once upon a time. She carried a paunch lending to elastic corduroy pants, Birkenstock mules, and a stretched turtleneck under a shapeless cardigan. No makeup, which didn't matter to me one way or the other, but she could've done more with her hair, which she'd left to spill down in a messy and unattractive bed-head sort of do.

However, on a kitchen table she'd laid out coffee and biscuits with honey, butter, and strawberry jam. "Fix yourself something," she said. "Plates right there. Then come on in the formal dining room where there's more room."

Callie started to pass, and I gave her a light frown. When you visited farmers who offered refreshments, you accepted. I slathered a biscuit—surprisingly warm—with all Ms. Simmons had to offer, poured a coffee, and entered the dining room.

The early American table showed scratches in its finish; the chair backs dull from being pulled out and pushed back in. Clear plastic had been stretched over the upholstered seats to avoid the obvious beating the table had already endured. Stacks of folders, notebooks, and two shoeboxes were heaped on the table top. A dusty silk flower arrangement had been pushed to one end and out of the way.

Ms. Simmons sat on one side; the material had been laid out facing us on the other. Magazines and assorted bags were stacked on the two extra dining chairs set back against the dark, aged, oak paneling. Someone's mother's china cabinet held dulled dishes from a long-ago era. Not that I was judging, but the St. Clair Simmonses didn't appear to entertain much.

But she'd made muffins, and the aroma helped to mask the dankness.

"I appreciate you tolerating us," I said and introduced myself again. "This is Callie Morgan, my assistant. I take it Mr. Simmons got called elsewhere?"

Not a lie about Callie, but mentioning I'd brought a cop would only interfere with progress.

"He's off pretending soldier, teaching people to shoot, or doing something with the farm," she said, not giving us her name. "I never know which."

I couldn't read whether she felt put out or not. "So," I began, "do I call you Mrs. Simmons?" Already read her name in the file—Sally Gruber Simmons.

"That's fine," she said, the only warmth in the vicinity coming from that pan of biscuits in the kitchen.

So, Mrs. Simmons it was. "Do you keep the records or does your husband?"

"I keep the household records. Here's mine." She motioned to one shoebox. "And he keeps the other ones. Mind if I work in the kitchen while you're doing this?"

She left and I handed the household shoebox over to Callie. "Just look for anything abnormal. And if you can find any of these notebooks that keep track of them, help yourself."

Callie gave the paper a once-over, then me. "You want me to really do this?"

I softly snorted. "Think about it like income taxes. I'll take the farm stuff."

Being late in the calendar year, the shoebox overflowed with tickets, receipts, and notes jotted on slips. "Haven't they heard of spreadsheets? Quicken?" Callie asked.

I opened a notebook marked *1st Quarter.* "Depends on the farm."

Wasn't long before I spotted a number of bills for an exorbitant amount of food, beer, and booze in the farm file, not the household file, and I called for Mrs. Simmons. She poked her head in the doorway, saying nothing.

Holding up a notebook, I expected a mistake. "I see a bit of money on entertaining in the farm business. Are these receipts in the wrong place?"

"Well, shit," she replied. "Those aren't supposed to be there. Those belong in his hunting club file. That's from when St. Clair hosts war games with another club. And the hunting parties, and whatever other chest-thumping crap he does out there."

A third set of records conveniently not here. The cost on three bills was a couple thousand. Not a huge expense, but strange, and for anyone who was behind on his debt, more than he should've been spending.

"Can you go get the hunting club records for me?"

"Aren't here," she replied. "He keeps those at the trailer. Those receipts you got there got crammed in a shirt pocket. When I do the wash, I check his pockets, and when I find papers, I throw them in with those others there."

How about that coincidence? "Do you ever attend those events at his trailer? What are they like?"

She drew up her nose as if smelling a stench. "I stay out of that stuff. Wives forbidden."

"This is for local clubs just getting together? What, like tailgating on his hunting place?" I asked.

"He calls it courting." Mrs. Simmons did a pretend curtsy then rolled her eyes. "Some of those folks come all the way from Georgia, and they expect seafood."

I'd attempted to match receipts to notebook entries. There were more receipts than entries, and we'd just learned why. Nothing noted about maintaining Mini-Hawk, like the wire, the dog food, the employees toting the AR-15s unless they volunteered for the rush of personating soldiers.

Seafood on the handful of tickets came from Beaufort. Seafood wasn't cheap, but damn, was he feeding a football team? "Goes to Beaufort a lot, I see."

"Seems so."

"Any other records in this house?"

"Nope. That's it."

"Thanks," I said, then went back to the receipts, making little stacks. I could see myself after-hours, building a spreadsheet of my own before this was over. When we confronted St. Clair, we'd ask for an accounting from his *other* records.

After another half hour, I held up a paper, leaning over for Callie to read it. Just under five hundred dollars spent at a boutique, and upon closer scrutiny, the items appeared to be lingerie. Most definitely a shirt pocket ticket saved by the wife. I was curious whether she'd actually read it.

"He obviously does more than one kind of courting," Callie said.

Nodding toward the kitchen, I asked, "Think it's hers?"

"Would like to think so, but . . ." She trailed off with a shrug.

"Mrs. Simmons?" I called again.

She appeared, looking a tad more perturbed this time. "Yes?"

"Did St. Clair tell you to include the receipts or just put out the notebooks and folders?"

"Just the notebooks," she said. "But I know that my household expenses might not make as good a sense without the tickets, so I put both out there. Hell, his were in a drawer where I toss those I find in the laundry. I put them in a shoebox to make it easier for you."

Which begged the question, "Do you ever look at these records? Like this one?"

She strode over and took the paper, reading it like it was a chapter long. "Son of a bitch." A storm brewed from that stare. "He's still at it."

I didn't have to ask what *it* was. "So this . . . clothing isn't for you? Or bought by you?"

"Hell, no. He told me he'd quit chasing skirts," she shouted. "I don't farm. I don't even work a job outside the home. He don't talk to me, and he leaves me stuck out here. No telling when he comes home, but does he expect dinner when he does? Hell, yeah." The ticket shook in her hand, bouncing with her rant, and I was tempted to grab it before she crumpled it into a wad.

"All he's got is land," she continued, her jaw tightening and adding unbecoming angles to an already homely countenance. "Wastes his dollars messin' with his guns and boys and dogs . . . and back to his whores he said he'd finished with."

Worried she'd trash the ticket, I held out my hand. She returned it, and I quickly snapped a picture in case this ticket got gone. "Any chance the girls are more for his visitors than him?" I asked.

"What's the date on that ticket?" she asked.

The print was tiny, but I found it. "August twenty-five of this year."

"Ha," she announced. "He didn't have no party in August. What does that tell you?"

I didn't answer.

She jabbed at the table, and I almost spread myself across the receipts for fear she'd scatter the order I'd painfully sorted. "And this don't even count what he keeps at the trailer," she said. "He probably don't want you seeing that. The beer, the liquor, the seafood, and cigars."

Her finger made a final sweep around the table. "When you get done with that shit, think you could update me on what you found?"

Depended on what I found, but I agreed nonetheless. "Um, sure." But I wasn't revealing anything serious for fear she'd unload on him . . . or tear up the evidence. I'm sure I could compose some sort of sanitized oral report when we finished.

"Well, the household expenses seem in order," Callie said.

"Damn right." Mrs. Simmons left the room.

"That was fun," Callie said, deadpan, once the wife was out of earshot. "Don't be surprised if we hear on the evening news that she shot the bastard."

"She does have an ill temper, doesn't she?" I murmured.

"Can't blame her."

I pushed a different stack of paper at Callie. "Let's get done. Think you can look at farm expenses? Just ask me if something doesn't make sense."

"Sure," she said. "My interest would be what's he hiding in that trailer," she added.

My phone vibrated on the table with a text. I'd silenced the device to keep a better ear on where the wife was in the house.

"Speaking of temper . . ." I said, reading the message.

"What?" Callie asked.

"It's Savvy."

"Who?"

"The Community Manager I told you about earlier. Savannah Conroy."

With a twist of her mouth, Callie began reading the first farm notebook. "Thought y'all were buddies."

"Doesn't stop her from coming at me. We're in her neck of the woods, and it appears she's adamant about meeting us at the office."

"How adamant?" Callie asked, focused elsewhere.

"Like, Get your ass over here before I rip you a new a—"

"I get it," she said. "We going now?"

I toyed with the idea of jumping up. Savvy had that much control over people when she reached DEFCON One but I wanted to finish up here first. I didn't trust Mrs. Simmons as far as I could throw Mr. Simmons, and I didn't want to have to return.

But if Savvy wanted to be involved, I'd get her involved. For instance, how familiar was she with St. Clair Simmons's activities of late, and why was I finding out about Mini-Hawk and its extracurricular festivities in Simmons's dining room instead of from her or her staff?

# Chapter 11

*Slade*

TOOK US FOUR more hours to sift through the papers at Simmons's dining room table, and as sour and put out as Ms. Simmons tried to be, she still set a plate of some sort of muffins on the table toward the end, refilling our coffee cups. Then she sat. Maybe to rush us through. Maybe curious as to what was taking us so long.

"What's the deal?" she ultimately asked.

"Well . . ." I pushed the papers to the side. "He's too loose with his spending, isn't fully accounting for where his crop went, and I can't tell how he bought a tractor." I left off that we'd be pursuing his hunting club. No reason to tell her as she'd most likely tell him. I wanted to do that myself.

She held her cup in both hands, blinking. "Figures."

"Do you know where his beans and corn were sold?" I asked.

"Thought he planted truck crops this year," she said. "I just saw tomatoes and squash come home. I put up a butt-load of those in the freezer."

I wasn't sure what to do with that intel. Farmers didn't flip from row crops like cotton, corn and soybeans, to truck crops like vegetables on a whim, and the file said nothing about a change of farming strategy. The wife understood zilch about her husband, and he hid his activities from her just in case. What the hell was going on with this guy?

St. Clair Simmons had included nothing in his records about equipment. Like how he paid for a brand new 6 Series John Deere utility tractor. Nothing fancy. Maybe thirty thousand. Did our missing crop pay for it? Or did something else foot the bill?

"Whatever he planted, how do you think his crop did this year, Ms. Simmons?" I asked.

"Okay, I guess. Didn't say one way or the other. If he didn't make a dime, he'd be too proud to tell me. If he made a fortune, he'd not want me to know so he could spend it as he liked."

A marriage made in heaven. While I initially thought she was a waste of our time, she had enlightened us to some of his extracurricular activities, and the fact he may have records of same.

Any entity, farming or otherwise, kept records as a matter of course these days. Even Hells Angels filed tax returns. Crooks were accountant-smart these days, or rather the smart ones were. Capone was caught for tax evasion instead of the hundreds of dead bodies he caused. And since everyone kept records . . . .

The classes, the firing range, the advertising, and yes, even the hunting parties, gave Mini-Hawk an air of legitimacy and records I could get my hands on. I suspected that's where he poured the majority of his financial resources. IRS wouldn't care if he funded Mini-Hawk as long as he reported the income on his returns. Ag, on the other hand, did care.

My phone buzzed again. Another text from Savvy. She waited in the Walterboro office, asking when we could meet her there. After her first text, I considered her simply possessive about her turf and annoying. Now I had questions. She should be reporting crap like this to me, not the other way around, or getting to the bottom of it herself and dealing with him. In particular a guy behind on repaying fifty thousand dollars and change.

I pushed my chair back and organized papers into stacks.

"So what now?" Ms. Simmons asked.

"I'll take these with me, if you don't mind. If Mr. Simmons had been here, I'd have questioned him and probably gotten better clarification on the inconsistencies." Then I handed her my card. "If you think of anything, or if Mr. Simmons wishes to get in touch, there you go. Just tell him we're not done and seriously need to meet."

Another shrug. I believe I could tell her he had the plague, and she'd shrug. St. Clair had definitely tarnished the shine off his wife. Too bad she did what he told her, because her name was beside his on every loan paper. She'd go down with him if it came to that.

We walked back through the living room, arms filled with shoe-boxes and notebooks, when we heard tires arrive on what had to be a decent-sized vehicle. We went out the front door as the Ram pickup parked a few yards to the side of my truck. Callie and I hesitated on the porch, but St. Clair remained in his vehicle. We moved to mine and deposited the paper in my truck's back seat. The farmer put a phone to his ear and gave us the back of his head.

Nope, he had no desire to meet us.

Callie hopped up in her side, but instead of getting in, I walked over to his window and knocked, motioning for him to lower it down. When he didn't, I knocked again.

"What?" he said when the glass came down, a stale, earthy, minty aroma of chewing tobacco wafting out. Sweet truck, but that scent would take up residence in the upholstery, a nice little free gift with purchase for whomever bought it next.

"We had a meeting," I said, firm.

He lifted one corner of his mouth. "You said get my papers together."

"Some were missing." I didn't miss a beat. "Your wife couldn't answer questions, so I'm taking them with me. Come see me if you want them back."

The sarcasm drained from his phony grin. "You can't do that."

"Here's my card when you're ready."

When I hadn't quickly returned, Callie had eased out, and from the edge of my vision, I caught her behind the truck. St. Clair didn't.

"Take the card, Mr. Simmons. Neither one of us has time for games."

At least this silly type of game. Apparently games meant something else entirely on Mini-Hawk these days, and St. Clair heavily entertained that new direction . . . to the detriment of his farm, which he didn't seem to care two cents about.

Callie appeared to my right. "Everything okay?"

St. Clair laughed, a sandpapery rasp. "And what would you do about it if it wasn't, half-pint?" He laughed again, bringing the sound up from his gut.

Surely he hadn't forgotten her uniform and badge from the day before. I stepped out of her way, unable to read where this was going.

"I'd help make things right if needed, but never mind," Callie said. "We done, Slade?"

"Yep." With her to my back, we headed for my Ford.

But St. Clair hollered before we got around his bumper. "Got a question, Ms. Slade."

*Congrats on remembering my name.* I returned, motioning to Callie to wait where she was. I didn't want to mess with the flow of information.

He leaned on the open window instead of getting out. I guessed he liked sitting higher, looking down. "Did I hear that the dead girl's name was Bright?" he said.

With the mother having been notified yesterday, I figured the news had made the rounds already. "Yes, it was."

A grunt of sorts escaped him, and he dropped his gaze. No comment.

"Anything else I can answer for you?" I asked, hoping to glean more.

His truck door opened and I stepped back. "Just wanting to know who died on my land," he said. "Young girl, I heard."

"Twenty-three."

Some head shaking, but then he raised that head and made serious eye contact. A current ran down my back. "Got caught making out? Some boyfriend did it, didn't he?"

Like he dared me to disagree.

"You'll have to talk to law enforcement, sir. I wouldn't know."

Peering through his passenger window at my truck he tipped his head. "Thought she was law enforcement."

Callie stared back hard.

"Open investigation," I said. "You understand."

"No, I don't . . . but I will." He got out, backing me up, and headed toward the house with no more conversation.

Back in my Ford, I cranked up. Callie kept her attention on him. "What'd he say?"

"Wanted to confirm who Jasmine was. Seems he'd already heard, though. Wanted to know how she died. I said ongoing investigation."

He went inside. "See?" I said. "I appreciate the backup, but you didn't need to protect me. There wasn't a problem. I had it under control."

"I know." She leaned on the console between us. "But you had a man who already believed himself some sort of Alpha dog, and if he had firearms at his double-wide, he had them in his truck, most likely an easy arm's reach of where he sat."

I looked over at her, puzzled at how unphased she was. "But he made fun of you. Saw you as no threat."

"Which suits me fine. Underestimating me makes him lower his guard. Where we headed?"

"Um, the Walterboro office," I said, now envisioning St. Clair with a firearm in his lap, then worried where it was when he got out. I hoped she didn't tell that to Wayne. "We're headed to see Savvy and pick her brain. Ask why she didn't see any of this coming." I drove another mile. "You really think he had a gun?"

After a long exhale, she launched into another private lesson for me. "Slade, we have a dead girl. We have a militia of some form. Your guy has been challenged and runs the risk of losing his property to the government. All of that should make you think twice before confronting him on his own land."

She stopped just short of telling me not to poke my nose where it didn't belong. Like Monroe, like Wayne. Come to think of it, like a half dozen other people, including my mother. She didn't. Instead, she laid out the wisdom. Left it hanging in the air for me to absorb.

Maybe because this time my nose belonged here. This was an agriculture case that was one hundred percent my business, and though there was a bigger picture I wasn't seeing yet, it was mine to pull together.

St. Clair Simmons didn't act a damn bit worried, but he couldn't just stray from his financial obligations like that. He knew that this problem would catch up to him. Which I read as his certainty for some bigger payout . . . big enough to gamble on whether we'd foreclose his place before he cashed in on whatever it was.

Was I reaching? Maybe. Right now, however, I headed to confront my Beaufort girlfriend. She might attempt to fuss at me, and she could try, but I needed to blister her more.

"Explain how the rank works here?" Callie said. "You work out of Columbia, for the state's head honcho . . ."

"Monroe Prevatte," I said.

"And you are or aren't Savvy's boss? I'm trying to get a feel on how much push-back to expect when we see her. You talk like her boss but then talk like you have to tread carefully. Which is it?"

My relationship with Savvy wasn't straightforward, but it hadn't always been that way. From the outside looking in, I could see the confusion.

"I'm not directly her boss, but I rank higher. I work at the right hand of the State Director. When I enter an office, staff are in essence answering to him. I'm the troubleshooter, the investigator, the person who shows up when things go wrong, which explains what you saw when we met Connor and his people. How they jumped to when I asked."

Callie got the explanation from her expression, but I wanted her to understand why things were different with Savvy.

"Once upon a time Savvy and I were equals, just in different parts of the Lowcountry. She's been around longer than I have, but I rose higher. We've successfully, at least thus far, preserved our friendship in spite of our job differences. Whether it's her or any other manager, though, it's a courtesy for me to let those like her know when I venture into their territory, and it's understood that they follow my directives upon arrival."

"So the lines blur sometimes," Callie said.

"Yes, the lines blur."

That was still too simplistic an explanation for my particular relationship with Savvy, but how could I succinctly explain my long history with her? Our years reached back to when I left college and she trained me. We grew into hard and fast friends who recognized each other's powers and each other's Kryptonite. And when we butted heads the sparks flew.

No doubt Savvy awaited inside. Who else with a federal job would dare flaunt a car they couldn't obviously afford? Her dead ex-husband bought it for her the month he died, attempting to woo her back. He'd died deceiving her, so she had no qualms about keeping the car—sure opened a farmer's eyes when she pulled up in a silver Mercedes Benz convertible.

We walked into the Walterboro office to find her leaning over the shoulder of a technician, her bra size not exactly a secret under a hugging sweater. She peered up critically at us before she straightened, a slo-mo effort to do nothing but project her displeasure.

The entire office hushed and watched.

I crossed my arms. Callie raised a brow, attempting to read the scene.

"Cut the crap, Savvy," I said, then laughed. "Fine. If I've got to say you look good before I warrant a hug, then I'll say it. You're gorgeous. Haven't aged a bit. You probably still set Beaufort on fire every Friday night."

Her green eyes twinkled and couldn't hold the contempt. "Miss Almighty Executive came to the boondocks to rub elbows with the rest of us, huh?" She scooted around the desk, meeting me in the middle of the room with a smothering hug.

This was my buddy from way back. When agriculture had dragged itself into the current century by finally hiring women to deal with farmers, we'd weathered chauvinism together for going on two decades, me fighting it with words and reasoning . . . her fighting it with her looks and audaciousness, daring any man to test her mettle. United, we could be formidable.

"This is Edisto Beach Police Chief Callie Morgan," I said, drawing Callie to come closer.

"She's pretty damn awesome."

"Nice to meet you and all that," Savvy said with the briefest of glances, "but excuse me a sec. There's a bigger issue here." She grabbed my left hand. "What the hell is this?" The last word rose up in an almost squeal. She jerked my arm up to show the room my ring, beaming as if it were her own. "Look what our Special Projects Representative has gone and done! Can we get an applause for this miracle of miracles?" She dropped her hold and clapped, the staff following suit. Then she gave me another hug. "Damn, I'm so happy to see that happen. I was about to think he was fair game for me."

She held me at arm's length, something I'd have to get accustomed to as the news spread, I figured. People looking at me like I'd grown horns or changed color thanks to the engagement. Noting a genuine tear in her eye, though, my insides fell at the circumstances that brought me here. Made me feel like a dog.

So I gave her my best girlfriend smile to make the best of the moment before the case potentially put us at odds. She was pretty, even at forty-six, her birthday one week and five years ahead of mine. Native American bone structure and skin tone from her grandmother, the tight clipped frosted curls from her father's Irish side. The combination proved striking enough for Savvy to have modeled in her twenties and thirties, and while her forties put that hobby behind her, I found her crow's feet and laugh lines still stunning. Savvy could dress, too, while my off-the-rack slack coordinates fooled no one into thinking I was fashion forward.

Savvy then remembered Callie. Barely over five-foot, Callie had to look up at Savvy's eight inch advantage, but the static energy between the two caught me by surprise, raising the hair on my arms. Callie shoved a hand out first. "Nice to meet you. Slade says you're a force to be reckoned with."

Savvy accepted just as strong. "She's never mentioned you, but I'm sensing there's more to you than your size four jeans."

"You should see her in uniform," I said, for some reason feeling the need to dilute the greeting. "Or chasing bad guys. We worked a case together, and since I was down here, she offered to assist."

Savvy's assessment shifted from casual to professional. Callie's assessment had been and remained the professional measurement of a chief.

"Let's take this to the conference room," Savvy said.

We entered a room barely containing an office table for ten, no windows, and a small square cabinet in the back with a Keurig awaiting use, water available from the ladies' room around the corner. Savvy, every inch the Beaufort manager, let us enter first, shut the door, then motioned to chairs. However, before our butts hit the seats, she uttered,

"What the hell are you up to in one of my counties without as much as an update?"

I wasn't surprised at the whiplash crack as her tone shifted. Callie's shoulders tensed, but she held her tongue, a trait of hers I'd come to appreciate. One I had plans to study and maybe emulate as the opportunity arose.

My other friend had no such restraint, and this was one of those times I had minimal patience for her need to lead a charge.

"Wayne's partner is dead, Savvy, so cut the crap." I settled into my chair. "Sometimes it's not about you. Jasmine was checking on St. Clair Simmons, and we're not sure how things fit together. You may not even need to be involved, but we won't know until we talk. Plus, I've seen enough of St. Clair Simmons's enterprise to have a string of questions to ask you."

She sat, undaunted, and crossed those long legs of hers. "Thought it wasn't about me."

"Why haven't you stayed on top of St. Clair Simmons's payments?" I asked.

"We treat him no differently than any of the other farmers," she said.

Callie spoke up. "How many of your farmers have converted from soybeans to firearms?"

Savvy hadn't any quick-snap comeback for that one, and she had enough intelligence not to argue blind. We'd said enough to tell her she was in the dark, and Savannah Conroy wasn't ignorant enough to fight without ammunition.

"My office missed some things, I take it," she said.

"More than a few," I replied.

She stood abruptly from her chair, mission-oriented, and I recognized her need to snare her office manager and put him on the hot seat.

"Don't, Savvy," I said with just enough volume to not be heard outside. "We don't know how deep or how far this goes. We didn't involve you for a reason, but now that you've plowed your way into this case, hold up, sit back down, and listen."

# Chapter 12

## *Callie*

CALLIE SAT ACROSS the conference table from a woman Slade had described as somewhat of a Super Woman in this part of the state, but she wasn't seeing it yet. Instead she harbored serious doubts about Savannah Conroy . . . about her being the *all that* that Slade spoke of.

She would hold out passing full judgment because Slade had a decent sense of human nature from what Callie could tell. But being too close to someone could cloud perspective.

Callie also had no concept of Agriculture's employment standards. Between her own case last August, and now just over a day of this one, her association with Slade had taught her that Agriculture handled way more money than she imagined, therefore providing a wealth of potential for mismanagement and crime. Farmers could be criminals like everyone else. Until she got a better feel for how these people and their world functioned, best she pace herself and study silently.

"I know St. Clair didn't pay us last year," Savvy said.

Slade countered. "And what are the chances he'll come in with one whopping check to bring it square this year? I didn't see enough crop receipts to pay for his living expenses, much less pay back the money borrowed to put seed in the ground. You sure someone's not looking the other way?"

Her collar bones stiff and squared, anyone could see Savvy fought not to take the remark to heart. "What makes you think St. Clair different than any other farmer caught by the weather? I seem to recall Connor stating St. Clair delayed one day too many putting his combine in the field, and the rains caught up to him. The remaining beans rotted. Connor inspected them before St. Clair tilled them in and gave up on his harvest. And what do you mean by militia? You make him sound criminal." After an overabundance of body language, she gave a scoffing, I-can't-believe-this shift of her head. "Man's just not that incredibly bright, if you ask me."

"Let's sift reality from bull. Try not to take this personally, okay?"

Slade's friend reared back. "This coming from you?"

"Especially from me."

Still not a fan, Callie registered Savvy as a woman who felt you needed her permission to criticize her work. She might be intelligent, but she deployed a sarcastic defensiveness making Callie wonder why Slade felt so aligned with this person.

"First things first," Slade said. "Did just Connor put boots on the ground? Or did you as well?"

Savvy quieted. A decent manager would think twice before throwing her staff under the bus. A selfish one would do it in a heartbeat. The answer was important.

Slade didn't give her time to respond. "Just Connor, huh?"

Savvy's expression showed a hint of remorse, and a tinge of regret, with maybe some deductions of her own. Callie's opinion rose a tiny bit. Finally, the woman said, "St. Clair Simmons was his responsibility."

"Did Connor favor St. Clair?"

"No."

"Did you?"

"No. No need to."

"We should never have a need to favor a borrower, Savvy."

"What's Connor's record with y'all?" Callie asked, realizing a few sharp questions might play best coming from her. "How well do you trust him?"

Savvy frowned. "He's worked for me for three years. Never disciplined him."

"Discipline or not, has he ever given you reason to question his decisions?"

"No."

"Has he shown a difference in behavior?"

"No."

The woman spoke too quickly, not even thinking about her answers, in complete defiance.

Slade slid a hand across the table and rested it on Callie's forearm. "Hold on. We're not ready to go accusing staff."

"We're not ready to exonerate them either," Callie replied. "Whether you call it failure to do his job or a deliberate cover-up, it appears one or the other occurred."

Slade removed her hand as if disassociating.

"To be truthful," Callie continued, gaze bouncing off Savvy, "we're premature meeting your friend here."

Green eyes pinched, Savvy leaned forward. "Who the hell do you think you are?"

"Stop it," Slade said. "Both of you."

Callie sat back, more than happy to have played the bad cop, turning the reins over to Slade. If she was right, Slade would now be able to press more, focus her questions and worry less about the friendship. Nothing she hated more than wasting time.

And Savvy would cooperate with Slade to avoid Callie.

Slade began anew. "Savvy, are you aware of Simmons's hunting compound out there? That he's spending more time training people how to shoot than he is farming? That's what we're calling militia, maybe for lack of a better word."

"Had no idea," Savvy replied short and tight, a bite-me stare on Callie.

Slade waved her fingers. "Attention here, please. Have you inspected his farm, his equipment, or his crop in the last year?"

Savvy reluctantly turned full attention to Slade. "Me or my office?"

"You, personally."

"No, I haven't."

Slade kept her expression nonjudgmental. "When's the last time you did?"

"Maybe two years ago. Connor's good, and besides, it's why you have staff, so you don't have to touch every account."

Good. Slade had slipped into an interview, and while not recorded or formal, it was getting the job done. They could revisit something more formal later.

"Connor's from Colleton County, right?" Slade asked.

"Yes."

"So he'd be more aware about St. Clair's business," Slade said. "*Now* you can go fetch him."

Savvy left the room, this time not quite as hot as before.

"Can you rely on her?" Callie asked.

"A thousand percent," Slade said. "She takes some getting used to, but you want her on your side. She has her moods."

Callie looked at her phone. "Never would've noticed. And I don't want to step on your toes, but . . . ."

"But what? Let me have it."

The phone went back in Callie's pocket. "This is your realm, but I'd have queried Connor first, without telling him I was coming and without having Savannah in the room. Might've talked to him before we went to

Simmons's place this morning, too, in order to get a feel for what he senses Simmons is about. You already saw a new tractor last night, not to mention the compound, so Connor's insight might've served you well when you went to the farm today."

"He could have also tried to con me."

"All the same, you're better equipped if you seek the target last, after you've fully armed yourself with the facts."

Slade sat stoically, and Callie wasn't quite sure she'd ticked her off or if Slade was recalibrating. Slade wasn't formally trained but had shown some experience in the field. Callie, however, had a substantial quantity of both . . . just not with farmers. She'd arrested people of various professions across the spectrum, though. White collar and blue. Educated and not. The criminal, the insane, and the incredibly stupid. She'd never seen professional investigative techniques get in the way of running an investigation.

Slade seemed to think the agriculture culture and answers came first.

"Then there's the issue of jumping when your friend called," Callie continued. "She could've waited."

"Wait a second . . ."

Callie waited, but Slade seemed turned around in her thoughts. Guess she expected she rode with a cop as a physical backup but not mental. A lot of folks assumed cops acted more than thought, and few understood the depth of a detective's perception of people. Or the value of a training officer. She doubted Slade had ever really had one of those. But she deserved one, and Callie had kept her mouth shut since yesterday and struggled to be nothing more than a traveling companion.

"You sent her out there to retrieve this guy," Callie said, motioning where Savvy turned the corner. "And who says they aren't getting their stories straight?" She could see how Wayne butted heads with his fiancée on the job.

"You're wrong," Slade said.

The door opened. Savvy sported a baffled pout. "He stepped out."

Slade stood and headed out to look for herself. "What do you mean he stepped out?" She peered back toward the main office like Connor might appear and Savvy just missed him. Irritated, Slade asked, "What's on his calendar?"

"One appointment he marked cancelled," Savvy said, flushed, her embarrassment loud and clear. The woman's office manager had jumped ship during a time she couldn't possibly need him more.

Hands on hips, Slade wasn't pleased. "Is he in the habit of driving off like this?"

"No," Savvy said, the calmer voice of the two now. "He's not."

"Is his car gone?"

"I ran out to see if I could catch him, but it wasn't there," she replied. "He left a leave slip on his technician's desk. Told her it was deer season and he was hitting the woods to put meat in the freezer."

Slade nudged Savvy into the conference room and closed them in. "With his boss right here on site, he goes deer hunting without your say-so." Slade waved at Callie and herself. "With the two of us arriving to research one of his accounts . . . an account we'd already passed on to the IG."

"I'll deal with him," Savvy said.

"Darn right you will," Slade replied. "Tell him to get his pea-brain back here. He can't be far, and he darn sure isn't up in a tree yet." She jabbed an angry finger at the carpet. "He gets back here now, today. If he doesn't, he's AWOL, without pay." Slade tried not to look over at Callie, the I-told-you-so opportunity too easy. She didn't want to see it on Callie's face. "Text him. Phone him. However you want, but tell him to return to this office. I'll be waiting."

Savvy already had the phone to her ear, but she soon hung up and tried again. After three tries, she held out the device. "He has his phone turned off." Without asking, she began texting. "Let me also talk to the others," she added, still typing as she left to see the others.

"Just a sec," Callie called. Savvy turned.

"Is Connor married?" she asked.

"Recently divorced," Savvy replied. "She found someone else about a year ago. Since there were no kids, she admitted to the adultery, so it only took three months. Slammed him hard."

"Where's he live?"

"With his mother, last I heard, but I've never gotten into his personal business too deep. I've tried to let him alone about it."

Callie motioned in the general direction of the staff. "Also confirm his address with your people," she said. "A single guy can live anywhere."

Savvy looked to Slade for approval, got the nod, and left. Callie saw there was an actual chain of command after all.

The government-issue clock read four.

"I'm calling Wayne," Slade said.

Callie lifted her own phone. "I'm calling Raysor." When Slade showed a disconnect with the name, Callie added, "That *round* Colleton deputy who works with me at the beach. He's related to half this county." Raysor's ear stayed to the ground gathering up Colleton rumor, and he might have a better idea about Connor's whereabouts. And his ethics.

The Colleton County Sheriff's Office had aided her in many a situation coping with Edisto Beach issues, and now seemed the time for her to give back to the county. She wouldn't ordinarily give a tinkers' damn about a farmer not farming right, but Wayne's dead partner tipped that scale. Until Slade or Wayne tossed her to the curb, she'd use her connections to help. She was changing her job title from babysitter to partner.

Jasmine Bright, assigned to investigate the man, died on Simmons's place. The man envisioned himself as a two-bit soldier of fortune. Then the Ag employee who'd made the loans to Simmons had chosen to scram rather than answer to his higher-ups.

Deer season had not a damn thing to do with his departure.

# Chapter 13

## *Slade*

BEFORE WE LOST more staff, I drew each one aside, and told them quitting time wasn't a factor until each had been interviewed. Unasked but appreciated, Callie used her phone as a recorder, reading in the intro and closing information each interview required as I queried the three about Connor and St. Clair Simmons.

The temperature in the room had risen a few degrees with the small conference room's door shut and its rotating occupants radiating fear. We left Savvy out of the interviews for obvious reasons, and I felt as sorry for the staff stuck waiting with her as I questioned my next *victim*. At least that's how their facial expressions registered the events.

While Agriculture had need for investigators like me, like Wayne, the average employee had no working knowledge of what we did, nor the crimes committed under Ag's umbrella until they were sucked into an investigation like this one. These three women, a clerk and two technicians, felt gob-smacked as to why I arrived with a cop in tow, why their regional boss Savvy showed unannounced, and why their immediate leader vanished, leaving them to twist in an unknown ill wind.

Who could blame them for not trusting us? We'd made the person they did trust run for the hills.

Sometimes it took an investigator asking the right questions to scratch their memory and bring issues to light. We had to tap their mental databases before they scattered for the day, got together and muddied each other's thoughts . . . or contacted Connor.

Callie and I queried them about St. Clair Simmons, the consensus being he was a harmless county resident who pretended to be bigger and badder than he was. They stated few in the community took him seriously, either, and with the cloudy purpose of Mini-Hawk, folks thought even less of him. A man going through a mid-life crisis, one described.

However, he owned enough property to be respected among the rural landowners, meaning he maintained his land and paid his taxes, keeping developers at arms' length. He held only a minimal reputation as a solid farmer, so when he shifted to teaching hunting, survivalist, and firearms classes, no one seemed much surprised.

"Have to hand it to them," Callie said as we let the last employee leave. We'd told each of them as they left to take an extra hour off sometime this week. "They believed enough in Connor Boone to follow him blindly."

Whether that was good or not remained to be seen. Depended on why Connor took off, and whether any staff had been a party to whatever reason why. "Since he wasn't too upset about St. Clair being behind, they weren't either," I said. "They assumed he had things under control, or had some sort of plan with Simmons. I'm not reading intent in any of them."

I finished a comment on a pad, preferring to see my words than rely on recordings that could get erased or corrupted. "Their lives aren't accustomed to bad things, Callie. That's on cable TV. Even when he abandoned them, they believed that his disappearance had to be important. They live in a bubble."

"Yes," Callie said, "but once backed into a corner, they agreed he probably hadn't gone deer hunting." She checked out the Keurig on the corner table, peering inside, then decided against using it. "Ever seen them interview neighbors of murderers? *He was a nice guy. I'm stunned he could do such a thing.* His personal life's screwed up." Callie came back to lean on the chair she'd obviously grown tired of. "That can send anyone down the wrong path."

Boy, could I walk that walk. Callie had a dark history, so she could talk that story, too.

*That poor man*, the three staff kept saying about Connor. More of a boy to them since the youngest was easily a decade older. He'd been beside himself for the last year, they said, after his wife dumped him. Surely that contributed to the stress they'd witnessed these last months.

His employee fan club hadn't been much help to me, and from Callie's expression, her.

Callie went to open the door. "Mind if I air out this room? Anxiety can really stink up a place. They were horrified that Connor left them hanging."

But they hadn't thrown him to the wolves yet, either.

Savvy peered in. "Can I enter? Everyone's gone."

"Sure," I said.

As Callie had warned me, I'd seen Savvy as a complete ally, full of the answers I needed with no doubt as to what she said, which meant I'd wrongly assumed her staff was on a tight leash and completely aboveboard. Connor scurrying off had surprised her more than it had me, leaving me concerned about her awareness of activities in Colleton County.

But with her being sideswiped and humiliated, she'd cooperate to the *nth* degree. I understood that much about her.

Savvy picked up St. Clair Simmons's file.

"Don't think anything we're looking for is in those pages," I said, studying my notes.

She slapped the folder shut. "Then how can I help?"

"By telling us things that aren't in the file. Whether you agree with your staff." I slid the notebook around and across to her to read her staff's comments.

A few moments later, she slid them back. "That's exactly how I perceived him. Simmons, too."

"What's *not* in the file about Simmons?" I asked. "Or *not* in those interviews about Connor? Think."

Callie watched, chin propped on the heel of one hand. Wasn't sure I had the patience to be her. And I kept feeling judged.

"Like what?" Savvy said.

I shrugged. "You tell me."

Callie leaned forward. "Like reactions. Like personal life. Questionable behavior that stopped you even for a second but you discarded. What others whispered to you in line at the store. Gossip, disturbed routine. How's anything different today than a year ago, since that seems to be a pivotal moment in Connor's life . . . and coincidentally timed with St. Clair not paying the first time?"

I hadn't thought about the year's similarities like that.

As I ripped off the interviews and gave the clean pad to Savvy, a knock sounded at the outside door.

I went to the entrance to find Wayne standing on the office stoop taking note of the parking lot. "Callie still with you, I see." Her patrol car remained at the end under an oak tree. "But why'd you get Savvy over here?" Everybody recognized that car and the license tag that said, of all things, SAVVY, and she'd parked it right up front, next to the entrance.

"She just showed," I said under my breath. "She and Callie are inside. Everyone else is gone. After what happened today, Callie pulled in her Deputy Raysor who's supposed to be on his way."

Insuring the lock wasn't engaged, he drew me outside. "Why, what happened? We don't need a herd of people on this."

"First, Savvy texted, upset we were here for Simmons without advanced notice."

"Well, hell, Slade, she can get over that," he said.

"By the time we got here from Simmons's place, she was waiting for us, but that's not the real issue."

He scratched a gnat from the side of his neck, waiting, no surprise at Savvy's conduct.

"Connor Boone, the local guy who managed the Simmons's account, took off without getting permission, waiting until I had Savvy occupied before he did." When Wayne didn't say anything, I assumed he had to think about this.

"If you recall," he said, "she underestimated her staff in Beaufort, too."

I hadn't wanted to say that aloud . . . to him or to her. No doubt she'd already thought about the two who'd manipulated records and money right under her nose before. She almost went to jail for the fraud except I took the case personally and, after dragging Monroe down there to assist, solved the mystery. We'd saved her ass, and I doubted she slept a night without reliving some part of it. A knife scar across my ribs reminded me.

Monroe was now boss to both of us, and he was the last person willing to take chances. How he'd view Savvy as a manager if this went badly remained to be seen. As the state kingpin of Agriculture, politics could alter his vision. She'd update him only if he summoned.

"We left texts and messages for Connor," I said. "He's not answering. With you running in one direction and me in another, I wasn't sure where to take this until you got here, so I didn't send anybody to his house."

Wayne's curious stare spoke loudly. Since when did Slade wait for his advice?

But a dead agent trumped a lot of things, and with it being Wayne's dead agent that sort of put me in my place. I might fight for how I wanted to investigate my cases, but he had the right to approve or veto me this time.

His eye caught the ring he'd put on my finger, and the corner of his mouth gave a twitch. The reminder gave him a positive moment amidst the sorrow, and he let himself be happy for a second.

I hadn't had time to be thrilled, to feel engaged. Not in these circumstances.

A Sheriff's Office unit turned in, dipping hard at the driveway due to the heavy foot behind the wheel. With a sharp right, he parked one over from Callie's unit, and the car creaked as he relieved the vehicle of his weight.

"Deputy Don Raysor," Wayne said, meeting him partway with outstretched hand. "Glad to see you again. We were about to head inside."

As they entered the conference room, Savvy grinned big at Wayne, but her smile dissipated at the sight of Raysor and his uniform. Regardless, Wayne strode over for a hug, Savvy gripping him extra hard while offering her condolences for Jasmine.

Then from both their sudden grins, she must have whispered something in his ear that had to be congratulations.

"Now that all the law is present and accounted for, how're we doing this?" I asked.

"Let Savvy stay for a while," Wayne said, which appeared to soften Savvy's nerves. "She can order the pizza, too. Is there a drink machine around here?"

Savvy leaped to her feet. "I'll place the order. They're only around the corner, and the Coke machine is in a vestibule outside the next office over. Only takes coins but we keep a cursing jar in the front office. Happy to rob it."

She left to place the order.

Wayne shut the door.

We updated Wayne and Raysor. Simmons's activity was suspicious. Connor's reaction was overly suspicious. Savvy seemed in the dark, which surprised Wayne. Disappointed me. Without words Callie made it clear she didn't trust Savvy, and Raysor held his words. I still trusted Savvy but was saddened by her innocence.

With the hodge-podge of opinions scattered around the room, we conceded to the biggest badge for the next step.

"I have a preliminary coroner's report." He pulled out his phone to read, and to my surprise, he slipped out reading glasses I'd never seen.

"Wait, what are those?" I asked.

He peered over the top of them, and I hushed. On second thought, I rather liked the look, the black frames matching the dark in his salt and pepper beard.

"The anaphylaxis stands as cause of death. Time of death around three a.m., give or take. Toxicology will take a few days. Also some bruising on her left upper arm." He held out his phone hand and motioned to the area with the other. "Around here."

"Did she fight with someone?" I said.

"We don't know what it means," he said. "Did she hit her arm fighting the hornets?" He sighed big at the end. "We'll find out after the full autopsy."

We quieted, everyone surely envisioning their version of how that scene spun out. The panic. The suffocation. The wonder about whether another being participated, or worse, watched without assistance.

To me, bruising high up on her arm meant someone else was probably there, but I kept quiet. Wayne hated when I came to conclusions without every tiny step proven in fact. "What about her mother?" I asked. "You going to tell her the particulars?"

"No, I'd rather wait until we have more information." He removed the glasses.

My stomach grumbled, and I mashed my middle to quiet the noise. Wayne looked fatigued after two nights of snatched sleep, and suddenly my muscles felt the lack of *zzzz's* as well.

"Spoke to ATF, too," he said, which jerked me back from my physical needs. "Mini-Hawks is an LLC and has a firearms license. Had an agent from ATF Regulatory go through the inspection reports. No sanctions for noncompliance. Only had a smattering of gun sales, mostly from people who took the Concealed Weapon Permit courses."

"So not enough to pay his farm debt," I said, ever attuned to the farm aspect of things.

"Not even close," he replied and leaned against the wall, hands in pockets.

"FBI take any sort of interest?" Callie asked. "I know a guy."

"Yeah, I do, too," Wayne said. "But no."

She frowned. "SLED?"

The South Carolina Law Enforcement Division served as our state version of FBI. City police and sheriff's departments relied heavily on their forensics. Wayne nodded and delivered the bad news. "They're doing the toxicology, but as you probably know, a fast turnaround is two weeks at best."

"More like six," Raysor said, speaking up for the first time. Callie agreed with a weak smile, the respect evident between them.

I had to say it. Everyone thought it. "So are we saying nothing's being investigated about Jasmine?"

The sadness in Wayne's eyes spoke before he did. "SLED and Colleton County have been out there hunting for signs to say differently, but with this coroner's report, I'm afraid it's probably going down as an overzealous girl having an accident."

That made sense, except—"At three in the morning?"

A hard knock sounded and Savvy swooped in with two large pepperoni pizzas. "Here, take these," she said to Wayne. "Hope nobody's a vegetarian." Then she disappeared and returned with an armload of soft drinks and water, enough for twice our number. "Wasn't sure what you guys wanted, so I just got enough to have choices."

She doted on everyone, overly eager to appease, and she didn't sit and participate until she'd met our needs. As we ate, conversation turned generic. Talking about a dead woman while downing slices and Cokes seemed inappropriate.

Especially a woman whose death might not be avenged, a fact we were trying to absorb. I didn't think anyone at the table honestly bought the hornet attack. Radar was going off in all of us. It certainly didn't feel so cut-and-dried to me, and from the looks of Wayne, he felt the same.

"I've been thinking, y'all." Savvy spoke low, respecting the mood. "Earlier Callie said to think about gossip."

From the quick crease of his brow, Wayne had no idea what she meant. Raysor showed no interest other than in his paper plate of food.

Animated, clearly showing a desire to make up for earlier, Savvy wiped her mouth and shoved the crust on her napkin to the side. "St. Clair Simmons is known for having a girlfriend. That's kind of what you meant when you said think outside the file, right?"

"Maybe," I said. "We did find lingerie receipts in his farm records."

"Seriously?" Raysor said. "This guy really *is* a dumb f—"

"Don," Callie interrupted, quashing the word.

Savvy kept going. "And he goes to Beaufort a lot, right?"

"Saw the seafood and booze receipts for his hunting parties, or whatever they are," I replied. "From Beaufort."

Callie tossed her napkin on the plate. "So who's the girlfriend? She might shed some insight."

"They've changed over the years," Savvy said. "But it's not like they're hookers he orders as needed. Word has it he's held onto one for close to four or five years."

"Who's word?" Callie asked.

"Really? You said gossip," Savvy said with an irritated stare, then returned to her story. "Doubtful they ate in public, and if I were him, I'd use that motel over near Frogmore and avoid Beaufort eyes. That one and one other on Lady's Island."

"Yeah," Raysor said. "I'm sensing a romantic McDonald's back at the room." He gave us an eye roll.

I snagged my pad again. "Got a name?"

Savvy threw stink-eye looks at Raysor. "I haven't seen her, and nobody knows her name."

"Well, the wife can't tell us anything." Callie turned to Raysor. "Heard of any of this?"

The deputy came up for air from his third slice. "He keeps a mistress, and he don't flaunt her in Colleton, so what Legs says over there sounds right."

Savvy snapped her head toward me in amazement. "What rock did he crawl out from under?"

I gave her my best let-it-go look. I'd heard him address Callie as *Doll* without her dismay. If he could police well, I cared little what nicknames he threw around. Especially since his attention was on pizza and not the woman.

Wayne shifted in his seat, stretching his legs under the table. "How do you even know that, Don?"

"These are my people," Raysor said. "My kin work in almost every establishment in this county. Just saying if he's smart, he'd take her to Beaufort with him where he feels more . . ." He gave a coy flip of his hand. ". . . discreet."

"His wife hasn't left him after years of knowing he sleeps elsewhere," I said. "Not sure an adulterous reputation matters much."

"Oh, he'd be discreet," Raysor said. "A lot of women get even around here."

That bit of news quieted the room.

Wayne chuckled sadly and went for his Coke. "You ladies asked for gossip and you got it. Now what're you gonna do with it?"

But Savvy had me thinking. "St. Clair has a girlfriend he can't date here." I held up a second finger. "He goes to Beaufort to get seafood for whatever it is he does at Mini-Hawk."

"See gas tickets from Beaufort in that shoebox?" Callie asked.

"Quite a few. But what else is Beaufort known for?"

"Boats," Raysor said.

I shook my head.

"Military," Savvy said.

I pointed at her like a gameshow host. "And what do you find around the military?"

"Firearms and ammunition," Wayne said, slowly sitting up.

Nothing was spoken as we studied each other, waiting for the next person to come up with a new connecting piece. Nobody did.

"I thought we had something there," I said, disappointed.

"Still, hold onto all that. But don't lose sight of the mission." Callie held up her two fingers. "We figure out why St. Clair Simmons hasn't paid his debt, and figure out why Jasmine Bright was in his woods. What can we do toward either or both those ends?"

"Talk to Connor, and talk to Jasmine's mother," I said. "Then after that, revisit St. Clair."

Raysor threw his soiled paper plate in the empty pizza box. "If I were you, I'd seek out the women."

"Women?" I asked.

Savvy blew out a breath. "Jesus, who is this guy."

"Yeah," Raysor said, ignoring Savvy and stretching out the long syllable into two longer ones with his Lowcountry drawl. "Women. The mysterious girlfriend and Connor Boone's ex. People . . ." He scanned the room in mockery. "Surely you've learned nothing talks louder than an incensed female. Make 'em mad about a man and they'll spill every thought in their head."

Disapproving, Savvy laid arms on the table, directly across from the deputy. "How have you kept your job—Scratch that. How have you lived this long with that caveman attitude?"

Raysor only tried to humor her with a look down his nose. "Tell me it won't work."

"But we've already determined we don't know St. Clair's girl," I said.

He laughed, then laughed again. "She don't know that, though. Gossip got you this far, let it take you the rest of the way."

Wayne set down his bottle. "I'll grant what Don says makes sense, but we're missing the obvious."

"Yes," I said. "We should be looking for Connor."

"Unless he's independently wealthy, he'll show up sooner or later," Raysor said. "Man needs his job. I say check out the women first."

Nobody could argue with that, but we could add a third woman to the list . . . Jasmine's mother. How had she not known her daughter was coming home to visit?

# Chapter 14

## *Slade*

THOUGH UNHAPPY with the decision, Savvy accepted our instruction to remain behind and maintain order at the Walterboro office in case Connor didn't return the next day . . . and call ASAP if he did.

"Can I interrogate staff?" she asked.

"She sure sounds like you," Callie uttered, leaving the room.

"I'll leave that up to you," I replied to my old friend, a brief look at Callie. "Just don't scare them into quitting because Monroe would have a conniption fit. Remember he's your boss now." A fact Savvy had as much trouble remembering as I did. The two of us had always run over him, and here he was on the throne.

Callie and Raysor decided their work day had concluded, and I didn't much blame them. Raysor left for his place barely two miles toward town, and Callie headed for the beach. "Gives me a chance to check on my office," she said. "I'll hold your room. Take your time. I'll leave the alarm off till you get there."

She and Raysor would return the next day to stroke his relatives. Those at the sheriff's office, the courthouse, maybe, and any other location Raysor deemed might have a relative ripe for gossip-mongering. He was intent on that strategy of his, that if the girlfriend heard enough talk about her boyfriend's questionable business, maybe to include concerns over a dead girl, she might step forward. Or at least bitch loud enough to be spotted. Or the overturned rocks might uncover a lead to the girlfriend.

Wayne and I decided to handle Connor's ex tonight. As oddball as our team was, Wayne and I held the only proper authority. Our official case being St. Clair. The unofficial case being Jasmine. With the third not-yet-criminal issue of Connor's disappearance also fitting squarely in agriculture's bucket of unsolved items.

So Callie and I shifted partners. Hadn't had much time with Wayne, so I relished the change.

Savvy locked up the office, and we saw her to her Mercedes. From the fog of our breath, an expected cold front had arrived, its icy gusts likely stripping the lingering orange and red leaves off maples and oaks before night was through.

The aroma of hamburgers wafted over from a Sonic Drive-In across the street and down a hundred yards on Robertson Boulevard, the neon harsh against the evening sky. Seven thirty meant dark after the loss of daylight savings time.

"Connor's ex's name is Rebecca?" I'd reached Savvy's car and wanted to make sure my facts were straight before she left.

"Maiden name was Ingle in case she took it back," Savvy said, "but she went by Boone last I heard. Connor wasn't chatty about the break-up, but word has it she kicked him to the curb and kept the house. Receives alimony on top of her job, which to me is plain wrong."

We saw Savvy off, and once her taillights disappeared south toward Beaufort, the parking lot took on a desolate ambiance, the lone street-light offering minimal security amidst the shadows of twenty-year-old trees and their windy sway. Wrapping my arms up close, a shiver pierced and lingered. The temp had to be in the thirties, and my heavy coat remained locked in my truck in the back lit corner.

"Can't believe we're alone," Wayne said, wrapping an arm around me.

"Love you, too, Cowboy, but your car or my truck? I'm freezing my butt off."

"Mine belongs to the government," he said. "Might as well use their mileage and gas unless you're talking about other than driving."

After retrieving my coat from my truck, I insured nothing stood out that a prowler might consider worth breaking in to snare, and locked it up tight. I fully expected to find frost on the windshield in the morning.

Wayne dialed up the heat in his vehicle. "This arms-length pretense that we aren't an item wears me out sometimes." He tapped a finger on his cheek. "Don't you dare buckle in without giving me one right here."

Stretching, I reached to oblige. He twisted to plant his lips on mine, and that's all it took. That first long, deep kiss became another, and our hands wandered under coats and shirts to find flesh, and we let ourselves enjoy a hard and fast ten minutes of lust with our clothes on.

What had felt inappropriate last night, due to Jasmine's death, seemed overdue now.

His heavy sigh warmed my neck. "We need to get going."

I sighed back.

He buckled up, but we remained parked with him staring ahead.

"I'm sorry how events spoiled things, Slade. We've had no chance to really talk about us. Or do any of the planning stuff that's supposed to be fun."

"Supposed to be?"

His mouth squirmed to the side. "Not exactly the right words."

"I know what you're trying to say, Wayne. But since you brought it up, which planning are you talking about?" I shifted my feet directly under the heater on the floor. "Planning a wedding or planning our life?"

He hadn't expected that. "You make it sound ominous. I guess both."

Wayne prided himself on being a strong, collected soul, but in our sideways chats about becoming something more permanent, we'd never delved into the details as to how his life would fit into mine. Or mine into his. My life was way messier with two kids, a house on the lake, and a live-in-sister. He managed a bachelor's life in an apartment. We always spoke in ambiguous terms like *I hate leaving you to go home* or *maybe one day we won't have to do this,* when we parted after a date. So easy to say when you didn't have to deliver on that pretty sentiment.

Still, as dedicated as he'd been in waiting for me, I'd envisioned him the mature, got-his-facts-together half of us who preserved a wedding day image in his head along with an ironed-out honeymoon. But me? I'd been afraid of opening the darn ring box for eighteen months, much less considered how to share furnishings, update insurance beneficiaries . . . set dates.

His unexpected nerves suddenly became my nerves.

And one stupid, unspoken thought kept rebounding around my skull. Years downstream, what would we say when people asked at tailgate events or dinner parties, *How'd you two get engaged?*

And we'd say, In a fancy restaurant, of course. With wait staff and diners holding their breath when Wayne left the box on the white linen tablecloth. You know . . . the night his partner died.

Like having your birthday on September 11, or your mother dying on Christmas Day.

"How are we approaching Rebecca?" I asked, tucking into my coat for warmth, not wishing to delve into a personal conversation that could last till dawn.

"Depends on how much she still cares for him," he said, instantly back into investigative mode like it was the more comfortable place to be. "Follow my lead, okay? No ad-libbing guesswork."

Yep, we were back to normal.

Took twenty minutes to find the subdivision, and another few to circle around to the correct street. The oldest house couldn't have been more than five years old from the size of the shrubbery. The developer had leveled the trees, sold off the topsoil, then stair-stepped the lots to accommodate slabs. Nothing natural about that sort of construction, but they sold fast enough from the lit sign flaunting *Phase Three - Open for Contract.*

Three blocks and still looking. How long *was* Marion Street?

Wayne slowed. "There, in the drive. Isn't that a white Ford Ranger?"

"Sure is." I spoke softer like it mattered we didn't spook our quarry. Fate had indeed come down on our side.

Wayne parked at the curb, blocking the truck, something I wouldn't do with my beloved truck under any circumstances. A government car maybe, but not my pickup. Exiting, we strode to the front stoop like guests for dinner. Even in the evening dark I felt open and exposed. There was a reason I never lived in subdivisions. Nosy neighbors. Surely one or more of these houses had already noted the ex-husband's vehicle in the ex-wife's drive.

With no lamp shining on the porch, the lit doorbell button showed the way. I reached to ring the bell, but Wayne held me back. "Listen first," he whispered, head turned to the right. "And like I've told you before, don't stand in front of a door before it's opened. Move that way." Which put me to the right and him to the left.

He had a habit of doing that at elevators, too. Like someone might let loose a shotgun when it opened. I'd hate to live in that man's head.

Voices raised inside, and I turned to interpret the commotion. Two voices duked it out. A male and a female.

"Can't understand what they're saying," I whispered.

"Shhh."

The shouting escalated. "I said leave," said the woman.

A thump on the back of the door, and I flattened against the brick. Wayne rang the bell then rapped hard. "Police. Open the door."

Surprisingly, they obliged. Or at least the woman did. The man wasn't to be seen.

"Ma'am." Wayne stared around her, hunting for the second party. Then behind him into the yard toward the truck. Back at her. "Are you Rebecca Boone?"

About my height, give or take, and she had her dander up judging from the breathing. In leggings and a long sweatshirt, her sneakers gave her a gym-loving appearance. Half of her still hid behind the door. "Yes,

I'm Rebecca, why?" The last word had a bite to it. "*Who the hell are you?*" sort of nailed her attitude.

His left hand folding back his coat, Wayne revealed the badge on his belt. "Federal agent."

"Oh," she said, taking it down a notch. "What's the deal?"

*What's the deal?* Deja vu hit me of Wayne setting foot on my porch what seemed like a lifetime ago. An agent on my doorstep had stunned me speechless.

"We heard an argument." Wayne stepped in, but she wasn't backing up. "Where's your husband?"

She amazingly held her ground. "I'm no longer married, and I don't know what you mean."

"Dump the whole *Gone With the Wind* deal," I said. "Sounded like a romper room in here. Where's Connor?"

Rebecca's eyebrows pinched, then her whole demeanor changed. "Oh, hold on, y'all." She giggled. Giggled! "I think I can solve this dilemma. Come on in."

Inside, gas logs burned in a tiny fireplace, a flat screen hung above the mantel. She lifted the remote from an end table and returned the sound to a Jason Bourne movie, the volume remarkably high for my taste.

"I muted it to answer the door," Rebecca said, hands clasped with the remote against her chest, speaking up to be heard over the chase scene. "Sorry you had to yell, but I didn't hear you. I was doing yoga during the movie, and—"

Wayne grabbed the remote and hit mute.

"What about the thump?" I asked in a raised voice.

She shrugged. "I'm not very good at it."

Wayne spun and returned to the front porch . . . about the time I heard the truck engine.

Unable to back out of the drive due to Wayne's strategic block, Connor had backed to and fro enough to skirt across the lawn and cross the curb to Marion Street, in the direction we drove from.

Wayne ran shouting. "Connor Boone! Stop! Federal Agent."

Connor stopped, all right. His window rolled down, he took a split second to aim a nine millimeter and shoot the front and back tires of Wayne's car.

Wayne drew his weapon only for Connor to get gone too fast . . . and to realize the neighborhood was too full of windows able to catch stray bullets.

Rebecca shoved me to the side. I bounced off the brick corner into holly bushes, while she leaped the two steps to ground level and onto the grass, her remote in a fisted grip. "Connor, you idiot!" she screeched.

Neighbors no longer hid their curiosity, watching from every lit up porch for six houses either direction and on both sides of the street.

Wayne strode back, hard purpose in his steps. "You," he ordered Rebecca. "Back to the porch."

He abruptly stopped at the bushes and assisted me to my feet. "What do you want me to do?" I said, picking off prickly leaves stabbing through my pants legs.

"Watch her," he said, huffing, half-angry, undeniably frustrated as he extracted cuffs and slapped them on her wrists behind her back.

"What did I do?" she cried, as he made her plop her butt on the cement step.

"You assaulted me," I said.

Wayne punched numbers into his phone. "If she runs, do whatever it takes to throw her down."

Wow, that was a first. I almost wished she'd give me the chance to leap into action.

Rebecca's lips pouted. "This isn't fair."

"Just stay seated," I ordered, moving to stand guard behind and to the side of her.

Wayne said nothing about going back inside, so here we'd stay, possibly to see if Connor circled back. He might be craving to finish what he'd started with his ex or curious what we did with her. So far he'd proven the idiot Rebecca touted.

Wayne dialed 911, relaying his identity, Connor's name, and the tag of Connor's truck. No way he could've seen it the way Connor drove off, which meant he noted it when we arrived. I should have.

The way temps were dropping, the night air might frost leaves by morning, but the chill seemed to impact Rebecca none. She kept staring off in the distance where Connor'd disappeared, no longer enraged about the cuffs. "I'll just be damned," she kept saying, then peered around at me. "Did you see what he did?"

"The whole neighborhood saw what he did," I replied, wondering what the hell got into a man who'd had the reputation of a quiet, clean cut, reliable guy.

"Maybe the mother f-er is finally trying to grow a pair of balls." She looked up and behind at me. "He's a different man."

I stepped back, about to remind her she would land in her own holly bushes if she tried to touch me again.

"Only owned a rifle for deer hunting," she continued, gushing. "Kept trying to get him to buy a sidearm or at least borrow mine to go get his concealed weapon permit." A soft sigh. "He went and got it on his own. Oh, Connor."

She'd clearly worn the pants in the family . . . or ex-family, but the redneck honey had developed a fresh, half-cocked admiration for her ex-husband. I hoped she enjoyed prison visitations, because the man who'd moments ago been only an Agriculture employee with an administrative issue, had graduated to breaking federal law. He'd fired at a federal agent, destroyed government property, and interfered with a case. Internally, he'd done what most employees didn't realize could put them in serious jeopardy: refused to participate in an investigation.

I'd wanted to give him the benefit of the doubt when he ran off after Savvy, Callie, and I showed up. He could've had a valid reason. This much authority could've really rattled him, but I didn't care what his reason was now. I had enough clout to insure his job was toast, and I'd make sure of it with Monroe.

Wayne hung up from 911 and made a brief call to Raysor. Neither man was much for long-winded conversation.

"Raysor's coming with another deputy to take our statements and give us a ride back to your truck," he said. "He's sending a wrecker for my car." That he said to me, but when he turned to Rebecca his tone hardened. "What were you two arguing about in there?"

She didn't even try to use the movie cover again. "He wanted to hide here for whatever reason."

She wriggled, starting to rise. I placed a foot on her cuffs to plant her butt back on the stoop, meriting a wicked stare over her shoulder.

"He's hurting for money, I know that," she said back to Wayne. "He's behind on his alimony."

"If he stayed here and didn't have to pay rent, he could better afford to pay you," I said.

"Just what he said," she exclaimed, only I was joking.

"Has he mentioned St. Clair Simmons?" Wayne asked.

Rebecca made a mashed up, quirky thing with her mouth, like there wasn't much to say about that. "A farmer. Connor's talked about him some. Considered a redneck in these parts."

The pot calling the kettle . . .

"Did he like the man? Dislike him? Do business with him? What?" I winced hearing my drawl deepen from my exposure to her.

"Seemed to be okay about him. Connor liked his place."

"So he socialized with Simmons?"

Wayne was letting me go with this line of questioning, an ear on me, his eyes on the street.

Rebecca seemed not to care about the subject. The puzzlement on her face clearly showing she wondered why any of this mattered. "The man owned land and Connor always wanted to own land like that. He went out there. That's about it."

"Connor must be afraid of something to want to hide here," Wayne said, half-hidden in the dark. "What do you think that was?"

"Can't exactly say," she replied. "He can be a pussy. His biggest weakness." Tucking her legs, she laid her cheek on her knees. "But damn, the way he popped your car tires has me rethinking that favor he asked of me. I've missed him."

Wayne gave up on her and rested against the brick, avoiding being obvious. Neighbors still ogled but not as many as before. We'd left the porch light off.

"Can I go inside?" Rebecca asked. "I'm cold."

"No," Wayne replied, curt. About that time a Colleton County cruiser pulled up, and not far behind them came Raysor. Wayne pushed off the brick and met them partway.

Rebecca peered over her shoulder at me. "Why's your man so mean? I don't deserve handcuffs."

"You aided a wanted man, and if given the chance you'd call him," I said. "And we've been waiting to see if he'll cruise by checking on you."

Damned if a soft look of affection didn't take her over. "You think so? I was a hint disappointed he'd left me to deal with y'all by myself." She laid her cheek back down on her knees. "Can't believe the bastard still loves me."

Holy bejesus.

The guys studied the G-car's tires, listened to Wayne, then came over to interview Rebecca, taking it inside.

"Want me to wait out here and watch?" I asked.

"No need," Wayne said, on the threshold. "Not so sure one of these houses hasn't already phoned Connor to tell him we're still out here. Regardless, he'd have to know we've put an APB out and flagged him as armed. He's not coming back. He's hunting for a hideout."

I followed him in, and he launched into Rebecca before I had time to shut the door. "Do you realize I could lock you up for twelve, maybe eighteen months? Is that what you want?"

Rebecca stood firm, though, hands still behind her. "Believe it when I see it."

The deputies chuckled all around, and her sneer at them only added to the show.

"Tell you what I'm willing to do, though," Wayne said.

"What, we're dealing? I'm not turning him in, no matter what."

"Phone Connor," he said, ignoring her remark. "Pump him up about how turned on you were by his fine shooting. You were, weren't you?"

"Damn straight."

"Good. Ask him where he's staying so you can come to him. Do that and I'll lessen the charges."

She thrust her chest out. "I will not be a traitor."

He motioned to Raysor. "Then take her, Deputy."

She backstepped into one of the deputies. "No, no, wait."

"Wrecker's here," said the other deputy. "I'll go handle the car," and he left.

"Time's running out," Wayne told her. "No reason both of you should live behind bars."

Gazing at the carpet, she agreed, justifying it as a safety issue so Connor didn't get shot as a fugitive. *Whatever worked in her redneck brain.*

After the deputies' car departed, along with the wrecker, only Wayne, I, and Rebecca remained. Raysor said he'd return when requested.

We wanted the scene back to normal, in case Connor swung back by.

Wayne retrieved Rebecca's phone and held it before her, on speaker, as the call went through to Connor.

"They've left," she said when he answered. "You can't come here, though." Her eyes held on Wayne trying to read how far she could go. "I love you, baby."

"You sure they're gone?" Connor asked.

"I'm sure. You went and got a sidearm, didn't you?" she said, and Wayne nodded she was doing fine. "You've been practicing, too," she said. "Damn, what a rush watching you shoot out those tires."

"You think so?"

"I know so," she said. "Two shots, two kills. God, I love you, baby. I miss you."

"I miss you, too." He sounded pitifully forlorn.

"Where are you?" she continued. "I'll come to you."

She pulled off the act well, most of the conversation legit. I tried to silently relay being impressed to Wayne, but instead he mouthed *Get me some paper.* I grabbed a random piece of junk mail on an end table along with a pen. As I held the paper still, he wrote while still holding the phone to the woman's ear.

"Sorry, 'Becca, but I'm too hot to come over there right now," Connor said. "And you'll only get in trouble coming to me. I'll cause you nothing but grief."

Wayne held up his note for her to read.

She read it. "I'm afraid for you even more, Lover. They might hunt you down . . . even kill you. Please, let me come to you. We have to see each other."

"Sorry. I love you with all my heart, 'Becca, but I can't put you in harm's way. Too much has happened."

He disconnected. She looked at us with tears in her eyes.

Almost ten years of agriculture service under Connor's belt, if I recalled correctly. Even if he had cut St. Clair slack in paying his debt, Connor would've been better off hanging around and coping with the fallout. He'd have gotten nothing more than a reprimand at best.

He could've listened, seen what we uncovered, noted our concerns, and made excuses. Made us maybe see his side. There were many reasons farmers didn't pay properly, many of them rational, and we had ways of extending payments. Connor bolting screamed that he considered himself in trouble before we did. Now he was on the lam. In my opinion, and in Wayne's, too, Connor worried about way more than his farmer paying late.

Raysor returned, collected the three of us, and toted Wayne and me back to the county office . . . Rebecca to jail. Waving bye to the deputy in the November chill, standing beside my truck, I bet my winter coat Wayne wanted to see St. Clair Simmons's compound first thing tomorrow morning.

Because visiting St. Clair Simmons's place at night had already proved a deathly endeavor for Jasmine.

# Chapter 15

## *Callie*

THE LIQUOR STORE owner was drawing his shades when Callie drove up asking for a favor. He gave her the eye when she set a fifth of Woodford Reserve on the counter, but she cared little. There would be bourbon on her kitchen bar awaiting Wayne and Slade when they dragged in, regardless what certain residents on Edisto thought about their chief's drinking habits.

The couple indeed dragged in. Close to midnight. The day Callie'd spent with Slade had been long enough, so they had to feel whipped putting more hours in.

She'd found Slade to be the more wordy of the pair and patiently listened to how the evening had evolved. The shooting. How Raysor had locked up Rebecca Boone. How Connor was still loose.

Slade hadn't wound down as much as Wayne. "And Wayne told Raysor to spread the word about Connor being wanted by federal and local authorities for several violations," she said, speed talking. "Assaulting federal agents with a firearm, attempted murder, eluding arrest. A couple other charges I can't remember. Labeled Connor armed and dangerous. And had them say he was aided by his ex who remains in custody."

Laying on the charges. Good. "Raysor will have it in the newspaper if I know him. Someone in his family has to own it."

"Nice," Wayne said, some circles under his eyes. "The Colleton Sheriff's Office will be hunting him everywhere, with a BOLO out to SLED and neighboring counties. Nice," he repeated, then hushed, sinking into a bar stool.

But Callie pulled him back into the conversation. She'd lost a partner in Boston . . . befriended others who'd lost partners. He didn't need time to wallow. Being engaged was best. "You're headed to the Simmons's compound in the morning I take it? Be glad to tag along if you feel you need another . . . body." She avoided the use of *badge* for Slade's benefit.

Slade grinned and let her get by with it, refilling her low-ball glass before catching herself, stopping in mid-fill. "Wait, this is bourbon," she said. "And good stuff at that."

"Your sleuthing skills never cease to amaze me," Callie said.

"Thought you . . ."

"Shouldn't drink? I don't melt in the presence of alcohol, Slade. Look here." She took the bottle and then Slade's glass. "I'll even pour it for you."

But she couldn't deny the temptation perched on her shoulder, the urge to lick the lip at least. Callie pivoted to refill Wayne's. "Need me tomorrow or not?" She suspected Wayne was reluctant to share the loss weighing him down.

He filled his mouth with drink before answering and exhaled through his nose after the huge swallow. "How much credence do you give Raysor's theory about flushing out the girlfriend?" he asked. "Is that worth bothering with?"

Callie assumed her place at the third bar stool in old sweats and a long-sleeved tee. Socked feet. She'd grown fond of these two, and they fit into her house like family cousins. "Ordinarily I'd say he enjoyed gossip too much, but the fact that this woman is a secret in a county where secrets don't hide easily tells me her relationship might not be welcomed amongst her people. Wary enough to keep her tryst from her closest friends, I'd guess. And another thing . . . she might legitimately love the man."

In a world of facts and clues, riddles and covert ways, the law could underestimate the depth of love.

Slade seemed not sold on the remark. "She might not be so steadfast to a man she learns killed someone."

"Unless she's the type who'd do it, too," Wayne added.

Callie smiled from behind her glass of ginger ale, turned it into a laugh to match Wayne's so-damn-appealing half-grin.

"What does this girlfriend have to lose?" Callie continued. "Maybe everything. And think about this . . . why is she satisfied with being the mistress instead of the wife? Is it the most she can achieve with him? She'd be the one he most likely shared his secrets with, I believe."

Wayne swirled the liquid in his glass. "I'd appreciate you going with Raysor then, if you don't mind. If this affair is the best kept secret in town, then she can keep anything tight-lipped to include what happened to Jasmine."

"People talk in bed," Slade said.

Wayne finished off the last of the chips in a bowl they'd slid back and forth across the bar top. "Is there a double meaning there?"

"No, and I don't mean it literally, silly," she said. "It's just that you let your guard down with your significant other. It's part of the joy of a tight relationship. Trust. Violate that and no telling how a scorned party will spread talk."

"So we better not break up?"

Slade blew out in frustration. "Not what I meant."

But her logic was sound.

"So tomorrow's plans are . . . ?"

"You do your thing with Raysor," Wayne told Callie, carrying his glass and the empty chip bowl to the sink. "Slade and I will visit Simmons. I believe we need to keep his visitors solely from Agriculture from now on."

"You going unannounced?" Callie asked. "How will you know which place he'll be?"

Slade, done rinsing her glass, came around the bar, her eyes a tad bloodshot from weariness. "My guess is he's less likely to be with the wife he can't stand anymore."

"True that," Callie said. "Well, y'all try to get a full night's rest. I might be gone when you wake up. I'll leave the alarm code on a pad in the kitchen if you don't mind setting it when you leave."

The two retired to the guest room, Wayne letting Slade enter first.

Callie loved seeing them together. They meshed well, but Slade wasn't fully appreciating what she had. The ring was a nice step . . . a huge step, but they weren't in their twenties anymore, and time was fleeting. God knew she appreciated how time was fleeting.

*One time.* Just one time Callie'd entered Seabrook's bed. Then the next day he was dead. They'd held each other apart, maintained a stupid arm's-length relationship, leaving her with a short memory of that lone night, and an image of him taking his last breath on Pine Landing Road.

She'd let her head override her feelings and paid a price with no refund.

Which is why she'd said what she did about the girlfriend. When you threw love in the mix, your strategy had to change. Feelings factored in, making predictions less accurate and more elusive. That's how Seabrook had died, recklessly chasing a lead for who had murdered his deceased wife.

Wayne was shrewd putting her with Raysor. The boisterous deputy might miss the signs, not grasp the nuances of how a woman would think, even discount some hints as too emotional when emotion was exactly what they wanted here. Enough emotional tugs to make this woman come out of hiding.

The girlfriend might be a mistress, but it still pained Callie a bit to use a lover's feelings against her. However, Jasmine died. The coroner nailed the cause of death, but not the why. There had to be some reason she was in St. Clair Simmons's woods during early morning, and if someone else was involved, they were damn cold-blooded or losing sleep, making either a precarious unknown.

# Chapter 16

## *Callie*

CALLIE SLIPPED OUT of Chelsea Morning early, choosing to wear her uniform this time since she'd be with Raysor, and arrived in Walterboro by eight thirty. He waited for her at the Cracker Barrel on Interstate 95, off Sniders Highway on the south side of town where the hubbub might be enough for cover, letting them speak in a corner and not be as noticeable.

"I don't know your people, Don," she said, sipping her coffee, always black for expediency's sake. "Where will we find them and who are we asking? Honestly, I'm not exactly sure how to proceed with this."

"Doll, I got this. Throw a dart anywhere within the 29488 zip code, and you hit my family. Our ancestors carted their wagons over here eight generations ago, and there ain't a bloodline in this county that doesn't have a drop of our blood in it." He mashed his ample gut into the table, leaning over it. "We keep up with each other's business. You can't keep secrets in the Raysor Clan."

Wonderful legacy unless you treasured your privacy. Callie assumed her job was to channel, maybe even corral, Raysor's energy, which was no easy task, particularly amidst his own kind.

The waitress arrived with their order. Eggs and bacon for Callie. The Country Boy Breakfast for Raysor, which held more carbs and calories than she cared to count. "Best meal of the day," Raysor said, scooping out three pats of butter onto his grits, two more on each of his biscuits.

Her waistline anything but tiny, Josey—as her apron read above the three embroidered stars she'd earned—cocked a hip and studied the table hunting for missing items. "Anything else I can get you?" Then she winked at Callie for a reason she could not decipher.

"Yeah," Raysor said. "You familiar with this man?" He held up St. Clair Simmons's driver's license picture.

"A farmer. Lives off Old Coon Road. Likes hunting and stuff." Then she hunkered her shoulders. "Why, he done something wrong?"

"Nothing serious," he said. "He got a girlfriend on the side?"

Callie feigned casual interest in her coffee cup. *Nothing like being blunt, Don.*

"Ain't my business, Don," Josey replied.

"Ha," he laughed. "Since when is anything in this county none of your business?"

"Since my momma chewed me out for spreading rumors about Randall."

Raysor raised a brow. "Auntie overkilled on that one. Randall deserved that. He might not have stolen that car he'd borrowed, but he stole the washing machine out of the owner's trailer. You just got your item wrong."

"Yeah, but a car's worse. You cops know that."

"Again, what about the girlfriend?"

Josey shrugged. "He's been known to have one. I never saw her. Never cared to."

Raysor changed photos and held up another. "Know this guy?"

"Good-looking," she said and took it to study closer. "Looks familiar, but can't place him." She handed it back. "He a victim or something?"

"That one has issues. Call me if you see him."

"Looks nice enough to me. Who's this over here?" She motioned to Callie. "Hey, honey, I'm Josey."

"Callie Morgan. Police Chief from Edisto," she said. "Nice to meet you."

"Oh, Don," and Josey clicked her tongue. "Proud of you. Y'all need more coffee?"

She refilled the cups before they said yay or nay, and she left with another wink.

This winking business had happened once before, when Raysor and Callie worked another case, and she'd hoped it was an anomaly. "Why's she winking at me, Don?"

"She winks," he said. "It's just what she does."

"That was more than a habit. She thinks you're dating me, you lug."

He waved the thought aside. "They aren't used to seeing me dining with a woman. Every female in the family thinks they need to matchmake me. Don't give it no mind."

"And another thing," Callie said, lowering her cup and jabbing a finger into his sleeve. "*Does he have a girlfriend?* I expected a more subtle line of questioning from you."

"Straight is sometimes all these people understand, Doll. Plus, it's less suspicious. Makes it seem like nothing but run-of-the-mill stuff and they don't get scared about it. If we make St. Clair or Boone seem like Public Enemy Number One, you get a different reaction."

She needed a lesson on gossip spreading, apparently.

They ate in silence, only because Raysor held an intense devotion to his meal. Finally he threw his napkin down. "Got several stops to make. Been thinking about which kin would have the most intel, and it narrows down to about six. If we don't have anything by number six, I got a dozen more to choose from, but we've got to check on Wayne's car at Walterboro Ford, first. Told him I'd get back to him on when those tires would be changed."

Callie didn't ask why a call wouldn't work. This was his town.

Turned out the Ford place was on the other side of town on Bells Highway, at the corner of Robertson, down from the Ag office, and Raysor's nephew worked back in the garage. Both extended hands at the sight of each other, but when they parted, the bulky, oil-smeared beast of a man gave me a once-over and winked at Raysor.

Not again.

Hoss said the car would be ready around one. Raysor texted Wayne, then in surprise, watched his phone ring in his hand. "Y'all give me a second, will ya?" he said, walking off a few paces.

Hoss grinned big at her, the two left awkwardly alone, then he tilted his shaved, shiny dome in the Raysor's direction. "My uncle's a nice one, isn't ihe"

"Raysor's a good man," she said, not wanting to lead anyone down a wrong path.

"He's single." He clicked his tongue to nail his message.

"Um, so I heard."

Hoss leaned down. "I can put in a good word for you. I'm by far his favorite nephew."

"No, I'll handle my own affairs, thanks."

Crap, why did she choose that word?

Which must've made him think. He backed up a step. "You aren't married, are you?"

Callie just shook her head, not wanting to step into quicksand again. What the heck was so important for Raysor to leave her here like this? This was the third relative she'd met in her life, and each felt some burning urge to marry her off to Don.

She more than welcomed his return. "Sorry," he said and pulled out

St. Clair's photo again and picked up where he left off. "You know this guy, Hoss?"

The mechanic didn't take it for fear of messing it up, hands working a rag from his pocket as he peered at the picture. "That's St. Clair," he said, then looked quizzically at Raysor. "You know who that is, Uncle. My brother hunts deer on his place. Ann got her CWP there in one of his classes. And Rennie got a damn fine price on a Glock from him. Says you can get a better deal with St. Clair than Walmart."

Raysor waited to see if ol' Hoss had more to offer.

"What you asking for?" Hoss asked.

"Hunting his girlfriend," Raysor said, even more blunt than with Josey.

"Thought he was married."

"Ever stop you from having a girlfriend?"

Hoss reddened up to the top of his hairless skull. "Ain't no need for saying that."

"Tell me about the girlfriend," Raysor said. "His, not yours."

Hoss glanced at Callie to see how the revelation had impacted her. She acted like she didn't care, which she didn't.

"Just rumor," Hoss said, scouting the car bay for coworkers. "But he meets her out of town. Not sure she's even from here," he said. "Beaufort, I heard. But whoever it is, she's been his regular for a while."

"What's a while?" Callie asked.

Hoss almost jumped at my entering the chat. Raysor nodded to Hoss that he could safely answer. "Well over a year is what I heard," he said.

"Sure he doesn't court more than one over there?" she asked.

"Pretty sure."

"What does that mean?" she asked, aiming to continue as long as he would talk. "How could you know anything about her, yet never seen her nor learned who she was? Sounds like nonsense to me."

Hoss didn't like that. "We're confident who to believe and who not to around here, Chief Morgan. We may not know her but we know him. St. Clair likes to think he's loyal, you know? His wife's a piece of crap, so he's transferred that loyalty to his girl. My two cents anyway."

Sounded like he was excusing more than St. Clair with that explanation. Callie moved closer so she couldn't be heard past Hoss's ears, though she had to look up a foot to do so. "Sounds like you know the man way better than you first said. You talk to St. Clair much?"

Hoss shook his head. "Haven't ever talked to him. It's just what they say."

"Who's they?" she asked, moving into him even as he leaned back a step.

The nephew gave a pleading look to his uncle. "Who is this woman?"

"A badge," Callie said. "Answer me."

Raysor nodded again. A man of few words.

"Just *they*," Hoss said. "You know, the guys at the range. Whoever happens to be there practicing at the time. But no one's ever seen her, which is why I think she lives in Beaufort. At least that's where I'd keep her if it was me."

Callie suspected he spoke from personal experience as well as the rumor mill, and when Raysor didn't challenge the hunky guy, she assumed he believed the nephew, too.

"Now," Raysor started in again. "You know this one?" He showed the other photo.

"Oh yeah. That's Connor Boone." Hoss grinned, like he was proud of getting a question right. "Seen him at the range."

"Well, we're hunting him. You have any idea where he might be?"

There went the smile. "No, man. Just shared hunting stories with him while shooting. Why, what he do?"

"It's more what he didn't do," Callie replied, handing over a card. "And if you see him, call us immediately."

He held the card up and read every word then gave another confused look at Raysor. "Do I call her or you?"

"Damn, Hoss. Just call one of us, okay?" Raysor slapped his nephew on the back. "Ask around to these guys that work here, too. We need to collect Boone. We need to talk to St. Clair Simmons's girlfriend. Two things. Think you can park that in the right spot in that hardheaded noggin of yours so that you don't get confused?"

"Yes, sir."

Like a 250-pound child.

Callie and Raysor began to leave.

"Uncle Don."

Raysor walked back to the man.

"I like your girl."

*Good Lord.* More people seemed interested in her than why the cops asked questions about St. Clair Simmons and Connor Boone.

"What was the phone call about?" she asked at the car.

"Sounds like Slade and Largo done stirred something up. Couldn't tell me much on the phone, but I had to behave like we had a team waiting to swoop in on Mini-Hawk."

Hand on the door, Callie froze. "What?"

"Role playing, Doll. Just some muscle-flexing," he said, getting in. "He'll tell us later, I'm sure."

# Chapter 17

*Slade*

WAYNE AND I LEFT Edisto Beach the following morning, my F-150 crossing Scott's Creek around eight, the day gray and muggy cold, thick with dampness. Callie was already on the job per her text, and we set her house alarm as asked. I drove, relieved to leave the paradise everyone seemed so in love with. In only three years I'd almost drowned in salt-water twice, and living within sight of it was the last item I'd ever put on my bucket list . . . though this morning the fog kept it pretty much hidden as we put the town in our rearview mirror.

We weren't five minutes into our drive through that jungle-bordered two-lane when Savvy rang my cell. Bluetooth channeled it to the truck's speakers.

"Please tell me you found Connor," she said.

"Still searching," I replied. "Why, what's up?"

"He broke into the office last night and rummaged through papers."

Wayne gave me a skeptical grimace. "He's the manager, Savvy. He has a key."

"Okay, well, you're right, but he was in here."

Savvy could embellish, but we'd told her nothing about the event at Rebecca's house last night. Need-to-know mattered amidst an investigation, and Savvy had a way of taking information and molding it to use as she saw fit. She protected her turf. If she leaked to a staff member, they would then get in touch with Connor or offer assistance, and I'd hate for one of them to trip into something they wish they hadn't.

"What was he there for?" Wayne asked, speaking over the road noise.

"Can't tell, but he went through people's desks and forgot to lock back up. He logged on his computer." A break in the conversation made me think we'd lost signal, then she came back. "Was waiting for you to ask me how I knew."

"How did you know, oh wise one?" I asked.

"There's a time record every time someone logs in."

"Thank the technician for me." Savvy was about managing people and juggling the federal dollar, not technology.

"Smart-ass, but yes, I had her check. He signed in shortly after four in the morning."

"Researching stuff on St. Clair?" I asked.

"No."

Wayne stared at me strange. "Then what did he do?"

"Worked on about eight other farm files. Logging in like he was catching up on his work."

"Weird," Wayne said. "Did he damage anything?"

"No," she said. "It was like he came in normal . . . just in the middle of the night."

"Well, if he shows up, and he just might, call 911 and then us," he said.

Silence on the phone. "911? Aren't we being overzealous? Connor's AWOL at worst, Wayne." But when Wayne didn't immediately respond, she added, "Um, what don't I know? Should I be concerned?"

"Do what I ask, Savvy." The edge in his voice left no doubt his remark wasn't up for debate.

"Excuse me, Cowboy," she said, picking up one of my nicknames for him. "But this is my office, and Connor is my staff. My job—"

"Your *job*," he said, in a tone I never wanted directed at me. "Is to protect the government's investment, serve the public per your regulations, and do what your higher-ups tell you to do to that end. Last I checked, Agriculture's Office of Inspector General had the authority to direct investigations and the staff needed in the task. If Connor Boone shows, and you don't call 911 and me, you are an obstacle and can be dealt with accordingly."

*Whoa.* This was not my Wayne.

"Take it down a notch," I whispered.

A snap of a glare silenced me, but only because we were on the phone with Savvy. I'd have not taken that attitude otherwise.

"Well." Savvy dragged out the word. "Sir, yes sir. Sorry to have stomped on your boot toes, Mr. Senior Special Agent Sir."

She hung up on him, which only beat Wayne hanging up on her by a nanosecond.

I tried to select my words, but none felt more right than, "What the hell, Wayne?"

"She wouldn't listen."

"She didn't have the whole story to understand." My decibels far outmatched his.

"She might talk," he countered.

"She might cooperate better."

"She should do what I say," he said.

"Or maybe do what you *ask*?"

He shut up, and we rode five miles with no more conversation.

The argument made me recall the feeling I'd had during numerous moments of my last marriage. Him right, me wrong, my comments not worth considering.

But Wayne wasn't my ex, and this wasn't like him. Jasmine had to be the reason for this atypical persona in the passenger seat of my pickup, but that didn't give him a free pass to go overboard on others.

"Consider apologizing to her later," I said, about five miles from the turn to Old Coon Road.

"Who do you think—"

"Who do I think I am?" Enough of this. "Is that what you were going to say? I'm your fiancée, for one. I'm your best friend, for another. But I'm also a key representative with the US Department of Agriculture when it comes to rural activities in this state and the liaison between your kind and mine. That damn badge does not come with the right to bully staff because you have a bad day. Who the hell taught me to coax people to cooperate instead of plowing through them?"

I tried not to yell. Honest to God I did. But by the time I reached that last sentence I'd lost my patience.

I attempted to take us back down a level. "We're almost to Mini-Hawk. Are we going in there with our heads on straight or half-assed? We're equal parties in this deal, but you know what? Even though I've met with him, studied his files, talked to the people on his land, even enjoyed the company of his wife for four hours, I'll give you this one today." I dipped my head. "You'll need me, but take the reins, Cowboy. Get whatever this is out of your system and be the general leading the charge. I'll be your lieutenant."

His expression showed a mixture of surprise and annoyance. There wasn't much to fight over because I'd conceded to be his shadow.

"But?" he said.

Admittedly, he could read me well.

"But you better not let that damn insolence get in the way of doing what's right for Agriculture, for St. Clair Simmons, for that matter, and lastly for Jasmine. Because I'll damn sure draw it to your attention."

You could hear both our breaths as we traveled that road. We were a half-mile from the entrance when I slowed the truck to a stop. "You sure you're good?" I was still somewhat miffed.

"I do my job, Slade."

"I don't doubt that."

Never in my imagination had I ever thought I'd be schooling Wayne and tempering his actions. I'd received similar words but never dreamed of delivering them.

He'd ridden on the edge a few times . . . the most dangerous cases where lives balanced on a razor. But he'd always chosen the right stance, letting his instincts and reasoning unite. This was not one of those times. I felt it. And not having been in this place before, I wasn't sure what to do except try to become him . . . him at his best.

This was the first time I could envision him screwing up, and I didn't like how that felt.

We pulled up to the squawk box at the entrance. Mashed it once. Twice. Nobody answered. Maybe they ran their militia on banking hours.

Screw this. I dialed St. Clair's number.

"What are you doing?" Wayne asked.

"We can't waltz in," I said, motioning to the various signs that had humored me before. "It's gated, and we trespass if we enter without his permission since he has the place well-posted."

No answer on the phone either, so I left a voice mail stating who I was, requesting to be granted entrance to the facility, stating I'd be waiting until someone showed. I threw the truck into park and waited. Wayne started to get out.

"Please don't," I said. "Jasmine died on this land. We can wait a while. Simmons'll send somebody."

Wayne stayed put.

Took maybe fifteen minutes for Merrick to reach the gate and sanction our entrance. He strode forward, alert, eyes on us. From his appearance, he hadn't been woken up to escort us, maybe pulled off wall duty though, I joked to myself. Assuming they guarded the place around the clock, which might be some membership requirement. Who could say what level of protection they exercised on Mini-Hawk?

"Same directions as before, Ms. Slade," he said, then motioned with two stiff fingers as had the young scrawny guy from before . . . Angus Godfrey. A big name for a not-so-big guy.

Wayne continued to glower. His focus, however, shifted to Merrick, and he sought to hold eye contact the whole way through the gate. Merrick showed no interest in either of us.

"Who's that?" Wayne asked.

"Merrick Cox. Right-hand to St. Clair." I took the same eastern turn to the parking area. "The one who showed Callie and me around to inspect equipment. Was none too pleased at the task, but he followed orders. He's older than the other two *members* or whatever they label them. Angus was so scrawny I could take him down, but the other could put us both on the ground with one arm, so watch him."

The dogs tore across the field as before, Wayne not pleased. "You and Callie shouldn't have come here."

"We handled things fine." I studied the dogs now slobbering up my door. "Reach in the glove box for biscuits. They're more likely to love you to death than take your leg off."

He did, lowering the window to judge their reaction. He tossed a biscuit out to each of them, and when they returned with their nubs wagging, he left the truck and tossed them a couple more.

"Now we cross the field," I said.

Scanning the vast openness that made anyone an easy target, he put a hand on me. "The hell we do. That's wide open. Where's the guy who let us in?"

"Merrick," I reminded, then moved to stand in front of him. "He'll meet us at the trailer, is my guess, but listen."

The dogs danced around us, sometimes taking a few seconds to cock their heads eager for another snack, a kind word, maybe a pat on the head.

"What are we doing?" I said, in a calming tone. "What's the game plan?"

Wayne continued studying the wide field. "We ask him about his debts and how he hasn't accounted for where his money went for starters."

"Agreed. I have my notepad. Then what?"

"Connor Boone," he said.

Again we agreed. We'd heard enough from Savvy and Rebecca to realize that Connor was more familiar with St. Clair than he let on.

But Wayne didn't mention Jasmine in his plan. He was winging things, too, and Wayne didn't wing things. He choreographed and entered on his own terms, but despite my reservation, we couldn't stand on the edge of the field and argue about what happened next.

"Come on," I said, headed toward the double-wide. "This is the way it's done."

Wayne obliged, but trotted to the front. "Stay behind me."

Winter rye rose to our knees, obviously cultivated from the even rows and consistency of the ground. Level. Easy to survey. Like I'd thought before, a headquarters ought to be tucked in the woods amongst the pines. Maybe that was the farmer in St. Clair. Maybe clear lines of sight were his interpretation of safety.

Nobody waited outside for us this time, though I felt eyes nonetheless. We reached the fresh, treated-lumber porch, which hadn't been here but a year tops.

Since I hadn't considered myself the least bit nervous until we stood at the door, I hated that I jumped when Wayne knocked with clear intention. I'd considered myself the more collected of the two of us. Apparently not.

Atwood, the huge ex-military-something-or-other, snatched back the door. He was breathing hard, staring harder from his six-foot-two tower of camo.

Unphased, Wayne flashed his shield. "Senior Special Agent Wayne Largo to see St. Clair Simmons."

I simply stood stupid, scared silly, wondering why this beast of a man huffed and puffed as if we'd already pissed him off.

# Chapter 18

## *Slade*

ATWOOD SHOWED us in, the trailer rather cool. "Mr. Simmons says to wait in his office." The heat kicked on as he ushered us down the narrow hall . . . or at least it seemed narrow from how his shoulders brushed both sides. We entered the same office as before, and Atwood started to close the door.

"We prefer it remain open," Wayne said.

Atwood studied Wayne, judging an adversary, then pushed the door back and left us.

"There was a secretary before," I said, like I had to contribute something.

"Part-time enterprise." Wayne walked to a front window, scouting the field, then moving across the room to peer out the back. "They park over on the edge of those trees. Suspect our big boy was told to hightail it out here, and he ran harder than he's used to in order to greet us. He might be built, but I doubt he jogs much. Not like he used to in the ranks."

That summation gave me some relief. "Good. He's the one I said would take us both out."

"This must be St. Clair coming," Wayne said, barely lifting one blind before letting it drop.

We heard a metal door open, shut, then boots take the hallway toward us. St. Clair Simmons entered, cheeks red and with more stubble on his jaw than I'd seen the day before. He slid the fleeced camo beanie off and onto his desk, but he left his thinning hair disheveled. No greeting, just a plop into his chair with somewhat of a moan, and before I could look behind me, I heard Atwood arrive to fill up the doorway.

"Y'all are bound and determined to be a thorn in my ass, aren't you?" St. Clair said. "Y'all saw the equipment and pilfered through the papers, so you can't say I didn't cooperate. What the hell else you want?"

"A check for your late payments to the government," Wayne said. "Then we'd gladly disappear."

St. Clair sneered, half-admiring Wayne's response. "And you are?"

Wayne laid his card on the desk and held up his credentials. "Senior Special Agent Wayne Largo. US Department of Agriculture's Office of Inspector General."

The whole spiel. The card stayed on the desk, its embossed badge clearly denoting law enforcement.

I always liked those cards.

"We would've ordinarily let the local Agriculture office handle your late payment," Wayne continued. "But too many other discrepancies have escalated your case."

There was the old Wayne. In his element.

St. Clair unzipped his jacket. Guess he figured this wasn't as quick a meet as he'd hoped.

"There have been inappropriate expenditures and missing crop sales," Wayne said.

"The paperwork I saw didn't account for either," I added. "You're listed as having soybeans and corn this year but can't show enough proceeds to cover the cost of putting them in the ground, much less harvest and pay your debt. Where'd they go?"

He deflated though not fearful, appearing more burdened by our persistence. "Like I told Connor, I delayed too long getting into the field and lost enough crop to make things tight."

I skootched to the edge of my chair. "Yet you sit here in this headquarters of a hunting club. Could the crops have been converted into some other enterprise, Mr. Simmons?"

He scratched his unshaven chin, taking his wanderings up to his sideburns, his mouth rather animated in its crawling around in displeasure. His hands held long-time signs of labor, the nails leveled more from hard use than by clippers.

"I really want to pay y'all," he said, not exactly answering my question. "But I couldn't. I can't. So I changed directions. Ag wasn't interested in furthering my preferred business enterprises, so I took what I could for planting and freelanced from there."

Guess he did answer me. No denial at all. "You're owning the fact you used federal funds for other purposes than you borrowed them for?" I said, sort of befuddled at the confession.

"Why not?" he said. "Listen, you know how hemp is taking off across this country, and I intend to get in on it when it takes off in South Carolina. With the attitudes in this state, we can't do more than industrial hemp. Not the CBD oil or medicinal weed," he added at the end, like that proved he'd been legitimate and aboveboard in his efforts.

"You need approval," I said. "Individuals have to be selected. And of course Agriculture couldn't finance it. The crop is too early and controversial for us to finance hemp."

The state had exploded with interest for the crop. However, for good reason, authorities carefully monitored how many farmers, where, and when. Regulations weren't sorted out yet for growing the stuff, much less financing it, but farmers craved its money potential, especially those who'd spent their lives scratching the ground to earn a living from simple crops with low profit margins.

And it was so damn easy for some of those plants to conveniently develop the THC level to make them Saturday-night-high marijuana. Just took one potent male plant in the field. A plant with low THC was hemp and legal. A plant over point three percent was marijuana and illegal, and they looked the same. A hemp crop could morph into something THC-laden, turning an Americana farmer into a criminal.

"So where'd you plant the hemp?" Wayne asked. "Let me remind you about lying to a federal agent."

St. Clair replied with smugness. "It's state jurisdiction, Agent Largo. Besides, I haven't planted any yet. I put into the state for approval, and I've been told to expect good news, but I need investors, which is my primary focus at present. In particular, investors with ready-made markets because from what I've seen, half the guys who planted this year got stuck without a buyer. So I turned entrepreneurial. I invested in this place to make money while inviting investors to hunt and hear what I have to say. Investors with markets."

I studied the interior of the double-wide, at the IKEA furniture in a tin-can office, wondering how anyone courted money with this.

St. Clair clearly read and interpreted my expression correctly.

"Been talking to several groups, and they aren't the kind to meet in a high-rise in downtown Columbia," he said. "A couple of them come out of Georgia. One in particular shows a keen interest, so I have strong hope we'll be in a different situation this time next year."

Sounded like hiding and slipping around to me.

"And when you have multi-state involvement that's how you make it a federal case," Wayne said, getting his comeback dig. "Why aren't they investing in Georgia farmers?"

"Georgia laws haven't caught up to South Carolina's." Then he scrunched up a cheek. "Or rather, let's say their laws are more restrictive. Farmers can't sell hemp except to processing companies, of which there are none, at least not yet to my knowledge. And they can't ship the product outside the state. But out-of-state producers can ship into Georgia. Crazy, ain't it?"

While I hadn't done a deep dive into hemp, the rumors ran rampant through Agriculture about the pros, cons, and the virgin, untested codes now on the books. No two states were alike in requirements, having enacted regulatory controls wrenched too tight in one state or too loose in another. Each state's agricultural departments attempted to figure it out from scratch. No precedents or much definition on what to do if a farmer broke the law. One farmer in Dorchester, who had extra seed, got arrested for growing plants on an unlisted field, but once they threw cuffs on him, nobody had any idea what to do with him. He was fined and cut loose . . . eventually. What kind of precedent did that set?

But I could say this much . . . the market was glutted from farmers rushing to plant hemp without solid places to sell. Hemp required a totally different method of marketing than corn or beans, but a profit of six to ten times that of soybeans made for strong temptation in spite of the risk. High mold or an above-level THC test could be devastating as the law required plants be destroyed.

And I still didn't understand how creating a hunting club attracted a hemp market, though. It was almost like he was courting a particular party.

"Hope you've done your homework," I said. "This is untilled territory. You could find yourself and your investors ruined in the course of one season. Wouldn't catch me riding in the front car of this roller coaster."

His chair creaked as he shifted weight forward. "But that's where the money is, Ms. Slade. Where the risk is greatest."

"But you owe us now," I said. "Won't they look at your financial standing?"

"A criminal background check. Credit report. No problems with either last I checked," he said. "Y'all haven't taken action yet, I see." His attention turning toward the door. Atwood had left, his weight challenging the trailer's floor from the groans.

St. Clair's middle rocked up and down with silent chortles. "By the time you people get around to taking any legal action, I'll have investors and a crop in the ground. Don't need your money with my partners, and I sincerely look forward to operating without you breathing down my neck with bureaucratic paper and these two-bit inspections."

"You'll be eaten up with way more inspections than we give you if you get into hemp," I said.

"But they'll be more interested in my crop than my payments," he replied, winking.

Wayne swept a lazy hand through the air. "And in the meantime . . . this?"

"Yes, income for the time being," St. Clair said. "People need to feel safe, and my job is to give them that sense of protection. CWP classes. Firearm sales, and feel free to check my license."

"Already have," Wayne said.

St. Clair's slip of a grin noted the challenge, then moved on from Wayne's dare. "Then you learned I was legit. Atwood Snipes is the draw," he said. "That big boy's got that military background and a presence that make people love him. Notably the women." Another wink, a habit that wasn't becoming. Like an old man trying to look sexy to a recent college grad. Just didn't come off right.

"This guy matters a lot, too," he said, motioning to the door.

Merrick stepped just inside the entrance, Atwood behind him. "Everything okay, Mr. Simmons?"

St. Clair stood, coming around his desk to throw an arm around his man. "This is Merrick Cox, Agent Largo. Practically runs Mini-Hawk and a longtime friend of mine. Retired from the ball bearing plant and needed something to do. We've been friends for, what, thirty years?"

"Longer than that," Merrick said. "Since high school. Was also best man at your wedding."

A loud guffaw flew out of St. Clair, amplified by the low ceiling. "Well, can't hold that against you."

"Tried telling you otherwise," Merrick said, his smile smoother and restrained.

I tried to envision Mrs. Simmons as a young girl in a wedding dress, but the visual fell short. Bless her heart in more ways than one.

"So Merrick works for you?" I asked. "And Atwood? What about the skinny dude that was out there the other day?"

He eyed me, and I could read him wondering if I was entitled to ask the question. "Contractors," he said after hesitation. "So I don't pay taxes. They split class proceeds with me. Get a commission for every firearm and new student. Seems to work out. They set their schedules."

A nickel-dime operation that could make St. Clair a living depending on how much exchanged hands under the table. Get him by until he could establish something different since he sure as heck wasn't making money with his crops. "Who does the farming?" I asked. "What little there is. Sure hope it's more than that rye field out there."

He peered down his plump, deep-pored nose. "Missy, I don't just stand around looking intelligent. I can drive a tractor. What I don't do gets done by seasonal help, and these guys chip in here and there. As a favor, you understand."

I just didn't see this fella being that ambitious to farm, run a gun club business, and execute a plan for a hemp empire. His middle-aged-ness, his midriff with handles on the sides apparent even through his layers, the way he wasted no energy in his movements. Maybe I was stereotyping. Some people were deceptive, and ambitious thinkers weren't necessarily athletes.

Wayne stroked his bearded chin with his thumb. "What about Connor Boone?"

Darn. I'd been waiting for the right opportunity to ask that.

St. Clair waited, looking up once at his men as though wanting them gone before he spoke. "Connor's the loan man with USDA, and I didn't have to tell you that," he said, apparently okaying the presence of the men for this conversation. "Why're you asking?"

Wayne stood, going back to the rear window where he could see the vehicles, like he was admiring the place . . . or hunting for something. "I don't know," Wayne said, peering back around. "You're not paying your loan, and he doesn't seem too intent on making you. When's the last time you saw him?"

"I haven't in ages."

Wayne looked over at the other men. "What about you two?"

"Don't know," Atwood said. "A recent class a few months ago. Maybe hunting. Don't keep a calendar."

Merrick mildly nodded in agreement.

I imagined these men grunting in cave man fashion, and the room began to smell male.

Wayne meandered back to his chair. "Connor ever expect a kick-back from you, Simmons? Ever look the other way when you sold crops? You know, so you could have money to maybe court those in-vestors?"

St. Clair said nothing.

"Had a run-in with Connor last night, by the way," Wayne said. "Seems he fancies himself more of a gunslinger than he used to, with credit going to you and Mini-Hawk per his wife."

That drew a humorous humph from St. Clair. "Can't help how holding a gun makes a man feel."

"Can't help what a woman thinks, either," echoed Atwood. "Especially an ex."

"Who said she was an ex?" My speaking up sort of jolted most of the room of testosterone.

All Atwood did was grin at me. Did Simmons seriously say women liked this guy?

Wayne bored a stare into St. Clair. "He shot at my car."

St. Clair didn't flinch. "Let me simplify it for you, Largo. Not my problem."

I'd witnessed flippant, ignorant, sassy, and stupidity in both witnesses and targets, but never seen someone go head-on with Wayne, who seemed to consider St. Clair for a moment.

"I'm getting the impression there's more to you than meets the eye," Wayne continued. "You're not the typical farmer in these parts, and I'm not sure what you've got your fingers in."

St. Clair's nonchalant shrug irritated me. "Don't know what you're insinuating, Agent Largo."

"Just saying," Wayne said, letting the pause hang there a second. "Just saying that serious behavior can merit serious time."

St. Clair's grin hardened. "Real words of wisdom. I'll be sure to write 'em down. Now, I've cooperated with you. However, I'm not so sure you're being upfront with me."

Sometimes we did this tit for tat with someone we interviewed, though not often. Wayne more than me. Each side waiting for the other to wear out or let down their guard, but they were inching into tenser territory, neither giving. I couldn't spot an opening to speak again, wasn't sure it would matter. Unsure whether I'd ruin whatever tactic Wayne had chosen to use.

I straddled the fence of opinion on St. Clair. He presented pompous and arrogant, and maybe he was planning a criminal enterprise with the hemp, but he hadn't gotten that far. I was almost up for going back to Columbia, processing a collection action for the missing crop money, and being done with this man. Almost, but Wayne had lost his partner and wasn't going home that easily, and when Wayne had doubts, I respected them.

He hadn't said it, but he thought Jasmine was murdered, with someone in St. Clair Simmons's universe having a hand in it. I wasn't so sure. How did someone sting someone else with hornets? My money leaned toward Atwood, but then, who said it had to be the big guy? Jasmine wasn't large enough to be a physical threat to any of them. She'd definitely been outgunned.

Wayne, however, seemed intent on starting with Simmons, almost treating him a hardened criminal. "Is Connor involved in your operation? Falsifying records and misusing federal funding can get you ten years, and he'd pay dearly for aiding."

St. Clair inhaled slow and deep. "This song you're singing bores me. Connor Boone is one of you. He hunts here sometimes and uses the range, took a couple classes same as a hundred others in this county." He raised his voice. "I don't give a *damn* one way or the other what you do with him, because my plans are the same. He's nothing special to me."

"By the way, your security's not as good as you think," Wayne said. "Per Conner Boone's truck about a hundred and fifty yards over at the edge of those woods, either you've got a trespasser or you're harboring a fugitive." He took out his phone and hit a number. "Which is it?"

I twitched in my chair at the thought we might've found Connor.

No comment from St. Clair. Merrick's gaze flitted to the window, then back to his boss, eyes narrowing.

Wayne held up his phone. "Deputy Raysor, you're on speaker. I'm here with St. Clair Simmons and two men who go by the names of Atwood Snipes and Merrick . . ." He looked to me for help.

"Merrick Cox," I said.

"Cox," Wayne repeated to Raysor. "Are you still at the rally point with those other deputies?"

"Yeah," Raysor said. "Just sipping coffee and enjoying donuts waiting for the word. How can we help you?"

"Hold on," Wayne said and turned to St. Clair. "Which is it? Is Connor Boone a trespasser or are you harboring a fugitive?"

St. Clair peered around Wayne to Merrick. "How did he get back out here?"

So they had seen Connor lately.

Merrick shrugged, taking his attention to Atwood. "I don't know."

The boss stood and jerked a finger toward the back of the trailer. "Go run his butt off."

"So," Wayne continued, still holding out the phone. "You've got a trespasser?"

"Yeah," St. Clair said. "We're not harboring anybody."

"You need our assistance with the trespasser? Got a half dozen men who can be here in a blink."

"You giving me a choice?"

"Yes," Wayne said, standing firm and staring hard.

"We can handle it," St. Clair said low.

Wayne told Raysor things were good and hung up.

I assumed Wayne had good reason to let Connor slip off, or rather, be chased off. He couldn't chase Conner down alone, for one, and he couldn't let me tag along. Then there was the couple hundred acres of woods the man could hide in.

Wayne continued staring at St. Clair, their thoughts so loud I could almost fill in the blanks. Each had words they wished to say but didn't.

In that silence I felt the need to say what Wayne was thinking. "Why did Special Agent Jasmine Bright die on your land?"

St. Clair Simmons's composure morphed from confidence to some sort of concerned realization. His color rose, replacing the momentary pallor. As several seconds dragged out, I wondered if I'd misspoken.

He eased forward, making me sit back straight and brace. I didn't have to study Wayne to sense his increased friction.

In dark defiance, the question oozed from St. Clair's narrow lips. "Are you accusing me of murder?"

"Did you *hear* me accuse you of murder?" I said, fighting to present boldly. The question wasn't out of line. As I struggled to maintain visual contact as I was taught, I equally fought not look to Wayne for an out.

Blood throbbing in my neck, I kept talking. "She died in the middle of the night in your woods. Why would she be on your property? Her arm was bruised from suspected restraint."

No denial, no shock, and no retort. Instead, St. Clair opened his desk drawer, extracted a business card, and slid it eerily toward me. "Call my attorney."

"We have a right to ask questions," I said.

"You have a right to live . . . until you don't." He stood. "Get off my goddamn place. You're officially trespassing."

Wayne stood. "You threatening a federal agent?"

Simmons stood. "You forget that you don't have a warrant, and I no longer give you permission to be on my place."

Everyone but me had stood, facing off. I didn't want to make matters worse, challenging people who toyed with guns, but I rose. It was time to leave, even if the only retreat was through Atwood and Merrick. From the electricity overwhelming the room, I seemed the only person wanting out.

The men kept waiting for someone to blink.

# Chapter 19

## *Slade*

THE FOUR MEN clenched like dogs stiff with hair raised, glowers hot and lasered as though waiting for one to make the first move so all had an excuse to pounce.

"Stop!" I yelled, arms out. Then without thought I extracted my internal badge from my pocket and held it up like I'd seen on television. The black leather wallet and plastic shield that interviewed employees for disciplinary action, meant squat when it came to locking up bad guys. But with any luck it would shock them back to reality. "Everyone zip it up and back off!"

I poked it back in my pocket before anyone could read it, then being more comfortable with my back to St. Clair than the militia boys in the doorway, I moved to leave. Reaching down deep for the chutzpah I hoped I owned, I pushed out enough defiance to get Wayne and me out of this double-wide. "Get out of my damn way unless you want to be charged with kidnapping a federal agent. Isn't one dead agent enough for you?"

"Nobody killed that girl," Merrick said. "She died from the hornets."

I threw attention at St. Clair. "While on a three a.m. stroll in his woods?"

"The why and when ain't our problem." The coolness in which Merrick spoke shot an alarm up my back. He was suddenly nothing like the bored, annoyed guy who showed Callie and me tractors and bush hogs. The contrast made my nerves dance.

Atwood assumed the chest-out stance of a nightclub bouncer. St. Clair crossed his arms from behind his desk. "Merrick is right," he said.

Jesus, these standoffs.

"Out of my way," I said.

They didn't move.

Wayne had risen when I did, but instead of following me, he leaned on St. Clair's desk. "There is no situation in which threatening us will bode well for you. Is that clear?"

Seconds passed between them.

"Let 'em pass," St. Clair said, and the men parted.

I slid through, smelling their scents, the cramped space permitting only inches between us. Wayne's cowboy boots followed, the footfalls serious. We made it to the trailer's porch, thankfully, unescorted. Someone latched the door behind us.

I certainly didn't feel like enough of a threat to them to warrant that.

The dogs came running from across the acres, tongues lolling, the planted rye parting at their chests and rippling around them. They were much more welcoming than the beings in the trailer.

Wayne took my elbow, his long legs taking strides that made me trot. "Walk to the truck. Don't look back."

My heart kicked the inside of my ribs, breath puffing like a steam engine in the cold morning air. "Nobody seemed armed." Then unable to heed his warning, I tried to peer back.

Wayne snatched me forward. "Don't," he said. "Don't give them the satisfaction. No doubt they're armed."

"So I'm supposed to let them shoot me in the back versus the front?"

A shrill whistle sounded, making two rises and falls. The dogs stopped in their tracks barely ten yards from us and assumed a stance.

"What was that?"

"Damn it, keep walking," Wayne said. "And don't run," he added, reminding me how badly I wanted to.

The rottweiler pair that had previously licked my windows for attention stood on stiff legs, eyes forward, frozen in wait for what I hoped was an order that wouldn't happen.

Twenty yards from the truck, a different whistle pierced the air. The dog statues became black streaks and made straight for us.

I didn't wait for Wayne to tell me how to save my own butt. I dug in and ran. But as we reached the truck, another whistle sounded.

This time I didn't look back, grateful to the heavens that I'd not locked the truck's doors. I leaped inside, waiting for the other door to slam shut before taking off, but it didn't.

Wayne had stopped and drawn his weapon, his sights on a dog. Like back in the trailer, he honed in on the enemy, daring them to make the first move.

"Don't—" I yelled then clenched shut. I didn't want to be some additional trigger with Wayne so too-damn-eager to put a bullet in something or someone.

But the dogs sat on the perimeter of the parking area, waiting. Not sweet, but not terrorizing, either. Still . . . watching. The last whistle had ordered them to stand down . . . but stand by.

My nerves jazzed waiting for the whistle to sic the dogs on Wayne.

He backed slow and neat toward the truck while I reached over and opened his door. He slinked inside and eased the door shut.

Only then did we dare catch our breath, the windows quickly fogging. I cranked the engine and put on the defroster, then backed out and left.

"Could've shot those dogs," he said. "*Should've* shot those dogs."

"Glad you didn't." I struggled to level my voice. "Not their fault." I prayed the gate was open when we reached it. Pondered running through it if it wasn't.

Angus awaited us, however, overseeing our passage. Once on a public road, I hesitated and glanced back. He'd vanished into the woods.

Then I backhanded Wayne in the chest. "What the hell kind of interview was that back there? You and Simmons acted like rival gang members or something. I about peed my pants."

"It was an act, Slade," he said, like I hadn't gotten the joke . . . but I wasn't buying it. The room had crackled with bravado and challenged manhood, the stuff that probably got these men so wrapped up in hunting clubs and war games to start with. The chance to go guerilla and egocentric.

It seemed to have sucked Wayne right in. Either that or Jasmine's death had eroded his thinking. I hadn't registered any of that as play-acting.

"I don't get the deal about building a hunting club to attract a hemp buyer," I said. "At least not the kind of hemp buyer that comes from a legalized operation."

"You caught that, huh?" he said. "Hemp might not be his focus. A higher militia maybe . . . we damn sure don't need that." He was almost mumbling to himself. "Gotta check with ATF . . . can't believe this slipped in . . . but those guys don't seem . . ." then I couldn't hear him as his words disappeared in his head.

I was lost. "Like some sort of fraternity? The little club dying to join the big club?"

But he was back deep in thought, so I hushed and drove back toward the main highway, hands tight on the wheel.

"St. Clair Simmons has no idea about what happened to Jasmine," Wayne said after a mile of silence, after the road noise calmed him down.

"How do you know that?" I still struggled to sort out that scene at the trailer.

Wayne was granite to me. He was my tether to reality when I went off half-cocked. In all we'd been through, some being near-death experiences, he'd proven the most collected. We'd clicked and melded, his even keel with my storm. I didn't like this new side of Wayne, him not being firm and solid in navigating the unknowns. He had to be sure-footed so that I could be daring.

"While you were watching and listening to Merrick," he said, almost sounding like my old Wayne, "I had eyes on Simmons."

"*You think?* Gee, I hadn't noticed." Their double-dog-dare staring contest wasn't easy to forget.

He ignored my sarcasm. "What did you see in him when you mentioned Jasmine?"

I thought back. "Disgust at the accusation, but also a flash of surprise."

"Exactly. And while you parlayed with Merrick, I remained fixed on Simmons. I believe he's in the dark about Jasmine's death, and definitely concerned it happened on his land."

Having reached the stop sign where I'd turn right to head to town, and with nobody behind us, I threw the transmission into park. Time to speak to him instead of to the road. "Sounds like a lot of mind-reading, Lawman."

"I mean it, he's oblivious."

"So I did little more than insult him."

"You made him wonder who else may have done it. You made him weigh the options," he said.

I tapped both hands on the steering wheel, trying to decide how to say this. "Murder isn't necessarily on that list of options, Lawman."

"Yes, it is." Matter of fact.

What should I say to that? "So if you don't think it's St. Clair, who else?"

"Any of those boys who frequent the compound," he said. "Might not've planned to kill her, but they did. Someone did."

Or someone didn't. "What's the motive?"

"That's what we're still down here to determine. And those boys weren't going to do anything to us," he said, and I sensed him changing the subject. "They were trying to save a modicum of pride."

"Says the guy who drew down on dogs." He was worrying me. "You didn't really see Connor's truck in the woods did you?"

"Yeah, I did. Or a truck mighty close in resemblance. But the two of us would be stupid hunting someone on hunting land filled with trigger-happy hunters. Don't you think? Better and easier to catch him someplace else. He's not going far."

Had to agree. "Well, St. Clair wasn't too loyal if it was him."

"Something else I wanted to measure," he said.

I wanted something else measured. "Ever think Jasmine did nothing more than try to get a jump on your investigation? That she eased out there to get a lay of the land, maybe discover something in advance to impress you?" His stillness wasn't easy to endure. "That her death was pure accident like the coroner said?"

"I'm not stupid, Slade." But he said it to the dashboard, not to me.

"Didn't say you were."

We sat still until I worried someone would notice the Ford truck sitting at a stop sign going nowhere. "Where do we go now?" I asked.

"I'm thinking about it."

"Well, let me make a suggestion," and I pulled onto the highway. "You didn't finish with Jasmine's mother. Connor sort of threw a wrench into the haphazard plan we had, and we still need to see Mrs. Bright. What's her address?"

He said nil.

"Even if she blames you for Jasmine, she merits another visit," I said.

He pulled up the address on his phone and set the GPS, anchoring it into a holder on the dash for my benefit. Then he scooted down in his seat best he could.

Wayne had to get over the fact Jasmine had taken things into her own hands and he hadn't been able to stop her.


THE MAILBOX SAID Bright, and someone had painted sunshine faces on it sometime back, but they still smiled. A dated, pale blue two-door sedan was parked in a narrow rutted dirt drive of a beige single-wide with chocolate brown shutters. To the side of the residence, a ten-by-twenty garden flaunted a healthy patch of deep green collards.

An artificial green wreath with white mums and lilies hung on the front door.

It was ten thirty, the seasonal cold almost cut through by a warm autumn sun. GPS had taken us to Sixth Street, a mile and half east of the Walterboro city limits. The dirt road was lined with assorted trailers, most tended, a couple with worn-out cars on blocks in back yards, but everyone's grass was cut. I pulled in behind the sedan and parked, but we didn't immediately get out.

"What are we asking?" I said, because Wayne hadn't spoken since that stop sign.

He heaved a deep sigh. "The usual. Did she know Jasmine was headed to the Simmons place when she left home. Did she know why. Is there anything we should know about Simmons that would make Jasmine want to go out alone. Her impression of Simmons. Was there any sort of history between Jasmine or her and Simmons."

"Let me lead this time, okay? You already made the death notice. You did your thing this morning with St. Clair. Give me this one," I said.

"Whatever you want, Slade."

"No, whatever we need to do, Cowboy. You'll be there to work out any kinks, but she lost her daughter, and I might be a softer touch being female."

He didn't argue or agree, but he did get out of the truck. Together we approached the front entrance, noting the neighbor to the left check us out from her porch. "What's the mother's first name?" I asked Wayne.

"Magdalene," he said. "They call her Maggie."

The woman who answered was about my age, dark-skinned, hair cropped close to her head giving her neck the attractive elongated Hepburn look that Jasmine had been blessed with, too. Premature bags hung under tired eyes. She hadn't been recently crying, but she'd done her share earlier.

She gave me a trivial second of curiosity, but upon seeing Wayne, her forehead furrowed. "I don't need you," she said and turned to me. "Either of you." I'd quickly joined his rank of the unwelcome.

"But we need *you*, Ms. Bright." I held out my hand. She possessed the manners to take it. "I'm Carolina Slade from the US Department of Agriculture. I often work with Agent Largo, and I met your daughter for dinner right before she left Columbia."

I'd rehearsed that in my head en route, trying for words that didn't say *the day your daughter died*. Dead, died, dying . . . avoiding them all.

"So?"

I cleared my throat. "We're investigating that night."

"Why?"

I caught myself scrubbing a nervous thumb in my opposite palm. "Because she deserves closure. *You* deserve closure."

"Ain't no such thing," she said, leaving the doorway open after walking deeper inside.

I had to agree with her.

We entered the home, smelling of old wood, worn rugs, and history and found her in the living room where she'd curled back up in a recliner under a cotton lap throw . . . where she'd probably been sequestered most of the day.

The thin blue carpet looked discount but clean. The Walmart voile curtains were cheap but ironed and hung to reach just above the floor. Jasmine's pictures from every stage of her life crammed every shelf of a pre-fab entertainment center. Her college graduation picture sat on the end table next to her mother's chair, next to a box of tissues and a glass holding what seemed like only melting ice. The faint lavender of a used-up air freshener reached us from somewhere, blended with assorted kitchen smells. Foil-covered casseroles littered the kitchen counter with a dozen liters of soft drinks lined across the back. The condolence food.

"May we sit?" I asked.

She grabbed a tissue. "Do what you like."

"May I call you Maggie?"

"Call me what you like."

Nothing easy about this. I tried to imagine how much she'd railed at Wayne when he delivered the news. Might explain part of his depresssion.

Side-by-side, Wayne and I perched on the edge of the sofa cushions. I couldn't imagine losing a child, and I almost had. Callie came to mind, with the losses in her life, and I sort of wished she were here telling me what to do. Was there really a right way to do this? Ask a mother about her dead child's motives so that we could determine for sure that she'd been too adventurous for her own good after entering a profession that prized a certain degree of just that?

"Would you like us to call someone?" I asked.

She snapped her focus onto me so quick I flinched. "Why, what new flavor of hell are you going to heap on my head that'll hurt me more than the death of my baby? They won't give her to me yet, you know that? I can't even bury my child."

Her words shredded my heart. "Maggie. We're here to rectify that. We're trying to determine how and why Jasmine died so we can close this case, so you can have her. There's nothing we want more."

She drew the lap throw to her tighter, but at least she didn't argue.

"Do you know why Jasmine went to St. Clair Simmons's property in the middle of the night?" I asked.

Maggie indicated through the blanket at Wayne, her glare confirming. "Because *he* assigned her some damn investigation."

"Did you see her before she left?" I asked.

"I'd stepped out," she said. "Didn't even know she was coming home."

That still surprised me. "Would she stay someplace else in Walterboro? With a relative or a friend?"

"Girl was grown. She could've stayed anywhere."

God Almighty, how did we overcome this monstrous barricade of animosity? I reached back to that dinner, recollecting Jasmine's words.

"Did y'all talk about what she hoped to accomplish? The reason I ask is that during our dinner, she was ecstatic about coming to see you. She seemed familiar with Mr. Simmons, and that her family would be proud. She described him as being *wicked*. Her exact word. Do you have any idea what she meant by that?"

"Wicked. How would she even know?" Maggie's tears fell anew. "She was twenty-three, Ms. Slade. That man's a farmer who's lived in this county for fifty years. Some like him and some don't. She's never been on his farm. She's never been to Mini-Hawk. You think guys like those would entertain a girl like her in their world? Redneck white is what they are, and the last person they want on their turf is some slip of a black girl . . . except for maybe the wrong reasons. I told her more than once not to go out there."

From our morning on Mini-Hawk, I wasn't surprised at his reputation, and Maggie's description of that bunch pretty much matched the one embedded in my brain. Might explain Jasmine's incentive in taking such a man down.

"What about you?" Wayne said.

Maggie hesitated, her rant sidetracked. "What do you mean?"

"You talk like you know something about the place. Did you have a past with Simmons? Or any of his people?" he continued.

Fury in her eyes, she bit each word as she spit them out. "You're blaming me for what *you* did? How dare you. What'd you send her out there for?" she yelled.

He shook his head, the pain showing around his mouth. "I didn't send her, Maggie. Honest to God I didn't. She told me she was spending the night with you. She seemed happy about coming. Trust me. I thought she was here. If I had any idea she'd planned to go out on her own I'd have never let her come down here . . . would've denied her the case altogether."

Maggie tried to read Wayne through her tears.

"You have no idea what pushed her to slip out there?" he asked.

But Maggie only stared and cried those silent tears, with no attempt to stop the drips onto her throw. "I raised her to be tough," she said. "She had no father and no brother to teach her, so I did it. Raised her to be independent and think for herself. Law enforcement was not my choice for her, though, you hear? But that girl set her mind, and the more I argued, the stubborner she got. Even became federal to hammer it home." Sniffling, she grabbed a tissue, and the picture with it, cramming it to her chest with one hand, wiping her nose with the other. "She couldn't stop proving to me she was right."

Releasing a sob, she tried to hold back, but her body shook as tears spilled one after the other, unabated. She buried her head in her blanket and cried, "If only I'd have listened to her. If only I had her here so I could tell her she was right all along."

A knock sounded on the door. I rose to answer it.

The neighbor we'd seen earlier rushed in. "What'd y'all do to Maggie?" Then at the recliner, "Oh, honey, come here." She moved to envelope the slender woman into her plump, ample bosom, cooing to her while staring daggers at us over the top of Maggie's head.

Wayne stood. "Let's go, Slade." Then to the mother, "I'm not buying she died by an act of God, Maggie. Someone at Mini-Hawk may have been responsible, and I'm not dropping this until I know for sure. You want someone to answer for this? So do I."

"Our condolences, Maggie," I said, before he could say more. He was already saying too much. "We'll talk to them about releasing your Jasmine."

We let ourselves out and made our way slowly to the truck. The curious peered from an open door in the trailer across the street. No doubt we were crap to these people who'd probably seen Jasmine grow into a beautiful, professional woman with armloads of potential.

Was this a simple case of a zealous young lady proving herself to her mother? If so, Wayne couldn't have foreseen this. Not in any way.

Another lady hovered at the door of the trailer on the right, clearly considering scurrying in slippers across the grass to Maggie's now that we were leaving. I sighed. We left with no more knowledge than we came with.

Would I talk to my mother about plans that were personal and meaningful to me? Not likely. I'd talk to friends, or my sister, and if I had one, a favorite aunt, maybe. Mothers could be judgmental, even while trying to look out for us, even while doling out their advice for our own good. Just ask my daughter.

Listening to Maggie, a seed of an idea had sprouted, though, loose and undefined. I wasn't so sure Jasmine didn't know more about St. Clair than we did. What if Jasmine was using her first investigation to get even for something else. What if that *slip of a black girl*, as her mother put it, had actually sneaked out there thinking herself oh-so-smart . . . and screwed up.

Were we screwing up by leaving? People helped you because they believed you or needed you. Maggie felt neither. She'd never get back to us.

So on impulse I struck out across the grass instead of getting in the truck. "Ma'am?" I appealed to the lady in the slippers. "May I speak with you a moment?"

Like a deer caught in headlights, she halted, comically surveying ahead and behind her, as if she had options to run and hide.

I handed her my card. "If you see anyone slipping around Maggie's, you call me. Call us."

Her gasp literally took her back a step. "She in trouble?"

"No, ma'am," I said. "We just want her safe. We're investigating what happened to Jasmine."

Gingerly she accepted my card. "Why? What happened?"

I gave a subtle wince, noting I couldn't say. "Just take care of her," I said, with as much sincerity as I could muster.

"Holy Jesus," she whispered, staring at my card. "You can count on me," she said, tucking the card in her tunic pocket.

Our little secret.

# Chapter 20

## *Callie*

CALLIE SAT IN Raysor's patrol car, listening to the phone conversation play out between the deputy and Wayne. Some kind of put-on talk about a fictitious team of able deputies awaiting the order to descend upon St. Clair's world. Wayne obviously with St. Clair. Of course Slade with Wayne. Her mind started what-iffing itself to death.

Raysor hung up, chuckling to himself a second. He started to put the vehicle in drive and stopped. "Want to head to Beaufort instead of seeing my sister?"

God help her, the incredibly nasty image of a female Don wrecked her thoughts of Mini-Hawk. "Um, not sure how to answer that. Depends on your sister, I guess." She erased the mental optics. "She have better insight than your cousin and your nephew? They're more interested in getting you hitched than talking about Simmons."

He bobbed his head. "And she can be more intense than the others about the hitching part. Hoss did have his moment back there, though, and if Beaufort is rendezvous central for trysts . . . I mean, think about it. You're absolutely gonna get caught in Colleton. Who craps in their own bed?"

Oh, these people and their visuals.

"You sure Largo doesn't need us to stick around?" she asked, the obtuseness of his call still nagging her. "Sounded like he needed assistance, Don."

She texted the agent even as Raysor spoke. "He had it under control. A total ruse," he said.

She had to be sure, but Largo texted back a thumbs-up. She didn't pursue further in case he was in the middle of something. She and Raysor were on their own.

"Didn't Savvy say something about certain motels in Beaufort?" she said. "While Beaufort isn't monstrous, it's still a tourist place. We can't waltz into every hotel and B&B and flash a picture, asking if St. Clair Simmons showed up for an afternoon romp in one of their suites.

Like that's not a complaint waiting to happen." Then she had a thought. "Pull over a moment."

He did. Savannah Conroy answered, and Callie put her on speaker. "Hey. Are you in Beaufort or Walterboro today?"

"Beaufort, unless you need me in Walterboro, in which case I'm halfway there. Why, what's happened?"

"Nothing's happened," Callie said. "If I remember right, you said someone like St. Clair would come to Beaufort for a bootie call but not in the town. Or did I remember that wrong?"

"You remembered right. Over toward either Lady's Island or Frogmore would be my guess. Either way there's a motel that would ask no questions but is clean enough to justify the trouble. There are other places in town, but not for a local who doesn't want to be noticed."

Slade's friend had a sense about her. A street sense of sorts, and if Beaufort was her turf, why not use her? "Feel up to riding with us to check them out?"

"I'd love it," Savvy said. "I can give you two or three hours."

Callie loaded Savvy's office address in the navigation and told her they'd arrive in a half hour.

"It's forty miles and the speed limit isn't friendly," Savvy noted.

"It is for us," Callie said. "See you then."

The Agriculture office was on the east side of things, in the Burton community. Savvy waited on the curb in pencil pants and a cashmere sweater that fit her where it counted. A puffy white jacket in the crook of her arm.

"Cuffing me, officer?" she laughed as Raysor let her in the back of the patrol car, and the presence of cage between her and the front seat occupants seemed to bother her none. She immediately captured a picture of her environs.

"Don't make me see those pictures on social media," Callie said. "I'd like to keep you on our side."

"Just capturing experiences," she said. "Now, head through town and stay on Highway 21. It'll take you to Lady's Island. We'll start with The Sand Dollar. I know the owner, but not sure he'd be there. He hates working nights, though, so we might luck up."

Raysor kept checking his mirror.

"What're you looking at, handsome?" Savvy said. "You wondering why I'm familiar with this place?"

"Something like that."

"Honey, if I want to hook up with someone, it would involve chintz, feather comforters, champagne, and breakfast in a four-poster rice bed, not one of these places."

"So you admit—"

"Unh unh, big guy." She held up a finger with a waggle. "You don't want to cross a line and say something you'd regret."

He slowed upon hitting traffic, having passed a Radisson, a Hampton, and coming up on a Holiday Inn. "So why wouldn't he stay at one of these?" he asked.

"Because someone like you might expect him to," she threw back. "You want to be on the other side of the city. Walterboro folks come to Beaufort often, but they don't often have need to visit the islands." She winked at him in the mirror. "You're in my world now."

Raysor drove past the massive live oaks bordering marsh, down Boundary street which right-turned into historic Carteret Street, then returned to being Highway 21 as they passed by the waterfront park and over the water. "Turn at the main light once you get off the bridge," Savvy said. "Sam's Point Road."

Raysor found it, and a couple miles in, to the right, situated as Savvy noted, sat The Sand Dollar Inn. Simple, two story blond brick with maybe sixty rooms, an eight-foot light pink sand dollar over the covered entrance. A slanted triangle sign stood near the road, the motel's architecture dating it to the late 1950s, but proper maintenance kept it appealing and eliminated the seedy appearance it might have otherwise had.

"Drive around it first," Callie said.

Savvy laughed from the back. "Well, nothing like a police car cruising slow through the parking lot to make people zip it up and cut it short."

But Callie noted cameras. Some in strategic places for vandalism, but not as many as she'd wish. "Let's go on in," she said, hoping to find better surveillance inside.

Raysor let Savvy out. "Let me do the talking," she said, leaving the puffy jacket in the car.

Callie came around. "Hold on. I'll take it from here."

Savvy's hand shot to her hip. "You have no oversight in Beaufort County." She snapped her head at Raysor. "And neither does he."

"Frankly, we're here under the aegis of Wayne's federal authority," Callie said, lowering her voice as someone left a second-floor room, peering over the edge at the law enforcement types gathered below. "You're with us as a courtesy."

Savvy leaned in, accenting the six-inch height difference. "Don't have a damn clue what an aegis is, but the fact is you may have aegis, but you don't have the intel. I know the lay of the land. People know me, and you need me."

"Then don't mention Jasmine Bright or Connor Boone when we go in," Callie said, tired of the haughtiness. "When I speak, don't interrupt."

Savvy bounced her eyebrows. "I can live with that." She strode first into the motel lobby.

Easy-to-clean Naugahyde chairs circled a large round coffee table with one long sofa against a wall of posters of past tourist events, which Beaufort had aplenty. The Film Festival, a Taste of Beaufort, the Shrimp Festival, and the Water Festival. The room softly glowed with pastel colors and cream tile floors. The wooden parts of the furniture were a light, yellowish oak.

The three approached the matching oak counter, a sixty-ish gentleman bending over some task behind the four-foot tall barrier. Didn't take more than a snatch of a peek for him to straighten and move the reading glasses off his nose.

"Savannah Conroy. I'll be damned." He reached over the counter with both hands.

Savvy slid one of hers in between them, with a sideways seductive look. "Carlisle Padget, I haven't seen you in a month of Sundays."

The sandy-haired man with a comb-over had already sucked in his gut, and the strain to hold it showed in his neck. "You either, girl. You're looking mighty fine."

She removed her hand, bent enough to rest her arms and sweater assets on the counter, and gave him a bold once-over. "You're looking damn good, too. Lost weight, huh? How've you been?" So went the social niceties about health and acquaintances until Raysor cleared his throat.

"Pardon me," Savvy said, backing up, removing poor Carlisle's close-up view of her endowments. "These are my friends. They had a couple questions, and I said you'd be the perfect man to answer them."

"Uh oh," Carlisle said in jest. "They haven't heard about us, have they?" Callie tried not to roll her eyes at the mutual giggling between Savvy and the motel manager.

Callie held out her hand. "Nice to meet you, Mr. Padget. Savannah speaks highly of you." She introduced herself then motioned at Raysor who was not humored in the least by Savvy's show. "He's Deputy Don Raysor from Colleton County," she said when he wouldn't.

"Why, you're a cute little thing," Carlisle said, leaning forward and looking down. "Care to sit over there in our living room so you can see better? Or the dining room where we've got a Keurig." He motioned to the back corner not twenty feet away as if it were distant.

"No, sir. This is fine," Callie said, long time calloused to the comments about her five-foot-two height. She pulled up a driver's license picture of St. Clair on her phone. "Has this man been to your establishment in the last few months?"

He took the phone and studied it, glancing once at Savvy for a read of what he should say. "I'm not sure." He returned the device. "We see every sort come through here."

"Can you query your system for a name, please?" Callie said. "St. Clair Simmons. Start with Simmons and we'll search from there. Probably checked in around supper time on several dates. With a woman."

He pecked on his keyboard, less friendly and no longer as comfortable in his skin. "Not seeing anything. You sure of the name? Could've used an alias. Especially with a lady friend."

Callie was afraid of that. "Anyone else we can speak to? Someone who might run another shift on different days and maybe met him?"

"Well, we change shifts at five," he said. "Assuming you had time you could come back. Like I said, nothing on the computer . . ." He quit looking at them, as though distracted by work backing up.

Callie didn't ask about camera footage. Not without some sort of date and time reference. Either the man wanted to cooperate or not, and the odds weren't incredibly good that this was the place. St. Clair could've just stayed at the Holiday Inn back on the main strip.

"Appreciate your help," she said.

"Oh," Carlisle said, reanimated and focused on Savvy. "I'm honored to help any friend of Savannah. When're you coming by again, gal?"

"I'm judging the Boat Parade next month," she said. "Can't miss me."

A smile. "I'll be sure to come by."

They left, Raysor releasing a disgusted heave-ho of a sigh as the doors let them into the light. "Feel like I need a shower to get rid of that guy."

"He's completely harmless," Savvy said. "But I think he's lying."

Callie'd sensed it, too, but they had another motel to canvas. If they fell short there, they'd be back. A clerk might be more apt to cooperate than the owner.

She wondered how much of a long shot this whole day was going to turn out to be.

"Where now?" Raysor asked after again locking Savvy in the backseat.

"Go back where we came and cross the highway," Savvy said as Raysor settled himself behind the wheel. "That's Lady's Island Drive. There's a sweet little motel named the Palms. The owner's not local, but the manager is."

"Sweet, huh?" he said, leaving the parking lot.

"What's your issue, Don?" Savvy asked from behind him, capturing his eyes in the mirror again.

"Just more of an old-fashioned guy who believes marriage ought to be sacred," he said.

"You're happily married I take it?" she said.

"Nope."

"Then how do you know how it works?" she asked.

"My parents," he replied.

Savvy laughed. "Like we really know the how and why we were conceived."

Callie let them go back and forth while she pondered St. Clair, yet again wondering if this chase for a girlfriend was worth the effort. She'd committed to Wayne for several days. Partly to watch Slade, and partly as the favor she owed him from their August case on Edisto. But the original case had grown in number and size. Connor Boone had screwed up administratively and shot at an agent. St. Clair misused federal funds. Jasmine died suspiciously. The three matters seeped into each other, lines and details muddy. St. Clair's mistress might be familiar with the particulars that touched all three events, but a girlfriend who'd hung around for over a year would more likely be loyal to her beau. Like Callie said back at her place, love was underestimated in crime solving, and had the power to distort everything.

"There," Savvy said. "On the left."

The Palms was not quite as austere as The Sand Dollar and had tried to a certain degree to emulate a more modern style—say, the nineties instead of the seventies. As before, Callie had Raysor drive around, making note of cameras. More than The Sand Dollar had and at almost every angle. Good coverage. However, that also lowered the chances that someone with clandestine motives would stay here . . . assuming they thought to look.

They entered, this time with the clerk standing at attention more for the uniforms than Savvy. Not that he didn't give her sweater a double-take. Clearly he had no idea who she was and didn't seem to care when she said she had an in with the manager.

A dead end though. Not the first blink of recognition of picture or name after spending fifteen minutes exercising an assortment of searches for a variety of names, to include John Smith, of which there were none.

"It's a quarter to five," Raysor said. "We going back to visit *Carlisle?*" Said with no slight dose of derision.

Callie limp-wristed a motion toward the highway. "We're here. Might as well."

He growled. "Well, after we get done, my belly's gnawing my bones, and it ain't waiting until we get back home. This is turning into a wild goose chase, if you ask me."

"Your suggestion, if I remember right," Callie said.

Savvy reached through the cage and wiggled a finger. "You get grumpy when you don't eat, don't you, boy? Tell you what. If we wind up empty-handed, I'll buy dinner. If we hit pay dirt, the bill's on you."

Raysor's grumble served as his response. He slowed for a light, then covered the couple miles back to The Sand Dollar.

Inside they waited for a lone man to register, who looked none too thrilled to be in the company of cops. The clerk, a young woman in her thirties, went above and beyond to serve his needs and keep him from carrying his bag and business down the street. Callie wondered if a date waited in his car.

He left with a sideways scowl at them, and Callie took the reins, wasting no time after a minimal introduction. "We were in here earlier speaking to Mr. Padget. He couldn't recognize the man we seek, but he said you might since you handled the evening shift. He assured us you were adept at querying that computer and had a memory that put his to shame."

The woman stood like a statue, trying to take in the mission.

"The man we're seeking is not in trouble as far as we know," Callie continued, laying her phone on the counter. "He's a source and isn't aware we're desiring his input. His name is St. Clair Simmons, originally from Walterboro, and he comes to Beaufort often on business."

"He missing?"

Callie forced a neutral expression. "Just hard to tie down." Appear sympathetic. Just uniforms doing a public service, for the greater good.

The clerk wrote down the name then hammered the keys. "I think I've seen him, just not by that name . . . nope. Not seeing that exact name. Goes by the name of Hawk, I believe." She typed some more. "Yep. He comes once a week. Not always on the same day. Sometimes misses a week, but he pays with cash and always asks for the same room. One forty-five."

Callie couldn't believe their luck. Savvy beamed.

"What's so special about that room?" Raysor asked.

After her straight-laced demeanor, the clerk finally grinned. "First, it's on the end, bottom floor. Second, it's as far from here as he can get. Third, the cameras aren't real good there. Wanna see?"

Holy Bejesus, this woman was too good to be true, assuming the guy was St. Clair. Callie wanted to hug her for offering them the first positive movement in their entire day. "Show me."

Callie left Savvy in the lobby and Raysor with her, hoping they didn't leave scars on each other before she returned. Back in the main office, which consisted of a room no more than ten by ten with a desk, a filing cabinet, and a table, the eager night shift manager took a few moments to find the dates that coincided with a Mr. Hawk.

Bending over the clerk's shoulder, Callie watched her skillfully backtrack through the security camera footage.

"Here's the most recent," the clerk said.

Distant and not the best resolution, but damned if the man didn't look like St. Clair. "Are you absolutely sure of that date?"

"Positive," she replied.

"Can you make me a copy of that?"

"Sure."

Callie snatched out her notebook, noting the dates and times of each appearance. "I might be getting back to you for a statement. And whatever you do, don't let anything damage these records, you hear?" Callie looked up. "Or do I need to call the owner for some sort of direction to cover you?"

With a laugh, the clerk replied, "I taught him how to use this system. Trust me. I got this."

Callie nodded in thanks and went back to scribbling. The odds of finding St. Clair and his honey staggered the imagination. Especially since the most recent date was the night that Jasmine died.

# Chapter 21

## *Callie*

"DO YOU RECORD license tags?" Callie asked The Sand Dollar clerk, who was now energized, her hand on the mouse ready to please after Callie's earlier compliment of her.

"We have a place to note it on check in, but he never did," she said. "Cameras?"

"You read my mind," she said, clicking, scrolling, hunting for a better view of the pickup truck's rear end. But St. Clair had backed into his parking spot at the end of the building, in getaway mode in front of room one forty-five—not once but every date the clerk pulled up.

So instead Callie studied the occupant who patiently waited for St. Clair to check in. The same woman each time. Wearing sunglasses. Visor down. Always departing the driver's side once he returned, on the opposite side of the motel entrance and away from the cameras.

"Know her?" she asked the clerk, who shook her head.

"Pull up those last four visits," Callie said, figuring they'd go back a month, plenty for what they needed. "While you're doing that, I'll step out a sec. Be right back."

She retrieved Raysor, and in an afterthought, gave Savvy the nod as well. If St. Clair's date was a Beaufort native, Savvy's connection to the place might give them a name.

"What do you think?" Callie asked once Savvy hugged the monitor.

Squinting, Savvy studied the pictures, shrugged as if nothing rang her bell. "Total stranger. But a lot of people live in this area."

She moved aside letting Raysor get closer. The room warmed with the four bodies huddled so close. Savvy wore something floral. Raysor just smelled of deodorant.

A bell sounded out front.

"I've gotta tend the desk," the clerk said, leaping up. "Be back soon as I can."

Raysor appropriated the free chair to see better. "Son of a bitch," he mumbled, eying one pic, then another. "She's black."

"What the hell, caveman?" Savvy spit the words, indignant more than before at the middle-aged deputy, only this time without the least splash of humor. "You got a problem with skin color?"

"No," he boomed back. "But I understand how the world works around here."

Which left Savvy speechless.

Callie sighed softly. "He's right."

Not expecting Callie to agree, Savvy's cheeks took on a deeper color. "Not exactly what I expected from you. Damn." She exhaled for effect. "And you're friends with Slade?"

Shutting the office door, Callie leaned on it, just in case the clerk was overly efficient. "Just hush a moment, Savvy. We have to think this through. Don," she said, sensing an urgency she hadn't felt since the day Jasmine died. "No doubt in my mind that Mini-Hawk's rank and file don't know about St. Clair's extramarital activities, and if they sense an affair, they have no idea with whom."

"Roger that," he said.

"You sure you don't know her," Callie repeated.

"Damn sure," he said. "But damned if they don't do a good job hiding her identity. Makes me wonder if she's hiding because of race or because of her name."

"Or just because," Callie said.

Savvy made her way between them, patience obviously not her strong suit. "What the hell is wrong with you Colleton people? It's like you're fifty-year throwbacks. If I'd had any inkling of an idea of your bigoted mentality—"

"Savvy, shut up." Callie wiped her face with both hands, then bringing them down to rest on her utility belt. "St. Clair is one of your borrowers. Were you aware of his affair?"

The order to hush didn't set well, and Savvy's eyebrow and prob-ably her temper rose. "I help farmers with their livelihoods, not their sexual escapades. Had I heard he had a girlfriend? Yeah. Did I care who it was? How old she was? Who liked it on top and if they were into B&D? Hell, no. And the *last* thing I cared about was race. Jesus, who cares about that anymore?"

Raysor rose, equally pissed. "Militia, you idiot. They care. And they don't ride the same train we do. Any of *that* getting through to you? And what they believe seriously matters here, just not for the reasons you think."

Callie reached over and gripped a beefy arm. "Don. Lower your voice."

He peered down at her. "I won't have her bashing my people." He stared over at Savvy. "And I don't like having a civilian this ignorant in the midst of this."

"It's a federal case," Savvy said. "More my business than yours."

He raised a finger at her. "Let's see how important you are when guns cut loose and bodies start dropping."

Savvy's mouth fell agape for a long second. "What the hell does that mean?"

"Means we don't have time for the bickering," Callie said. "Get in the car. We'll drop you off, Savvy, and get back to Wayne and Slade with this."

Feelings between them still raw, Savvy and the deputy left the building, leaving Callie to handle the good-bye and thanks. "Can you email me those pictures?" she asked. "The last thing we need is for you, Mr. Padget, or this motel to hold up a federal case."

The stunned clerk read Callie's business card and flitted across the keyboard, taking a couple minutes tops. "You got 'em," she said.

Callie told her to keep the card, offered thanks, and left.

A silent five miles later, they dropped off Savvy with a curt snap of a thanks, her offer for dinner silently rescinded. The remaining two headed back to Walterboro, Raysor's stomach rumbling beneath his vest.

"I was tasting that shrimp," he grumbled, mashing his gut.

"We'll try to meet up with Wayne and Slade to grab dinner."

"Yeah," he said, and they traveled in silence.

"The girlfriend issue might turn out to be nothing," Raysor said.

"Agreed," Callie replied, knowing full well that both of them invested hope in those pictures.

Each fell into their own thoughts for the remaining trip, Callie texting Wayne and Slade that they needed to talk, and Raysor grumbling to himself about narrow-minded people. Texts sent, Callie decided she'd bet a month's pay that if neither Raysor or Savvy could identify the girlfriend, that nobody on Mini-Hawk could easily ID her either. She suspected St. Clair's Beaufort trysts being as much about hiding the woman from his peers as his wife.

St. Clair was a fake, pretending to be a bad-ass. A good number of redneck hunting club rosters held any number of St. Clairs. They donned their camo, wielded weapons, and tackled the woods with their semiautomatic weapons like they were mercenaries hired to clean out the wilds of Kenya.

But how devoted would those closed-door guerrilla wannabes be to St. Clair's goals upon learning how progressive he was with his female fraternizations? The South might be working to progress beyond race, but not so with the alt-right and sundry other wing-nut groups. Callie had no real read on Mini-Hawk and its political beliefs, so she couldn't say for sure. Maybe they were white guys who just liked their guns and had nothing better to do. Maybe St. Clair had land, liked to hunt, and used his assets for an income stream until he could land back on his feet as a farmer. Could be there was no real militia. Could be they had a few black members.

But something happened to Jasmine. What had Jasmine misinterpreted, stumbled into, or dared to expose? She was a native of the area, most likely familiar with the environment. Jasmine had kept her intel to herself, maybe to impress her new partner. Maybe ignorant about these guys . . . and got in over her head.

Sure, she was stung to death, but why the hell was she out there to begin with, without Wayne, and at that time of day?

There were holes in this story, and they didn't all belong to St. Clair.

# Chapter 22

*Slade*

WAYNE SILENTLY got into the passenger side of my truck, not offering to drive. "Let's go grab a bite," I said. "When in Walterboro, one does barbecue. Dukes on Robertson. Awesome buffet. They have this cute, life-size pink pig in front—"

"Just drive, please," he replied.

"I'm just trying to help."

He sighed. "Yeah, I know."

At the end of Sixth Street we headed toward Robertson, which would wind us around to Dukes. Not a long drive, but too long to be taken in pure silence. I let him stew for a few minutes, debating whether to console or chastise him, when his phone chimed. He popped open the text app.

"It's Callie. They're leaving Beaufort. Says we need to meet and talk, maybe over dinner. Raysor's about to faint from malnourishment."

The remark drew a slight grin out of Wayne. His fingers flew over the keys. "Telling them we're headed to Duke's," he said. He waited for the quick chime back. "Don knows it. They'll meet us there."

At least somebody nudged conversation out of the lawman, and capitalizing on the moment, I perpetuated it. "Good. We can have coffee while we wait for them to get there."

But he didn't respond to me. I tired of his mood.

We reached the parking lot, pulling nose in under the double-stacked signs shouting where we were. *Dukes BBQ Here* on the top sign, then beneath it a pig with sunglasses standing in flames over the words *Here* [downward arrow] *Dukes Barbecue*. Not to forget the portable lit marquee at the road saying *Wed 11-8 and Thu Fri Sat 11-9*. The establishment damn sure didn't let you to drive by and not notice.

With impending dusk, floodlights shined bright, lighting up the Ford's interior as if I'd planned it. I pivoted to be more comfortable and to see Wayne better. To hell with coffee. We could wait here as good as anywhere else and talk without fear of listeners.

"We're doing the best we can," I said. "Jasmine was her own person."

He stared at the bottom sign, the one with the pig in sunglasses. "Her mother sure blames me."

"She's a mother," I said. "She has to blame somebody."

I'd never seen him this down on himself. He'd encountered guns, killers, and kidnappers. None shook him up this much.

Was it Jasmine's age? The fact she worked for him? Either could matter.

"What's wrong, Wayne?"

He wasted no time telling me. "I let my personal life cloud my thinking. As a result, an agent is dead."

Which made my thoughts race. His *personal life*. I was a strong factor in that category. "Care to elaborate on what that means?"

I hoped that didn't sound adversarial. I didn't want to pick a fight. That would indeed be selfish. God help me, however, I wondered if he regretted letting Jasmine go ahead to Walterboro so he could remain behind and propose . . . along with the overnight luxuries that came with the fresh erotic joy of being engaged. How much of that did he regret? But worse, how much would remain burrowed in his psyche until our engagement was inextricably linked with the memories of death, neglect, and remorse?

And no explanation on my part would remove that scar.

My left hand rested on the steering wheel. As pretty as this diamond was and as sincere as Wayne had intended the proposal, it had come with a burden.

"Think we need a do-over?" I concluded, instantly apprehensive at making his sadness about us.

"I'm not doing this here," he said.

I removed the diamonded hand from under the light, sliding it into the darkness of my lap. As long as this case was ongoing, and as long as there was a momma blaming Wayne for sending her daughter into harm's way, there was no proper moment to talk *us*.

But when would the proper time be? After Jasmine's funeral? After the case was closed? The next time I caught Wayne in a positive mood to only throw a wet blanket on it by dredging up the past?

Without a doubt, our hottest and most dynamic moments as a couple occurred at the peak of an investigation. There was something about the intensity of the chase that revved our motors. But just as those times energized us, they threw us into squabbles as we clashed on how to cope with human nastiness . . . often pitting one against the other. Add to that he worried about me, and I worried about him, though he never saw the reciprocity of that, but I'd saved his ass and he'd saved mine. Some of his worse anger occurred when I'd been jeopardized and he had no control. Wayne was always at his worst when he couldn't call the shots, couldn't make things better, square, right.

What the hell was I supposed to do with that? About that?

So we sat in the quiet. Him staring straight. Me staring anywhere but at him.

Hopefully Callie would be along soon.

An incredibly painful half hour later, the Colleton County SO unit pulled up on Wayne's side of the truck, and Raysor tipped a chin of acknowledgment as he got out.

Inside the restaurant, the heavy scents of chargrilled meat and vinegary sauces made us more hungry. We took the well-rutted floor path across the room to where thick, white ceramic plates were stacked at the ready. Three different people behind the buffet and six in the dining room yelled to Raysor before we got past the vegetables.

Callie moved up close to me. "How're we supposed to talk in here?"

"Yeah, even the salt and pepper shakers have ears," I said, following Raysor to the line.

We sorted through the pulled pork and hash, the grilled chicken and fried livers, homecooked sides, hushpuppies and banana pudding, and found a booth in the corner farthest from the door and buffet line. A guy at the neighboring table still welcomed Raysor, his wife asking how his mother was.

"This isn't going to work," I said.

Raysor tucked a napkin into his collar, fluffing it to cover his front. His plate doubled the volume of mine . . . tripled Callie's. "Who eats and talks anyway?" he said, and honed in on his turnip greens.

To fit into the four-person booth, Callie'd sat next to Raysor, with me next to Wayne. The two men wouldn't have fit on one side. Callie watched me, sensing my unrest. With a micro-movement shake of my head, I forked my mac and cheese. Like Raysor said, might as well focus on the food since conversation would be stilted and anything but private.

Raysor's radio went off. He turned it down way low and grumbled he was there, come back. Callie's phone rang, then Wayne's. I swallowed quickly, hoping for minimal noise so I could hear at least one of the replies.

"Damn it," Raysor growled and got out of his seat. He fast walked to the cash register asking for a to-go-box.

Callie slid out as well, taking her chat out the front door.

Wayne had a finger in one ear, listening to his phone with the other. With a quick tilt of his head, he conveyed we had to leave. He did an indecisive side-step thing with the waitress boxing up our food, and left. Since none of them was making sure we left with our paid-for dinner, I waited. The girl was efficient, and the door hadn't shut on Wayne before I was on my way, a bag of two dinners in each hand.

Dusk had turned to full night, the bright billboard signage basking us in a yellowish glow. Raysor and Callie were already in the cruiser. Wayne held out his hand for my keys.

"What?" I gripped the door and center console as he wheeled the truck around to follow Raysor and his activated blue lights. Raysor hopped on the four-lane, taking us west.

His mind on the issue at hand, Wayne drove at ten and two. "We fired things up today, apparently."

"With St. Clair?" I assumed that's who he meant since we were headed in Mini-Hawk's direction.

"With everyone," he replied. "There's a gathering of people on the road outside of Mini-Hawk. Supposedly a vigil for Jasmine. Last count ten vehicles and thirty people. More coming."

"How do they know it's Jasmine's people?"

"Maggie's there, and a deputy says these people are from that area of town."

Maggie had yearned to collect her daughter's body and felt she had mourning to do and nowhere to take it. Now it was spilling up and down Old Coon Road.

"As long as it's civil and on public land . . ." and I stopped there, sensing full well where this could go. I prayed Maggie's side stayed on the road . . . and Mini-Hawk's people stayed home.


WE ARRIVED TO what had to be twenty-five vehicles, cops and civilians, mostly civilians, and the night conspired to make the gathering appear more ominous. From inside the truck, I imagined noise, arguments, maybe even protest mantras though I saw no posters or placards waved around. When we left the truck, however, the quiet sent shivers up my arms.

The crisp, clear night sky spanned above, pricked with hundreds of stars, the forest black with only the silhouettes of pines and oaks. The temperature forced people to huddle, their breaths a sea of rising steam. A humming drifted through the humidity, almost muffled but in unison with a few unable to resist the occasional *Praise Jesus* or *Lord, Lord.*

New arrivals walked slowly to join the crowd that lined up and down the road, facing St. Clair's woods. Gracious, there were kids, too, families uniting to honor Jasmine. Hugs. Candles in some hands. Flashlights in others. Phones shining their lights. Waving, more humming.

The deputies stood around seemingly lost at the fact nobody was breaking the law.

Maggie had to be somewhere in the midst of all, buffered by friends and family, the center of the vigil.

Raysor waded through people to another deputy. Callie came to us. "Apparently we need to update each other. Whose tail did you pull?"

Wayne leaned down to her. "We visited the mother this afternoon. Maggie Bright is mighty distraught, and I believe this is the result. She or someone in her circle redirected their grief here apparently."

He straightened, but she tugged his shirt for him to lean down again. I neared them, arms over my coat, the nighttime air frostier. A crescendo in the humming led to someone wanting to sing hymn phrases, and Callie waited, listened to make sure there was nothing serious about to go down in the raised activity.

"We found the motel where St. Clair goes, but can't ID his girlfriend," she said. "I've got pictures in the car, but they're not very good. However, they were enough to surprise the hell out of us."

"Well, this isn't the place to point a finger and ask around," I said. "But Raysor knows everybody, right? He can go around town, talk to his kin to see if they know her?"

Callie gave me a mixed expression of disbelief and disgust. "You haven't met his relatives. And who's in those pictures . . . we'll hold that for later."

I let it go. "We believe Connor was out at Mini-Hawk this morning per his truck parked behind the trailer. When we said he was wanted, St. Clair seemed eager to give him the boot. That was that call Wayne made to Raysor, pretending the sheriff's office was prepared to enter the compound."

Wayne agreed. "Afterwards, a deputy was positioned at each entrance to the compound, though I imagine they're all here now instead." He scouted the swaying landscape of bodies. "I sure hope this group doesn't get much bigger. There must be a hundred people here."

Raysor made his way to us, and put his back to the crowd. "Look in the woods," he said low.

Though dark, the clear sky helped us see the shadows of men amongst the trees.

"Crap," I said, spotting Merrick amongst those in front. Though Atwood wasn't difficult to identify with his size, the rest were unidentifiable behind balaclavas. Creepy fingers crawled up my back, down my arms. What the hell were those men trying to prove?

"Got more guys coming," Raysor grumbled. "Town and county, but damn, only takes one crazy to set this place afire and put us on the news."

He was right. For now, thank God, the crowd on the road appeared wholly absorbed in their remembrance, deeply devoted to honoring their sister. The crowd in the woods stood defiant, almost invisible, guarding their land.

"Son of a bitch," Raysor whispered, looking over our heads. Of course we turned.

A news van barely parked before a man and a woman spilled out. They fast walked past us, beelining to the crowd.

Like that didn't have potential to turn a prayer vigil into a mob.

"Who's in charge, Raysor?" Wayne asked.

Raysor pointed over our heads. "Him, now."

Another Colleton County Sheriff's Office patrol car parked, having taken liberties with space on the road. Two men got out. The bigger man walked like he owned the place.

"Is that the sheriff?" I asked.

"Yep," Raysor said. "Let me introduce you."

"Is he a relative?"

"Somewhat."

Navigating the maze between cars, we reached the sheriff, though he was none too pleased to be stopped. "What is it, Raysor?"

Wayne thrust out a hand. He'd already met the head lawman when he first came to town. The sheriff recognized Wayne.

"I'm still your liaison with federal officials," he explained.

"Then come on," the sheriff replied, and they struck out. The sheriff, his entourage, Wayne, Raysor, and Callie.

Which meant not me, something I had zero problem accepting for once. Crowd control wasn't in my job description. "Wayne! Keys, please. I'll be in the truck."

Wayne tossed them the ten feet without question and turned. They disappeared into the masses, but in my watching them, I spotted someone staring back at me.

I reached in my pocket, took out my phone, and held it up over my head, waving it, hoping she understood. With people moving between us, however, I lost sight of her, so I returned to the truck, sliding the key swiftly into the ignition to turn on the seat warmer.

My phone rang, caller unknown. "Carolina Slade," I answered, hopeful.

"I said you could rely on me," a woman said, obviously tucked somewhere in the gathering. Singing rose next to her, around her. "Plus I told you I'd take care of Maggie."

The slipper lady I'd spoken to outside Maggie's trailer.

I started to reply with *You think a mob is taking care of Maggie?* but I restrained myself. "Not sure I understand what you're doing, Ms . . . Ms . . ." and when she didn't respond, I point-blank asked, "What's your name?"

"My name isn't important," she said. "What I'm doing is giving her an outlet for her pain. For my pain. For everyone's pain. She couldn't just sit in her house like that, and since you hinted that she needed taking care of, we organized."

Her interpretation of *taking care of Maggie* and mine were entirely different.

"That's wasn't my thought, but anyway, please try not to let it get out of hand, okay?" I asked, then when the chatter got louder, I added, "Maggie doesn't need a brawl . . . or a shooting."

Her voice rose louder. "We are civil, Ms. Slade. And in honor of Jasmine we wouldn't start anything."

Like Slipper Lady could stop a spontaneous brawl, and she couldn't read the minds of over a hundred people plus the deputies, each on edge.

"Well, stay safe. Keep Maggie safe." I started to hang up, then tacked on, "And please call me if you see an issue brewing."

She hung up and it got quiet. For a few minutes I sat in the front seat, trying to see Slipper Lady, spot Maggie, see where Wayne and Callie were . . . scan the crowd for anyone looking like trouble. I felt helpless sitting this far back, though, and amazed at how we'd gone from an engagement dinner at Saluda's to this.

A ridiculous idea popped in my head, scary. God help me, I wished I hadn't thought of it, because if I could so could someone else.

What if someone wanted to lay a wreath or light a candle in the exact place where Jasmine died? How would that go over with the Mini-Hawk men?

# Chapter 23

*Slade*

SOME RECOGNIZED the sheriff and parted. Others remained absorbed in their singing. A deputy handed the sheriff an old-fashioned bullhorn. He chose the nearest pickup and climbed up into the bed.

A portable spotlight aimed by the two journalists lit him up, which turned heads and had hands shielding squinted eyes.

"Ladies and gentlemen, my name is A. C. Roberts, the sheriff of Colleton County."

I recoiled as his voice boomed, the reverberation almost irreverent, but after tweaks with the mic, he carried on—still loud enough I could hear him at distance and through the window glass.

"My condolences to those who loved Jasmine Bright, and your desire to honor her memory is commendable. We respect your vigil. Please remain on this side of the road for safety's sake, allowing traffic an outlet." His non-occupied hand demonstrated directions. "And a gentle reminder that you refrain from entering this man's property. Please work with us. My deputies are here to assist."

Mumbling grew here and there, and I wish he'd shown up sooner, before the balaclava boys had made their appearance, because his timing almost coincided with theirs.

Sheriff Roberts lifted the bullhorn again. "You may recognize the black bands on some of our badges." He motioned to his own on his chest. "I've ordered the department wear them, because Agent Bright was a sister in blue. While she was one of you, she was also one of us. Everyone out here mourns her passing."

He said a few more eloquent words, ended on a solemn note with proper praises to the Lord, then thanked everyone for letting him interrupt their remembrance event and handed back the horn. He hopped down, immediately glad-handing everyone in his path while steering a route that I could only assume led to Maggie.

A deputy trailed behind, carrying two tall paper cups. People parted, and thanks to the spotlight following the sheriff, I saw Jasmine's mother just as Roberts handed her one of the cups, taking the other for himself. Then people closed in, and I couldn't see anything but the spot. Couldn't help but wonder how easy it would be to slip a knife in the sheriff in that throng. Would take only one disgruntled, grieving soul . . .

But that was me. Couldn't help thinking how any moment could turn criminal, and crowds scared me silly. My family relocated to the country, which provided a safer, more peaceful setting for me and mine. The tighter people packed in to live, the itchier my nerves.

The temp fell more; the air got nippier. Sinking deeper, I did my best to spread the seat heater over more square inches of my behind, back, and legs, wishing for a blanket. The sight of breath vapors rising from the horde made the cold feel colder, and my core couldn't get warm. Guiltily, I told myself to count my blessings. Maggie and so many others weren't thinking twice about the temperature. They'd stand out there throughout the night if their broken hearts desired, and law enforcement would follow suit.

Hands crammed into coat pockets, I surveyed the woods again. Mini-Hawk's delegation remained in guarded stance like statues, some almost invisible with the spotlight making the woods seem darker. No sign of St. Clair Simmons. A good thing and a bad thing, I guess. His absence might be deemed hardhearted, but his presence could incite the more outspoken of Jasmine's followers. He was damned either way, and I bet the sheriff told him to remain at home.

But St. Clair sending his ambassadors was about as bad. They creeped me out. In daylight, Angus was a twerp, Merrick a retired deer hunter, and Atwood a dated soldier trying to perpetuate who he'd once been, assuming he'd really been anything. Because you look like a football player doesn't mean you can play.

Even under the clear sky, luminescent three-quarter moon, and the television spot, the boys took on a supernatural presence. They seemed to perpetuate that image the way they hovered on the edge of being seen. Shadow figures. Had any of them had ever seen serious confrontation? I wondered which ones might crave it versus which hoped tonight would be over so they could go back to the trailer, maybe light up a wood fire, and while safe and sound brag about what could've gone down if this or that had happened.

"This" or "that" could happen so easily. The idea of a bold mourner slipping into the woods to the shack remained in my head. If everyone understood where on Old Coon Road Jasmine's death had occurred, they probably had heard the how. Old-time residents maybe had a first-hand memory of that shack, understood how old shacks would be a perfect place to harbor hornets. Instinctively, I scouted again for movement, but nobody crossed the line where the road paralleled the woods, honoring the sheriff's wishes. Maybe I was thinking too hard.

Then to my right, at the far end of the Mini-Hawk men, almost too far to be considered part of St. Clair's garrison and a far cry from the lit up crowd, I gleaned movement.

I skootched over to the passenger side to see better, immediately regretting the loss of the heated seat. The late-comer took a stance, gawking down the line of others to see if he was doing it right, then he stood against a tree and tried to blend in.

Which drew a grin out of me at his attempt to be ominous while being anything but.

He apparently caught Merrick's attention as well as mine, or seemed to. Merrick abandoned his post, headed toward the opposite end of the line, but disappeared into the darkness. About the time I figured he only needed to whiz in the bushes, he appeared behind the new guy . . . and frightened him senseless.

Merrick's hand clapped hard over his mouth, his other hand gripping the back of his neck to sandwich him in a hold. With a stiff move, Merrick's mouth met the guy's head, a severe message being delivered directly in an ear. The body language between these two guys spoke volumes.

With a snap, Merrick removed his hands and turned the stray around, ordering him to leave. Intimidated, the guy lifted his mask only for Merrick to grab it and jerk it back down, but not before I recognized Connor Boone.

I hunted in my pocket for my phone, dropping it on the pitch black floor. I bent down, grateful for the background image automatically coming on with movement so I could find it, and hit recent calls to find Wayne.

"Hey," he said. "You might want to leave—"

"Hush," I whispered hard, then felt a fool for thinking anyone could hear. Still, I hunkered to not draw attention to my phone's screen. "I think I saw Connor."

"Where?"

"In the woods."

"You think or you're sure?"

"I'm mostly sure," I said, feeling ninety percent solid.

Voices spoke, overriding the singing in the background. "Well, we've got a situation developing. Already excised one man from the crowd to a patrol car."

Disgruntled voices fell over each other in the background.

"Back up," Wayne said—not to me. "Raysor, have a word with that one, will you?" Then he came back to me on the phone. "Connor's not our priority, Slade. We have bigger issues."

"So ignore him?"

"Can't talk. If you leave, text me so I'll know where you are. Better yet, just go on back to the beach."

He hung up.

I quickly peered into the dark forest to regain my bearings on the two men. Merrick wasn't there any longer, and searching back up the line I spotted him walking behind his men, returning to his spot, I presumed. He had laser focus on the mourners who weren't so solemn any more. Connor, however, was gone.

The sheriff appeared to my left, weaving his way in and out of the cars back to his own, a deputy at his rear. Another television station appeared in a mid-sized SUV, the newscaster recognizing the sheriff, but after being denied access to the man by the deputy, he ran toward the light with a young man looking nineteen years old bouncing a camera behind him.

Guess the sheriff trusted his uniforms . . . and hated the press.

Returning my attention to the mass of people, I saw some arms pumping in the air. A guy in his thirties jumped into the same truck bed previously used by the sheriff and shouted, "Justice for Jasmine." He didn't stand up there long before deputies and a couple of the mourners ordered him down, hands grabbing him any way they could.

No way I was leaving. No way I could help with the crowd, though. However, one task remained that fell in my wheelhouse. Talking to Connor Boone.

The man was a wuss, behaving like a twelve-year-old trying to impress a girl by shooting tires, and now his hunting buddies by donning the garb and a firearm to pretend he served in someone's private army. All it took was Merrick's scolding for Connor to take up his toys and go home, so I rated his threat level minimal if not zero. He'd shot at our tires, not us.

Merrick returned to his original post, but moved a few yards closer to the ruckus. The guys in the woods kept eyes on the cops and crowd, measuring, awaiting orders.

I eased the door handle, then remembered to get my .38 out of the glove box. Not that it held any sort of advantage over the other firearms in this situation, but to have nothing in the presence of dozens of AR-15s and Glocks felt stupid. I hid it in my coat pocket in hope it stayed there until I locked it back in the glove box when I returned with Connor.

Leaving the truck, I nudged the door closed to avoid attention and backed against it. Squinting, I scanned the trees. Nothing where I last saw Connor.

Instead of marching straight over to where he'd been, though, I veered right, opposite from everyone else, and hugged the sides of vehicles, between vehicles when I could, and walked forty yards or so before crossing the uncrossable line into the woods.

I'd played this sort of game before, only in broad daylight in a forest outside the small town of Pelion. A drug dealer had snared my sister and Wayne, and the only way for me to get to them was hide behind one tree then another . . . and do it stooped close to the ground instead of up-right.

It was a darn sight harder repeating that move in the dark.

But on the bright side, Connor wouldn't be dependable in a fight, and had probably never been battle-tested. He was a milquetoast, hometown guy with a government job whose wife dumped him for being too passive. In Merrick's obvious opinion, a liability if the night went sideways. And Connor, having been properly chastised and belittled, had scuttled off with his tail between his legs.

I was pretty sure I could talk him in.

But as I crab-walked from tree to tree, I considered another theory. Connor would take up position out of view, ready to launch himself into any skirmish that sprouted. He'd pretty much lost his wife, his home, and his job. He had nothing to lose and everything to gain in his mind by sticking around since Mini-Hawk was probably all he had left in the world.

I didn't go straight into the forest, but instead took my covert move-ments at an angle, zigging sometimes. Thank God the ground was damp to mask the noise, but thanks to my klutziness, my jeans were soon wet up to my thighs.

A couple of car doors closed. The crowd growing or thinning?

The end guy of the lineup had tightened toward the guy next to him, watching the gathering. Must be more people, more tension. Good. Less attention toward me.

I moved until Connor stood about fifty yards to my left and back. I could stand, and even if someone looked in my direction, they'd never see me.

"Connor," I whispered, then listened hard. "Connor," I repeated, comfortable at not being heard by Mini-Hawk men.

I dared to walk farther in, whispering louder.

A rustle sounded to my right. I froze, suddenly fearing a second line of men as backup.

Instead, a masked man appeared from behind a tree ten feet away, back against the bark and sliding so I could see him. "Slade. What are you doing here?" Connor said in a raspy whisper.

"Saw you talking to Merrick," I said, moving another tree closer. "I want you to come back with me."

"Can't," Connor said. "I've crossed a line. I've chosen . . . this."

"What the heck do you mean by *this?*"

"I shot at a federal agent. They labeled me armed and dangerous, isn't that right? Heard people talking in town. That means someone might prefer to shoot me as bring me in alive."

A laugh bubbled up, and I forced it down hard and quick. "Connor, you shot tires, dude. However, we can go back and say you were showing off for Rebecca. That agent wasn't near that car. I'd be pissed as hell if I thought you'd seriously tried to kill Wayne Largo."

Connor didn't laugh. He held up his semi-automatic instead. "You think this is funny?"

Suddenly my choices were anything but.

"Um, no, Connor. It's not." I reached into my pocket, taking the gun grip in my hand. "What started out as you not making your client pay on time is deteriorating, and if you don't come in, you're messing up worse. You're not too deep in this that you can't get out."

"I'm already in deep, you idiot. You have no idea."

His tone told me I'd erred in judgment thinking I could bring him in alone. "Running is worse," I said.

In that tense instant, my crazy mind thought of the movies. Wayne brought it up all the time. The two armed people at a standoff, using an insane amount of dialogue that would never happen in real life. *Too much talk*, he always said. Yet here I was with Connor, both of us babbling. Both of us afraid. Only he didn't know I was armed. I wanted to keep it that way.

"Go and leave me alone," he said, and turned to leave.

"Connor, come on, dude. Put the gun down and do what I say. There's no way—"

He wheeled and spit two rounds at me.

My .38 came out like I'd practiced for a James Bond flick. Two rounds went right back at him as I dove, in an earnest attempt to burrow out of sight into the leaves.

There I stayed, hand tight on the .38, head planted into the ground, tasting decomposed plant matter. Afraid to see who hit whom and waiting for all hell to break loose from those other guns in the woods.

My heart climbed up my throat, my breaths so thin I couldn't hear myself breathe. Any minute someone could pull a trigger at my back, put a round into my head, or catch me in crossfire . . . maybe in addition to one of Connor's bullets that I was too adrenaline-pumped to feel.

I couldn't stop shaking. No way I could fake dead now, and seconds became hours.

Footsteps scurried at us, too many to read. "Drop the weapons and show us your hands," shouted a man from deep in his gut. Another yelled, then another, each making me flinch.

Head still in the leaves, I slid the .38 out slowly, pushed it into view of whoever they were, then balled back up.

Someone knelt beside me, taking the gun. "Ma'am? Are you hit. Ma'am?"

"Slade! Damn it, Slade!"

When Wayne's voice came within yards of me, I dared peer up, pushing to my knees. He caught me, rolling me to a seated position, a strong grip with one hand, his other searching. "Slade, look at me. Are you shot?"

He kept searching, and I didn't care who saw. Opening my clothes, he touched me in fast movements, frequently studying his own hands for signs of red in the beam of a uniform's flashlight.

Finding nothing, he placed hands on either side of my head, staring into my eyes. I winced as the uniform's flashlight followed, the direct brightness making me turn away.

"Slade, answer me. Are you shot?"

"Don't . . . don't think so." I could've been riddled with bullets and wouldn't have known.

Wayne hunted further for bullet wounds, prodding, watching for my reaction. We'd done this before, too, only last time it was shotgun pellets in Newberry.

Seemed we were developing a small town ritual I could do without.

"Connor," I said, then couldn't figure how to finish the thought.

Connor'd missed with his shots. He'd fired. So I'd fired. I didn't

have to look to know I'd hit my mark. Daddy'd taught me too well.
Wayne had honed that existing skill until hitting my target was in-
stinctive. You don't pull unless . . . .

Turning to where other flashlights shined and people hunched, I
asked, "Is he alive?" When nobody answered, I repeated the question
with pangs of panic, "Someone tell me, is he alive?"

"He's alive, but not sure how long," someone said. "Ambulance on
its way."

Men worked on him, stifling blood loss, I guessed. How much
blood? Where'd I hit him? I hit his torso. I swear I did. Isn't that what
we're taught? If you draw you shoot center mass? Neutralize the threat?

A wave of weakness washed over me. Wayne eased me to him. "I'm
having them look at you, too." His scrunch held me close. "Goddammit,
Slade, what the hell were you doing?" he whispered for only me to hear.

"My job," I managed to squeak out, no strength behind the words.
"You were too busy with the crowd. I wasn't."

The shakes returned. He hugged tighter.

"Are they going to arrest me?" I could only think of how Connor
contained two bullets and I didn't.

"Every damn person out here knows the difference between the
report of an AR and a .38," said another voice. Callie. "He shot first. I
think you're good, but no doubt there'll be paperwork and conversation." She knelt down, a hand on my back. "How're you doing?" She
rubbed circles across my shoulder blades.

"I'm not sure." And I wasn't. Shivers ravaged my arms and legs. She
rubbed harder.

"Well, good thing you were the better shot," she said.

Was I?

We were too close for an average shooter to miss.

He'd shot out the tires.

What if he'd only tried to scare me, and I'd read him wrong?

# Chapter 24

*Slade*

LIGHTS BOUNCED off us as the crowd quickly abandoned their vigil and vacated Old Coon Road. Cars turned and headed from whence they'd come with nobody wanting to be involved in a shooting at the Salkehatchie compound.

No sign of the Mini-Hawk crew. Not even Merrick, the bastard. He'd done nothing wrong so why not stand by his man? Of course St. Clair wouldn't make an appearance.

The ambulance arrived quickly, but not before the area had almost cleared, the red lights bouncing off the woods on either side with only patrol cars left. One EMT tried to look me over, but I refused, sending the help to Connor, feeling selfish to utilize a medical professional. The more hands on him the better.

Deputies pushed reporters back off the private property, one of them giving a brief statement along the line of, "still under investiga-tion." Oh, they hovered, drooling over seeing something bloody, but they were denied the satisfaction. Medics removed Connor quick and clean with no camera vantages. With no officers claiming the authority to converse with the press, and especially with nobody identifying the shooter, the news hounds scurried to catch up to the ambulance. Calls were made to deter them on the other end.

The quiet fell hard which allowed thoughts of regret to consume my attention. The stupid son of a bitch didn't deserve to die. No reason for Connor to consider himself public enemy number one either, but he sure did. What the hell was he thinking? He killed tires and let St. Clair miss his payments. Was this guy that naïve about what constituted dire crimes and breaking the law?

Had he accidentally shot at me?

Wayne kept speaking in my ear, assuring me, telling me that if some-one shoots at you, you return fire. Connor missed. I didn't. It could've been the other way around.

The laundry list of what could've happened invaded my reflection of the night, over and over. What if this . . . what if that? Mini-Hawk consisted of wannabes. I'd much rather they'd been well-trained mercenaries because they recognized real threats. These guys . . . they could've done anything.

I should've stayed in the truck. Why wasn't Wayne telling me I should've stayed in the truck?

More shivering. From cold, from instant replays, from self-reprisal. . . . Wayne had noticed and refused to take me *home* to Callie's without my being checked out at the Colleton Medical Center.

So here I sat on an examination table, Wayne at the edge of the curtain.

"How's Connor?" I asked, feeling silly in a hospital, worried that time wasted on me detracted from Connor dying two beds down or something. "Is he here in the ER?"

"They took him straight to surgery." A straight answer without giving me anything to read behind the words.

"Is he going to be okay?"

"We have to wait, Slade."

So noncommittal I wanted to scream.

"Can't you check?"

"Too soon. They'll tell us—"

"Check anyway, goddammit. Since when do you not push your way through and make a doctor talk to you?" He'd done it three times in my history with him, coaxing medical professionals to relax rules, spill details, have faith in him as one of the good guys. Why couldn't he use that talent now? I needed to know, damn it.

My hands shook and I slid them under my thighs.

I needed to know if I'd murdered anyone or not. No, not murdered . . . killed. Wayne says law enforcement can kill, but they don't murder.

In a flash Wayne was at the table, hands again on both sides of my head. Apparently my thoughts had spilled out of my mouth. My arms and knees twitched.

"He's not dead, Slade," he murmured up close. "They'd tell me." He crushed me to him. "It was a righteous shoot, babe."

"They took my gun."

"Customary. You'll get it back."

My cheek against his coat, I focused on his scent, and his rocking. I didn't want anything else.

"Knock, knock," said a gravelly voice on the other side of the curtain.

"Come on in," Wayne said, and I pushed back, not eager for anyone to see me fragile.

Raysor strolled in like he worked there. "How you doing?"

"Fine. Not sure why I'm even here," I said, smoothing pants that didn't need smoothing. "I wasn't shot."

"Hmmm, well, there are procedures for this sort of thing, I guess."

"I guess." The air turned thick with awkwardness.

"Well, just wanted to check on you," Raysor said, studying a chart listing flu symptoms. "Girl," he said, turning around rather quickly for him. "I gotta hand it to you. Somebody taught you well."

Wayne nodded, but I was too addled to grasp. "What?"

"Good shooting," Wayne translated.

Raysor's salt and pepper wiry brows rose and fell. "What do you mean, *what*? Two near the O-ring with a three-inch spread in the dark, is what I mean. From a quick draw, no less."

"Oh." Might as well take the compliment from a man who meant nothing but the best for me. "Thanks. Guess I did have good teachers. Don't remember some of it."

"A natural." The silence returned, enough I could hear Raysor's rough breathing. Having fulfilled his task and delivered his message, he shrugged. "Well, guess I best go before the white coats arrive and I get told to leave."

Which drew the first smile I'd managed to make since the morning. Callie had a good one in him.

The doctor had to have passed Raysor coming in. He asked a dozen questions, did a cursory check of my vitals and scratches on my hands, and released me. On the way out of the ER, I repeated my request like a looped recording. "Check on Connor."

Wayne opened his mouth, then he seemed to change his mind about saying there was no need. While I waited in the lobby, he disappeared to quickly return. "Still in surgery. These injuries take time."

Which only created the image of a dozen blue-masked people with sweated foreheads scrambling to keep Connor's heart pumping.

Somewhere in the hubbub, Wayne spoke to the sheriff. I'd missed that call, but he didn't go into details as we traveled to Edisto, which didn't feel right. Sort of like I'd escaped a bullet.

I weakly harrumphed at the ridiculous metaphor.

Wasn't terribly late, eleven thirty, but my limbs hung like fifty-pound icicles. My brain felt dosed on drugs as I came down off the stress.

"Oh crap," I said with a jolt of new awareness. "We've got to notify Monroe."

"Already did," he said. "He said update him tomorrow."

I didn't ask what Monroe said. Didn't want to hear. At least Wayne had the presence of mind to let my boss, the state director of agriculture, know that two of his employees had been involved in a shootout—with each other.

"They sending someone?" I asked.

"They've put you under my oversight," he said. "Mainly because I was already down here, and I refused to send you home while I remained here. My IG people will be kept informed while Colleton County people handle the case. I'll wrangle all that."

This sort of thing, not that we had these sorts of happenings, wouldn't normally enter my purview, so we were walking on fresh ground. Plus I wasn't thinking straight.

Wayne had gravitated from frantic at the scene to pensive in the hospital to overtly caring in the truck, which had me wary. I wasn't hurt but he behaved like I was. I fully expected a scolding, and he wasn't delivering anything of the kind.

I'd been shot at before . . . even stabbed. Once danger passed, he worried, he fretted, then he invariably cussed me out. There was a system in how he juggled lover and agent. I'd sort of gotten used to the rhythm of his internal clock and admonishments.

"If you want to talk, talk," he said. "If you keep to yourself, I'll understand that, too. You warm enough?" Not waiting for response, he upped the heater a couple degrees.

I just stared at this creature. The way he'd acted at the hospital, I was surprised he hadn't dressed me, carried me to my truck, and put on my seatbelt for me.

"I don't get it," I replied, never the one to want silence instead of conversation.

"Get what, Butterbean?"

Um, still nurse-maiding me. "Why didn't they question me on site or haul me into the sheriff's office? No statement? No interview?" Something didn't feel right. Like another shoe still waited to drop and I wouldn't see it coming. Home tonight . . . jail tomorrow? Something was seriously abnormal about shooting someone and being told, *we'll get back with you on that.*

"They spoke to others at the scene, and we'll have to speak to the SO tomorrow," he explained. "You'll give a statement, probably write it tomorrow from Callie's porch or, if it's too cold, I'll light a fire and we'll go over it inside. I'll coach you, quarterback it to insert the appropriate buzz words. Then we'll run it to Walterboro."

We were spending an entire day figuring out how to say I followed Connor, discounted his machismo, got shot at, and shot back?

A car came at us through the pitch, over the speed limit, probably not expecting to see us anymore than we expected him. As the lights met us, I cringed. I mean, fists on my forehead, recoiled.

Wayne slowed, hand over to grip my shoulder. "It's okay. Do I need to stop?"

Heart doing a samba, I took an accounting. Panting, pulse up, blood pounding in my neck. What the hell?

"I'm fine."

"Really?"

"Really, Cowboy. It's late enough as it is," I said, those few words leaving me hundred-yard-sprint breathless. Leaving me not wanting to talk anymore.

Soon enough I was happy to see that even after midnight, lights shined at Chelsea Morning. Callie met us at the door. I hugged her.

"You okay?" she asked, accepting me with a massage across my back like she had in the woods.

"Sure." I walked in, not wanting to see the unspoken language between Callie and Wayne.

Callie could've scurried around and doted on me, but she didn't, and I appreciated the hell out of her for it.

"Drink?" she asked as we shed our coats.

When I hesitated, she read my silence as a yes. She poured two lowballs, setting both glasses on the coffee table. Positioning herself in a recliner that engulfed her tiny shape, she curled up with a Blenheim's ginger ale, and I had to smile at the symbolic substitute for a gin and tonic that I'd introduced to her back in August. Her way of saying she had her own method of drinking with us. Silently showing she respected me and my need for medicinal alcohol.

Wayne and I parked ourselves on the sofa, and we lifted our glasses. She held her bottle up for an air toast. "To us and what we do," she said. "And may we never take it for granted."

I took in a mouthful. The doctor had given me a relaxant at the hospital, but since I'd yearned for bourbon at the end of the evening, I'd pocketed the pills. The Woodford did a lot better job of soothing.

"Tired?" Callie asked.

"Not in the least," I said, but leaned into Wayne, looking up at him. "Bet you're exhausted, though."

The slight redness in his eyes and the circles under them spoke clear enough. He lifted his glass. "One will do me in." He'd already drunk half.

Callie'd already lit her gas logs, the flicker tranquil, but the ping under my skin hadn't wholly disappeared. I'd pour myself a second in a minute.

"Why don't you go to bed?" I said to Wayne. "I won't be far behind you."

"I'll sit up with her," Callie added.

He upended his glass, patted me on the leg, and stood. "Believe I'll take you up on the advice." He left to set his glass in the sink then came back to kiss me on the head. "Don't stay up late," he said, then trudged to the guest room.

"He looks worse than I do," I said, rising to get that refill.

Callie sat with her legs crisscrossed in the recliner. "Personally, I can't tell much difference."

"Thanks." Glass refilled, I parked back on the sofa.

Fire should crackle, I thought, intently studying the silent orange and yellow flames. When it came to legit ambience, gas logs sucked.

"Slade?"

"Hmm?"

"Are you really okay?"

My gaze shifted from the fire to her. "Why does everyone keep asking me that when Connor's the one with bullets in him?"

"You're surrounded by cops," she said. "They see things from a different perspective. The one left standing is the one left carrying the load."

I watched the fire some more. "Wayne didn't get mad at me. He always gets mad at me when I do something stupid." I sipped again and shook my head, sucking on a sliver of ice until it melted. "I think I broke him this time."

Callie chuckled, then set her bottle on the side table and unfolded her legs, leaning forward in the recliner. Her feet still didn't hit the rug.

"You scared him," she said.

"Yeah, I get that, but he scolds when he's scared."

Callie crossed her feet. "You don't preach or lecture someone who's shot an opponent in the line of duty. You console and support. Nobody understands the weight of shooting another human being until they've done it. You are welcomed into a club that nobody wants to join."

"But I'm not a cop. And he's not dead. Wayne promised to tell me."

"You shot someone, though, and you're not far from being a cop," she replied. "You have the harder job, in my opinion. Never seen such a unique role. You do a lot of the work without the full authority . . . without the full force of the law behind you. Wayne sees that, which is why he hangs so close. Why he scolds a few lectures in hopes of better enabling you. Why he kicks himself when things like tonight happen."

My heart sank . . . or it was spent after the day, couldn't tell which. "I sort of tie him up in knots. Sounds like I'm more of a handicap."

Her comical grimace wouldn't accept my reasoning. "You only heard half of what I said. You're an asset. You dive into cases. You solve cases. I like you. Wish you worked for me."

Such a tiny woman sitting there offering counsel, and doing so from the heart, which touched me. Past compliments often came back-handedly from folks who only reluctantly admitted I'd done something right. My own mother simply deemed me foolish. "Um, thanks. Wish I worked for you, too."

"Nah," she laughed. "You're right where you need to be."

I was astonished at such open praise, brushed a tear and blinked the rest away.

"But you're in a bit of shock, Slade, in case you hadn't realized it. That's why they didn't interview you right off. Wayne took you to the ER not only to see you were okay, but to help you settle . . . and to buy time. The locals gave a professional nod to Wayne to see that you return with a proper statement. Feds carry a lot of clout, and he doesn't flaunt it, so they respect him."

I swear I should've known that.

"My guess," she continued, "is that he'll help you prepare a statement, you guys will take it in, and after only a couple of cursory questions, they'll take it as gospel. Like I told you on site, every uniform out there recognized by sound which weapon shot first."

"I shouldn't have carried the gun in my pocket." I laughed once. "Shouldn't have left the truck."

Callie shook her head. "You were trying to help Connor, Slade. And you were doing your job."

I didn't see Connor as a criminal like everyone else seemed to, but he'd officially made himself one. Violence hadn't seemed to be in his nature, and Savvy would agree with me. What had he gotten himself into?

Unless he wasn't the person I'd assumed he was, meaning I'd blundered following him into the woods alone. What wasn't I seeing?

"Following Connor was stupid."

Callie watched, passing no judgment.

Really, why had I walked into jeopardy like that? "I wanted to help him, distance him from Mini-Hawk and get him out of the trouble he kept stumbling into."

Which made Callie smile. "Did y'all have any conversation before the shit hit the fan?"

I appreciated her not saying *before you shot him.* "He said it was too late when I attempted to talk him in. Said *I'm already in deep. You have no idea.*"

"No explanation about what *deep* meant?"

I shook my head. "When I tried to tell him otherwise, he shot at me."

My drink was gone, and Callie remained on the edge of her recliner. The clock on the cable box read almost two.

"There's way more story to him," I said. "At least he can't run. Maybe tomorrow I'll go to the hospital—"

"Tomorrow you sleep late then do your statement," Callie said, rising. "Raysor and I'll go by the hospital. I've had some experience at this."

Palms up, I conceded. When I stood from the sofa, my weariness caused a stumble. "Whoa, too much drink."

"Too much day," Callie said and took my glass. "Go to bed. We'll talk tomorrow."

But I had something more to say. Something I hadn't admitted to Wayne that ate at me like a cancer.

"He should've hit me, Callie. Makes me think he missed on purpose."

"You can't think like that, Slade."

I slowly shook my head in disagreement. "Oh, but I can. Nobody sees me as armed. Connor had no reason to assume I hid a gun in my pocket, and there is no indication in his background that he'd kill an unarmed person in cold blood. He shot to my right. Nobody stands ten feet close and misses. Not with that weapon."

"So what do you think he was doing. Scaring you off?"

"Maybe." Fatigue owned me as tears returned. "I might've killed him when he only wanted me to leave."

"There are better ways to chase off a person than firing a gun," she said. "Particularly when he could've triggered World War Three out there tonight. If you're firing in the direction of people, it's not a warning. Unless you're brain dead or asking to be shot. He's not right, Slade. He's screwed up." She came to me, softly stroking her hands up and down my arms. "And you cannot predict people who are messed up in the head. The best you can do is protect yourself and those around you. Go to bed. You're too tired for this."

I hugged her, and she lovingly patted me until I let go. "Good night," she said. "Go sleep."

Bones like lead, I made my way to the bedroom, peeled off clothes, and crept under the covers next to the lawman, who slept dead to the world.

But when I closed my lids I saw Connor, and popped them open. A streetlight shined around the edges of the pulled blinds, and if I listened hard, I could hear the waves four blocks over. I took five deep, cleansing breaths, willing myself to sink further into the mattress, and tried again.

Again the gun flashes, my hand clenching to grip a pistol that wasn't there.

In hindsight, I'd always been on the receiving end of violence. Delivering it was not at all what it was cracked up to be.

# Chapter 25

## *Callie*

HAVE A FEW DRINKS, crawl into bed next to the man you love, and sleep until you wake up. If that wasn't an alternative universe for Callie, she couldn't say what was, but she wished the best for Slade in having those choices.

Callie got by on less than six hours sleep anyway, about right for tonight . . . one sans alcohol. She'd already texted Raysor not to report to Edisto in the morning, that she'd meet him at the sheriff's office, and they'd take her cruiser. As emissaries for Wayne and Slade, they had errands to run.

She pulled the yellow eyelet quilt over her and attempted to drift to sleep, her soul hurting for her friend in the next room. Thank God Slade efficiently used a weapon, but she was altered now, like the rest of them. Even if Connor pulled through, Slade was changed, but she had shot true. Callie'd seen the grouping. Wayne . . . tomorrow he could be more attentive to Slade, maybe that job would take some of the sharp off losing Jasmine.

She couldn't stop thinking as she stared up at the fan hanging dormant for the winter months.

She prayed Connor lived. Didn't matter how evil the person, when you assisted in a spirit leaving a body, your soul changed. Your nights became about sweated sheets and waking disoriented in a normal bedroom after dreaming of shots fired.

Connor's clammy, chalky appearance didn't speak well of his condition when they carted him off. His breaths a struggle . . . reminding her of the times she'd taken lives and watched them likewise gurneyed into ambulances . . . surgery a wasted detour to the morgue.

Gin came out on sleepless evenings like this when she had no alternative, no person, no excuse or obligation to take its place. She would not do so with her guests in her spare bedroom. Imagination made the taste lay heavy on her tongue, though.

She threw back the covers. Maybe a hot bath. Real hot.

Moments later, with lavender scent and water up to her chest, she attempted to relax. She owned being a borderline alcoholic, but also owned the triggers. She'd unearthed and disposed of monsters Edisto residents had never seen, and those monsters came with a price.

But no gin. Not tonight. Slade and Wayne needed her whole focus to take this case, these cases, these disjointed yet connected cases . . . to conclusion.

There'd been enough damage. The couple hadn't left her when she needed them before. She'd stand by them now.

THE NEXT MORNING, Callie picked Raysor up, noting his face was clad in a full-blown scowl.

A half dozen reporters hollered at him as he half-trotted to her car. "Do we have militia in this town, deputy? Is there going to be a Salkehatchie War? Do black residents need to worry about Mini-Hawk? Are there any other militia in the Lowcountry?"

"You people get on out of here," Raysor hollered. Their questions muted once he dropped into the passenger seat and slammed his door.

"Damn reporters," he growled, reaching for his seatbelt. "Damn parasites. Stupid blood suckers. Goddamn—"

"I get it, Don."

To reach Callie's vehicle, Raysor had navigated past a cadre of journalists camped outside the Colleton Sheriff's Office. Luckily he hadn't flipped one of them the bird.

She shared Raysor's less than favorable view of reporters and wasted no time leaving. "Let's take it down the street and park, then decide our plan of action for the day." She scooted down Mable T. Willis Boulevard to Highway 63 and took a left.

"It's making the Charleston news, you know," he said, still huffing from the escape. "Not doing a lot for our image. *Frontporch to the Lowcountry* ain't as quaint a nickname with snipers in the bushes."

"Pray it'll blow over," she said. "Edisto's gotten over the Russian mob, a serial killer, and a cop killer." The last one Raysor would recollect well. Seabrook. His friend and Callie's lover shot on Pine Landing Road by a deranged reporter. A moment in both their lives that cemented their distaste for journalists. A subject that made him stop fussing.

"How's the beach faring without us?" he said instead.

"Thomas and Marie have it under control. A blessing this happened this time of year."

"Slade okay?"

Callie hesitated on that one, but ultimately gave him an "I believe so."

"She shot good," he said.

"Slade shot great," she replied. "But it's eating at her."

"She'd be alien if it didn't."

"Just what I told her."

She parked at a convenience store, where a patrol unit wouldn't stand out. "Need a coffee or Coke or something?" she asked.

"Nah, just tell me our marching orders. The sheriff's trying to de-emphasize the shooting, by the way. Said it was a memorial, and somebody accidentally discharged their personal weapon. But then one of those reporters realized it was on Mini-Hawk. Another learned the memorial was about a dead federal agent . . . well, you can imagine the spin-offs. He's declined to speak to FOX, CNN, and MSNBC, giving the locals his watered-down version."

Good for the sheriff. "No mention of Connor?"

Raysor grimaced. "Oh, they mentioned Connor."

She should've watched the news, but she hated the media and dodged their work. Edisto Beach had remained detached from most media, and truthfully, she wasn't interested in the rest of the world's problems. She wondered if Slade's agency would deal with the press since Connor and the shooter belonged to them.

"But as you could see back there, the media still think they deserve more than they got."

"Screw the media."

"Yep."

A guy in painter clothes came close by the car, his truck back at the pump, and Callie hushed until he passed before talking again. "Who in your family does videography?"

"That would be Marvin and Marsha," he said. "He's a teacher and she stays at home, but both handle the photography business. He has an in with the school board and does the district's school pictures."

Head tilted, she waited for him to finish.

"And yes," he admitted with a silly side-to-side of his head. "They have the equipment, and I get them jobs with the local government."

"Okay, then. Think they can clean up this video that motel clerk sent? Maybe pull stills to help identify St. Clair's girlfriend?"

He snorted once. "We're still dealing with that, are we?"

"We follow through, Don."

Guttural acceptance came from his throat. "Then head that way and cross the interstate. Two miles then past the billiards place, take a right on Cane Street. Marsha will be there. Marvin's in school."

Five minutes later, they slowed at a hand-painted metal sign on chains at the drive, *M and M Photography*. The sky threatened to drop rain too cold to freeze but wet enough to chill a person to the bone, so they scurried from the warm car into a meager ranch style house on a handful of acres. The photography studio operated in a refurbished garage on the end.

Like the other Raysor relatives, Marsha carried substance on her frame, enough for two Callies.

"What the heck is going on in Salkehatchie, Don?" Marsha said in a slung-out drawl. "We don't have skinheads or revolutionaries around there. The news is making us sound like a bunch of ignoramuses. Sheriff doing anything about it? Everyone's gonna be watching how AC handles this, you know."

"Ain't nothing to it," he said. "Damn press."

"Might've figured. Hampton is calling everybody, asking what they've heard. Bet he's hounding the whole damn family."

Callie looked quizzically at Raysor.

"Distant cousin," he said. "Fancies himself a reporter. We don't tell him squat, and he can't write worth a damn. We try not to claim he's kin most of the time."

Marsha took the liberty of changing the subject before Callie could. "So, cuz. What is it? You never come out here unless you want something, and I'm busy today."

As instructed, Callie forwarded the video from her phone to Marsha, and the woman quickly zipped through it. "Poor surveillance camera." More flipping. Stopping. "Hmmm." Fast forward. Stopping.

Callie peered over the woman's shoulder. "Do what you can. Give us the best stills you can muster of that lady in the sunglasses." She laid out the photos the motel clerk gave her. "This is what the motel pulled off, but—"

"Give me two hours," Marsha said, swiveling around, parking her sight on Raysor. "I'm doing this for you, cuz, so any chance I get paid?"

Raysor walked around the room, studying equipment. "Depends on AC's mood," he said. "And the budget."

"Cheap bastard," she said. "He stiffed me on one job already. We're busy. What if I say no?"

He grabbed the chair arm, halting Marsha's swivel, staring at her like he meant it. "Said it yourself, you're doing this for me."

She stared him down. "My birthday's in January. Make the gift a fine one or I tell your aunt about your trip to Savannah."

A soft grunt. "That was years ago."

"Not sure that would matter to her."

"Bitch," he said.

"Bastard," she replied.

He quick-snapped his hand at the computer screen. "Just do it. I'm good for it."

That must've worked, because she shifted her attention to Callie. "He dating you?"

"We just work together."

"A woman might fix his ways." She hung on the end a bit, like she was giving Callie an option.

"We're gone," Raysor said, disappearing into the house.

Callie, however, gave her a hearty thanks. She didn't want Marsha changing her mind over something like manners.

"There's always a Sunday dinner at Aunt Rose's place!" Marsha hollered after her. "You're invited!"

Callie and Raysor drove off and made for the hospital and Connor. He damn sure hadn't died, not without notice to Wayne, who would've rung her. But if Connor indeed circled the drain, Wayne preferred to be at Slade's side, not Connor's. So Callie had offered to lay eyes on Connor and speak to medical staff. Check on security. Deputies oversaw what should be a semi-conscious Connor without the strength to escape.

The Colleton Medical Center wasn't a half mile from Duke's BBQ on Robertson Boulevard. Three stories in one part, the blond stucco facility had laid down parking for a hospital twice its size. Callie noted two SO patrol cars outside. One of those drivers better be guarding Connor.

ICU was easy enough to find, and a deputy hung over the nurse's station counter, chatting up two uniformed ladies. Laughing at the end of some story, he glanced to his right and cut the humor at the sight of Raysor.

Raysor strode over to the deputy, Callie into the hospital room.

Connor looked no better than he had in the woods.

"Connor?" she said, low enough not to disturb the neighboring rooms, but loud enough to awaken him. She wasn't sure how loud she was supposed to talk to someone unconscious. "Why are you running?"

No movement. Just a settled sleep despite being surrounded by the incessant beeps and buzzes of the hospital floor.

After one more attempt, she left, finding the deputy at attention to the immediate left of the doorway. Raysor had replaced him at the nurse's station, in the same pose, sharing a story. The women laughing with him the same.

"Don," Callie said.

He left the ladies with a snicker as one of them threw in a last remark, and he met Callie to walk a couple rooms down.

"What's the standing order on security with Connor?" she asked.

"Guard the room," he said.

"Visitors?"

"Guard the room," he repeated. "When people come in, the deputy . . . keeps guard."

Whoever placed the protection order fell short on brains. Connor was hiding out, and he ran before he ever shot at Wayne's car, so he was scared over something she, Wayne, and Slade hadn't figured out yet. That mystery left Connor vulnerable in that hospital bed. With Connor having had access to St. Clair's purse strings, maybe he screwed up in some role in a bigger plan.

She did an about-face and returned to the now ultra-attentive uniform. "Anyone come to visit today?"

"Yes, ma'am." He might not work under Callie, but he appreciated the insignia on the uniform.

"You noting the names?"

"No, ma'am."

Raysor came over.

Callie continued. "You recognize them?"

The young deputy gave half a nod, happy to reply in the positive. "All of them, ma'am."

"All?" she asked.

He counted. "Mr. St. Clair Simmons, Mr. Merrick Cox, Ms. Faye Harrell, and Ms. Sue Edmond."

Two ladies from the local agriculture office, Merrick from Mini-Hawk . . . and the man himself. "Come alone? Together? How'd they behave?"

Perplexed, the deputy dared a peek at Raysor before answering. Raysor stood like stone.

"Um, the ladies came together. They talked more to each other about how he looked, cried some, I think. Patted him on the hand and left. Reminded me of my aunts."

"The men?" she asked.

"Oh, they came separate," he said, again happy at knowing he answered right.

When he didn't continue, Raysor popped the man in the chest with the back of his hand. "Tell her about their visits. Damn, boy."

Though wearing a vest, the deputy kneaded the spot. "Um, St. Clair Simmons mostly stood and stared. Didn't cry, didn't talk, didn't appear frustrated. Just stood there. Wasn't in there more'n five minutes. Nothing to read. Almost like he was visiting a stranger. Merrick, however, pulled up a chair and stayed a while. Maybe a half hour?"

Callie waited for the rest.

"'Connor Boone,' he said. Said it three times, hard staring like he was hunting for twitches or flinches . . . like he didn't believe the poor sap couldn't hear. I mean, Boone's been laying just like that since I came on duty. He is definitely not in this world. Frankly, I don't think he's coming back to this world. Not after two bullets in his chest."

This guy wasn't making detective anytime soon. "He look concerned?"

"Sure," said the deputy. "Lifted the sheet and studied the bandages. Read the bag of stuff feeding the IV. Shook his head. That man's conversation seemed to be more with himself. After calling 'Connor' a couple more times and getting nothing, he put the chair back where it came from and left."

"Any reporters try to get in?" Raysor asked.

"Someone's managed to stop them before they ever got here, not that they didn't try."

Thank God for that much efficiency. "How about the nurses? The doctors?"

"What . . . I'm supposed to watch them, too?"

"You know them well enough to vouch for them?" she asked.

From the panic in his wide eyes, Callie had her answer. "At least get their names?"

"I, um," then he discreetly motioned to the station. "Those two ladies there. A couple people checking the machines and stuff. A doctor . . . Smythe, I think?"

"Thanks," Callie said and reached for her phone, moving a few yards off.

The deputy sort of paled. "Who's she calling?" He turned to Raysor. "What did I do wrong? Who's she reporting me to?"

Raysor bobbled his eyebrows. "Guess we'll have to wait and see."

Hearing that, Callie moved a few yards farther, waiting for Wayne to pick up.

"How's Slade?" she asked.

"Acting like things are fine . . . on pins and needles expecting a call like this saying Boone died."

"I'm at the hospital," Callie said. "Connor is labeled as Serious."

"Could be worse," he said.

"Still can get worse," she replied. "Listen, they only assigned a lone guard at the door. Not sure he's observing much of anything short of whether anyone shows up with a machete."

Silence a moment. "Son of a bitch. I should've clarified myself last night."

"You were preoccupied, and you relied on the sheriff. No harm, no foul, Wayne. It's dead around here, and the deputy didn't let anyone in without observing them, sounds like."

"I disagree. Had the phone in my hand and was about to call you," he said. "Not for publication, mind you . . ."

She stood firm, waiting.

"One of my ATF sources, a fed on the inside, provided an unexpected update. You remember me mentioning Birds of Prey?" he asked.

She remembered. "From Georgia."

"Yeah. They have a man on the inside who says the organization is sending someone over here. Heard mention of Mini-Hawk, but nothing more specific."

Callie's mind took off with what-ifs and maybes. Did St. Clair Simmons have a prior meeting arranged with the group or had Birds of Prey heard enough of the news to be concerned? Was this about guns or about hemp? Mostly, were they friendly or malicious? If they were of serious enough concern that they had an agent planted in their ranks, Birds of Prey wasn't just innocent farmers or hunting club organizers. They weren't just St. Clair Simmons on a more sophisticated level. They were coming about something that couldn't be handled on the phone, whatever that *something* was.

"Any idea when?" she asked.

"Left mid-morning," Wayne said. "I'm calling the sheriff."

She looked back at the two uniforms watching her. "And I'll straighten up the deputy here and the other one downstairs. When will you arrive?"

"As soon as I can eat up asphalt," he said.

"Slade?"

He let out a soft laugh. "You think she'd stay behind?"

# Chapter 26

## *Callie*

THE DEEPER MEANING of *stand guard* as explained by Callie took almost immediate effect. Within twenty minutes a partner accompanied the young deputy on the ICU and another on the ground level. No visitors for Connor... period. No phone calls... period. No acknowledgement that Connor was even in the hospital... period. If anyone did more than walk off when told to, the officers were to report, and they better be able to identify the parties when they did.

And no reporters. Even cousins.

A half hour after the secondary deputies assumed their places at the hospital, Wayne and Slade arrived at the Sheriff's Office. They passed the conference room where Callie and Raysor now waited, waved and entered another room, came back out just minutes later. Slade had turned in her statement.

"That statement must've been gold-plated," Callie said, kicking out a chair for Slade to sit.

Slade heaved a big sigh and plopped, the relief embedded in her skin. "Couldn't sleep thinking about it. Woke at dawn and started writing. When Lawman got up, I had it mostly done. This isn't my first go-around, you know," she said, almost quoting Callie's comment to her from the night before in St. Clair's woods.

"See the news?" Callie asked.

"No," Slade replied. "Why?"

Wayne sat beside Slade, half-listening, checking his phone. Answering someone on a text. "Because Jasmine, Connor, Mini-Hawk, and St. Clair are all over it," he said.

Slade snatched out her phone. "They mention me?"

"Not that I'd heard."

Wayne peered over. "Monroe's already rung me again. I filled him in and suggested he just blow off the press. Check your phone."

Slade put the phone to her ear for the voicemail, wincing at the recording. "I need to speak to him." She rose and retreated to the back of the room. Her body language clearly said her boss had answered in lieu of voice mail, and she leaned in the corner, talking inaudibly, hand covering the other ear.

"How's her boss going to treat her?" Callie said low to Wayne.

"He's worried sick."

A grump from Raysor. "Hope he doesn't give her a hard time."

"Maybe she could've just hid in the truck, but she saw an opportunity to bring Connor in," she said. "He's integral to this mess. You or I might've done the same."

"You or I are—"

"Quit discounting her, Wayne, and for God's sake quit comparing your badge to hers. If you don't want her around on cases I'm sure you can put a halt to her being there. But don't invite her then criticize her every move. She pours her entire being into this job, and she damn sure worships the ground you tread. So is she in trouble with the boss or not? And if she is, what can you do about it?"

He held a palm up. "I hear you." His stare gravitated to the back of Slade. "I probably won't have to do a thing. That man thinks she hung the moon." His mouth tightened. "And she thinks the world of him."

"He's a friend?" she asked.

"An old friend," he replied. "Who'd step in my shoes if he could, but is too gentlemanly to come between us. Makes him that much more of a friend to her."

"Then damn well appreciate what you've got," she scolded. "So is Birds of Prey a threat?"

He set his phone on the table, screen up to monitor the calls and texts. "Strong potential for it. My buddy said he knows the one coming. He's busted some heads in his day, and nobody has an idea who will be with him. This group has its own attorneys, CEO types, and an ample supply of talking heads, so who the hell knows their intention. Business? Damage control? If you had skin in this game and heard from afar that the mission had frayed edges and unreliable partners, what would you do?"

Callie didn't have to think twice. "Cut that partner loose, most likely. Cut my losses. Recover what I could."

Slade came back and pulled out her chair. "They want their investment back, or they want to straighten out their partner."

Wayne gave a slow-mo nod, everyone a bit more nervous about what was headed to Mini-Hawk's Salkehatchie compound, how long till it got there, and what was the real motive when it did. Business, pleasure, or correction?

"How long before they arrive, or does anybody know?" Raysor asked, his gravelly voice a caustic reminder of his presence. "And where are the feds in this?"

"They're not coming," Wayne said.

Callie sat up at that response. "What about your agency? I know you said they don't have a big force, but considering. Jasmine, Connor, even Slade. Three agriculture employees. Not that I fully understand your Inspector General's Office."

"We've had a lot of phone time, trust me," Wayne said. "But the less time they're here as boots-on-the-ground the better. You'd have guys in the field who haven't done field work in a decade, plus my agency doesn't have jurisdiction over murder and no homicide investigators. That's not generally what we do. I'm already on the ground as liaison, by the book. Our guys would be counterproductive, but they'll arrive for the optics, in time for the funeral. Jasmine's body is expected to be released tomorrow, by the way."

"They've always been a piece of work," Slade said, after a peek at the open door. "Never liked those guys, and yes, they prefer guys. Bet they treated Jasmine like a token."

A darkness spread across Wayne. "They're like you, Slade."

Slade reacted in kind. "Come again? I have nothing in common with those stuffed shirts. How dare you?"

"You're satisfied with the coroner's accident determination," Wayne said. "Convinced Jasmine was stupid and died from a bad decision."

"Hey," Slade started, but Wayne's exasperation spilled out everywhere, daring any of them to stop it. "Her death falls under coincidence, and you know my opinion about coincidences. Presumed you felt the same from what I've taught you . . . from what you've seen in our work. An accident on a target's property? No, ma'am. And I'll dog Jasmine's death until I'm satisfied."

The lashing obviously caught Slade off balance, but she rebounded. "Seems to be a lot of stupid going around these days, doesn't it, Cowboy? I feel your pain, but I can leave if you don't consider me an asset. Monroe just told me he'd rather I head back to Columbia anyway. Told him no, that there might be some off chance that you needed me, but hey, Lawman, if that's your preference, I'll hit the road right now. Say the word."

"Time for me to hit the head," Raysor said, slipping out of the room.

Callie diverted attention to her phone, but she didn't leave. She wanted these two to have to cope in front of her, because frankly, they needed to get their act together, and with a witness within earshot they'd have to think twice before letting fly with a hot retort.

The weight on Wayne was evident. Same for Slade. They struggled to be a hundred percent present for each other, unable to because of their personal pain and probably the insecurities that bit folks on the butt at times like these. They fell quiet.

"I'm not siding with them, Wayne," Slade said softly. Callie was proud of her friend making the first overture. "I'm saying that your people are cold, and they don't understand the field anymore. We both know how ineffective your higher-ups can be. I'm here for you even if they aren't." She stood and took the three steps to stand behind Wayne, sliding her arms around his neck. She laid her cheek on his head, gave it a kiss.

Raysor returned, was taken aback a second at the scene, then resumed his seat, prompting Slade to do the same. Slade unwittingly twisted that diamond, over and over.

They didn't deserve this. What a crappy way to start an engagement.

"ATF, or whomever, not coming might be a good thing," Callie said, sensing something positive needed saying. "The visit could be no more than talking hemp acreage, or the operational cost of the hunting club. The percentage Birds of Prey would glean off the top of the gross . . . the marketing strategy of the crop." Innocent, nonsequential stuff. Maybe a goodwill visit to tell St. Clair they were there for him. She kept tugging on the positive, wanting to believe that an entity on a federal watchdog list had nothing nefarious in mind.

But ultimately she couldn't fool herself, nor this team judging by the looks on their faces.

Nobody could deny St. Clair Simmons had a PR nightmare, a nightmare with the potential to sabotage his state license to grow hemp. Just how important was Mini-Hawk to Birds of Prey? Nobody could even guess.

"Do we have a guess how long before they arrive?" she asked.

Wayne looked grim. "Left over two hours ago."

"Jesus," Slade said. "They're over halfway here."

No comments, with everyone coming to the realization there was no plan. "Feel like we're only observers of whatever happens," she added. "Wish we understood more."

"The press," Wayne said. "Connor and Jasmine put Mini-Hawk in the news. Maybe Birds of Prey didn't want the notoriety."

His phone rang. He stared at the ID on his screen, then snatched it up and left the room.

With a noisy release of a sigh, Raysor spoke up. "If this Georgia outfit wants Simmons to grow hemp so badly, why didn't they just pay his agriculture bill? You can take their money, can't you?" he asked Slade.

Callie cocked her head. Probably the smartest comment Raysor'd made since this whole mess started.

"We would, but if I were those Georgia guys, I wouldn't pay it," Slade said. "Hemp is a costly investment in its own right. Who would bail out someone who hasn't proven himself yet?"

Raysor gave a short *hunh.*

She continued. "They're waiting for the state to do a background check, I'd say. They'd need someone clean to be their beard for the organization."

Slade let that seep into their heads. "I have another question, too. Birds of Prey lives close enough to have come down to check on things when Jasmine died, but didn't. Shoot Connor, however, and they scurry to get over here."

Raysor waved a flippant hand. "Like Wayne said, too much notoriety."

"But what the hell do they think they're going to do about it other than make matters worse showing up?"

Callie sat straighter. Slade was an agriculture expert first, but her investigative experience was sometimes forgotten. There was a reason Slade and Wayne tag-teamed so often. No agent let someone into their investigative world unless said someone brought skills or brains to the table.

"Keep talking," she said to Slade.

"Okay, I'm not you guys with badges, but—"

"Badges sometimes get in the way," Callie said. "Pretend you have a badge. Or pretend we don't. Just spill it."

Leaning on her elbows, Slade clasped her hands. "Let's say St. Clair is being used."

"Here we go," Raysor said, collapsing back in his seat.

Callie rapped on the table. "Hush, Don. Listen. Go ahead, Slade."

Slade shrugged. Wayne remained in the hall. "I don't know but what if he's a figurehead because he owns the land. He latched ahold of the hemp idea. What if that's the real gist of things? He really teaches firearms classes and sells guns to fund his farm. He checked out with ATF with his firearms license, remember? Plus, I used to deal with St. Clair a few years back. He's not a macho guy. What if he's the victim here?"

Wayne came back in, sliding the phone in his hip pocket.

"So did the kid die?" Raysor asked him.

"No." Wayne said, wearing a baffled expression. "That was Merrick Cox."

A stunned bewilderment fell on them, Slade the first to speak. "Instead of me? I'm the one he carted around the damned farm all day long."

"Because I stood up to them in the trailer, Slade. His kind won't call a woman."

Slade almost choked on a laugh. "Wow. Okay, so what did he want?"

He motioned to Raysor. "How about coming with me on this?"

"Come with him on what?" Slade asked.

Raysor asked no questions and got up, lifting his coat off the back of the chair.

A knock sounded on the half-closed door. Marsha the photographer poked her head in the opening. "Excuse me for interrupting, but they said my idiot cousin was holed up in here."

"We're busy, Marsha," Raysor said.

She held up an envelope, her jaw tight and eyes narrow. "You want the pictures or not? I gave these the primo part of my day. The least you can do is thank me for hand delivering them, you bum."

Callie jumped up. "I'll take them. If he won't say it, I will. Thanks so much." She peered back at Raysor. "And if he won't get you paid, call me."

Callie gave her a card, and Marsha handed over the envelope. "I like her, Don. If you let this one get away, you deserve to die a bachelor. And if you let her pay, I'm telling our aunt on you."

Raysor reddened. Validated, Marsha grinned and left, triumphantly waving Callie's business card over her head.

"Let's go, Raysor," Wayne said.

Callie opened the manila envelope and let the pictures slide out. "You might want to study these first. Don can fill you in on our day obtaining these after y'all leave."

Each person reached over and lifted a photo out of the pile.

Wayne studied the photo in his hand, turning it over for any additional identifying information like a name, time, or date. "What am I looking at?"

"St. Clair Simmons's girlfriend," Callie said. "Might not matter at this stage of the game, but we pursued it best we could. Found the motel in Beaufort, thanks to Savvy. Grabbed footage from the parking lot camera which was grainy, but Raysor's cousin cleaned it up a bit, I see."

"Good heavens," Slade said, peering closer at hers, then reaching over to see the one in Wayne's hand. He compared his with hers.

Callie exchanged a look with Raysor, stymied. "We couldn't identify her. Savvy couldn't, either, and the desk clerk said that woman always hid in the truck before going into the motel room with St. Clair."

"What's the date on these?" Wayne asked, holding his up.

"The week of Jasmine's death," Callie said. "To include the night she died. What am I not getting?"

Slade jabbed a finger at the woman in the eight by ten. "This is Maggie Bright, Callie. St. Clair's girlfriend is Jasmine's mother."

# Chapter 27

## *Slade*

"HOLY JESUS," Raysor said.

"Think they know?" I asked. "Mini-Hawk, I mean."

Wayne gave a clipped scoff. "What about Birds of Prey?"

Seemed St. Clair Simmons dated Maggie Bright, and apparently not on a test-drive sort of whim, either. *For years.* No wonder he met her in Beaufort for their afternoon delight. No wonder Maggie told no one in her circle. Those two seeing each other flew in the face of everything an alt-right quasi-militia stood for, and based on Jasmine's comments about St. Clair, anyone in her social circle and family would condemn her mother for fraternizing with the jerk. This was *not* a man liked by everyone. He was white; Maggie black.

Mixed race relationships weren't taboo in the South much anymore. South Carolina's last generation or two prided itself on progressive change. Still, change was hard and nothing was perfect. Like anywhere, there could be failures of enlightenment.

Why had the couple taken their relationship forty-five miles distant from family and friends? Mini-Hawk's connections, hatred of St. Clair, concerns about the mixed-race acceptance in the community, or something else responsible for the cloak and dagger game?

We swapped each other's photos, like a different picture would clear everything up or cancel out the other.

Who was aware of this? Characters ran through my mind from Atwood Snipes the linebacker to the slipper neighbor next door to Maggie. Angus, Merrick . . . heavens, St. Clair's wife. I couldn't envision any of those characters thinking this extra-marital relationship was made in heaven.

"What about Jasmine," I whispered, wondering how in the world could she not have been aware. Wayne massaged his temple, eyes closed.

"No way you could've seen this coming," I said.

"She never should've worked this case."

Nobody could argue with that, but Jasmine chose to hide her

conflict of interest. I could hear Wayne thinking, *I should've asked her. She was from this part of the state.*

Raysor grumbled and tossed his photo of Maggie on the others. "This is horseshit. We're chasing our own asses sitting here." He lifted his watch. "That Georgia group will arrive before we know it, and I'm assuming that's what's driving Merrick."

"You're right. We've got to go," Wayne said. "Slade, stick with Callie, please."

I dropped my photo. "Oh no. You don't get to leave without telling us. What's happening?"

Wayne shrugged his jacket onto his shoulders. "Merrick says he has information someone needs to hear about Connor, and he says it's related to Jasmine."

This stank to high heaven. "Doesn't sound right, Wayne."

Raysor's grouse of a stare said he was ready to leave.

"We're meeting him at his brother's house," Wayne said. "Halfway between here and Mini-Hawk."

Raysor grumbled, "I know it, and if we don't go now, we'll never make it."

Warnings went off in my head, ugly deep sensations worming down to my core. I went to Wayne, touching his coat sleeve. "How can you be sure this isn't a setup?"

After our earlier blow-up, he held his tongue and tried not to discount my concern, but I could read him. Everyone could. He was choosing not to talk so they could get gone.

"He could've drawn you in by mentioning Jasmine," I said. "He gave you no other hints?"

"Her death," he said. "He has an hour, and St. Clair expects him after that. I gathered he didn't want to be seen talking to me around anyone Mini-Hawk connected." He rested his hand on mine, and apprehension rolled through me that I didn't like. "It's opportunity we can't pass up."

I didn't ask to go with him. I'd only make matters worse meeting with a man who deemed me worthless, but letting Wayne loose went against every cell of my being.

"He's not about to hurt a federal agent, Slade, not with Raysor with me." Again the pat on the hand. "I'll update you and Callie after."

"Give me my keys then. I'd feel better if you rode with Raysor, and I'll need a car."

"You have Callie, and we need a civilian vehicle. Sorry. I'm taking your truck."

They left, Wayne's boots echoing on the linoleum until they exited the double doors.

Energy spent, I fell into a seat beside Callie and stretched arms forward across the table, dropping my head between them. God, he better be right that this was nothing more than clandestine information gathering. He did have Raysor, though. That was something.

But those Mini-Hawk guys loved their AR-15s.

I looked up at my partner. "What are *we* supposed to do?"

Callie seemed to be thinking hard, not immediately meeting my gaze. "I'm still trying to wrap my mind around Merrick," she said. "What's he afraid of?"

"Well, he and St. Clair have been buddies since high school. Is he saving St. Clair, or is he evading St. Clair? Is he acting on St. Clair's behalf or going behind his back?" Suddenly this case sank to a more complicated depth, like it had levels we weren't remotely aware of.

"Let's dissect this mess. You and me," I said.

Her silence gave consent.

"Just listen," I said, straightening back up. "Either Connor's a Mini-Hawk groupie, or he's been taken advantage of. Could've been forced to overlook St. Clair paying his debts. St. Clair bragged about us not being able to foreclose before his financial status improved, and if Connor was convinced, coaxed, or coerced to not collect the debt to buy St. Clair that time, that's enforceable."

"Enforceable against who?"

"Either . . . both."

"You envision Connor a pawn," Callie said. "Okay, I can see that."

"I believe he holds onto secrets. Enough to bother Merrick."

"The deputy guarding Connor said Merrick visited this morning. Tried to rouse Connor by calling his name, seemed undecided about something and left."

I nodded, feeling like I slowly stacked blocks, each time hunting around for one in the dark, where they were hidden, before finding one to pile on . . . not sure what I was building.

Connor chose to help St. Clair rather than do his job with agriculture. What was his mystery? Personal gain? Failure at his job we hadn't discovered yet? His divorce unraveling his mind?

None of which deserved two bullets.

Callie tapped my arm to draw me back. "Change gears a second. We just proved Maggie Bright was in Beaufort when Jasmine came home, which meant St. Clair was in Beaufort, too. Why did Jasmine go out to Mini-Hawk at three in the morning if he wasn't there?"

We just kept finding more questions. "Maybe she didn't know they met in Beaufort?"

Callie settled a stare on the pile of pictures. "You can't assume she was even aware about the relationship, Slade. She hadn't lived at home in at least four years. What if she was just an eager girl hoping to make a splash. Just a green agent getting a jump on her supervisor."

"We're getting mired up in the reeds again. As Raysor would say, *chasing our asses.*"

Callie rose and started a slow circle around the table for twelve. "Then we don't worry about Jasmine right now. Birds of Prey is more pressing . . . maybe. What if St. Clair isn't aware they're coming?"

I shook my head. "Sounds like Merrick knows. Someone's worried about something happening in an hour. Besides, we can't do a damn thing about a papa militia coming to scold a baby militia."

"No. And we don't want to get in the middle of anything like that, either." She leaned on the back of her chair and I draped forward at the table, twisting my ring. "I'm wondering if any of this matters," she said, giving voice to a surprising question. "Do we *have* to do anything? From my vantage, we can give this up and go home. You'll turn in Connor, of course, who'll do some time for sure, assuming he even lives, but the rest? Entirely out of our hands."

Callie pushed up off the chair. "Jasmine's officially listed as an accident. Only time will tell whether St. Clair pays his loans or not. I'm sick of beating this dead horse, but what the heck is there left for us to do?"

When she hushed, the room fell silent short of the central heat pushing through two vents. People walked out in the hall. Phones rang.

She almost had me believing her, but as much as Wayne flew at me about Jasmine moments ago, I couldn't write off Jasmine as a pure accident, either, much less a non-issue like Callie said. Most law enforcement discarded coincidences. They chased every clue and possibility until even the most outlandish reason was disproven before something as lazily convenient as coincidence was given credence. Callie'd been a decorated detective. She ought to know that.

I got up and walked to the rear corner, addressed the wall, and mentally ran over all of the information, returning to the moment the four of us first met at the Agriculture office.

We'd been chasing whatever red flag waved in our vision, from whatever direction, like we were bound to chase any and all red flags. Assuming, then doubting our assumptions. Leaping without tangibles. Groping at wind. That's what you do when a man or woman goes down in the line of duty. Right?

No.

We commenced this Colleton County insanity high on emotion when it should've been a more synchronized mission. The hub center of this entire mess was St. Clair Simmons. We were letting periphery distractions lead us astray and our pain about Jasmine blind us at times, but everything was integral. Jasmine, Connor, and St. Clair. Only we couldn't see how.

Staring at plain sheetrock, I took pulse-slowing breaths, allowing every bit of knowledge we'd acquired settle. Not that we didn't need the sundry bits of flotsam and jetsam we'd accumulated, but unless we stayed anchored onto the main premise, we'd let the details lead us further astray. Our own issues would cause us to fail. Regardless of what Wayne avowed, he wanted to have human intrusion to blame for Jasmine's death. Finding that proof was his driving force. Then throw in me. Since shooting Connor, I couldn't shut my eyes without seeing holes in his chest.

We were too close, too desperate maybe, but Callie wasn't right about quitting and going home, either.

Go back to the beginning. Tap those ruby slippers, Slade.

I pivoted around. "Remember what Raysor said."

Callie gave me attention. "I'm listening."

"He said talk to the women because they'd spill if they were pissed with their men," I said. "Someone needs to speak to Maggie, like we talked about before. I'd wager serious money that her daughter's dying on her lover's land threw a wrinkle into their paradise. She'd want answers, and she'd want him to find them. She's under a horrendous mantle of guilt, and I say we help her unload."

Callie's expression brightened with purpose. "Her last night at that motel was the night Jasmine died."

I pointed at her. "Precisely. Tell me that isn't eating at her gut? And Wayne said follow the money. What if he and Raysor coincidentally appeared at the Mini-Hawk gate when Birds of Prey arrived. That'd throw everyone off balance. We're still obligated to account for Agriculture's money. Gives him a reason to be there."

"That might cost St. Clair his business deal, Slade. I'm not sold on that one."

"No, think about it," I said, coming back to the table. "Coincidentally appear with Birds of Prey there. Wayne could still have questions for St. Clair, simply by the book for an Ag investigation. He could see how everyone responds. Get a better feel for the future of Mini-Hawk. Keep in mind, we still have to determine if St. Clair stole federal money earmarked originally to grow current crops, and even if he hasn't, we have to decide whether to foreclose his place. It's a textbook case, really."

*Textbook case* shot a zing of déjà vu into my heart. The term Wayne had used in deciding St. Clair should be the case for Jasmine to cut her teeth on.

"Dicey move," Callie said. "ATF has an undercover guy in place to think of. Criminals don't believe in coincidence any more than cops do, Slade. You don't want to endanger an agent."

Okay, she had me there. But I was on a brainstorming roll in the presence of a patient friend who happened to be a cop.

However, I stuttered on the next proposal. "In the beginning you emphasized we misread Connor and should've spoken to him first, before St. Clair." A wrong choice for which I'd punished myself the entire night. If we'd spoken to him more in depth, right from the start, he might not be lying in ICU. "If he comes around," I said, so desperately wanting to say *when*, "he still might have something to say. Something he might be desperate to get off his chest. Someone needs to stay with him."

Someone, but not me. I couldn't look that man in the eye if he regained consciousness. If he awoke and mumbled, asking for someone to listen, that person just couldn't be me.

"We also haven't spoken to Angus, Atwood, or the other staff at the compound. Just like Raysor thought a woman might speak against her man, I wonder about these guys. How loyal would they be if their boss lost a golden opportunity they'd banked on for the last two years? How invested are they in St. Clair Simmons?"

Then I heard Wayne as clearly as if he stood in the room. *Isn't that following the money?*

Snatching up my phone, I started texting Wayne.

"What are you saying, Slade? There's only the two of us, and I'm not taking you to Mini-Hawk to interview those men."

I could almost hear her channeling Wayne. What are you up to,

Slade. Don't con me, Slade. Don't go rogue on me, Slade.

Fingers typing like sausages, the words kept messing up. Too much to say on such a small screen. Too much to type, too much he needed to know before they met up with Merrick. St. Clair's men had livelihoods at stake, doubly so since their incomes banked on the decisions of both Birds of Prey and Mini-Hawk.

These secondary players might be more nervous. The secondary players would be more easily played.

Someone poked their head in the door, then surprised at finding us there, retracted. Voices gathered outside.

"Don't you even think about going to Mini-Hawk," Callie said.

Another person peered in. He spoke to Callie, probably since she wore a uniform. "Um, we have this room reserved for an operational meeting in five minutes?"

We hopped to our feet, my tapping throwing misspelled words out in order to conclude Wayne's message. Done. I continued speaking as we shoved chairs under the table. "I'll speak with Maggie, then. She dislikes Wayne and doesn't know you or Raysor. You can . . ."

"Babysit Connor Boone?" she said. "Not likely."

People squeezed into the room as we snaked ourselves around them to leave.

Outside, we ran into a moist cold, the flattened, gunmetal clouds almost hitting the tops of pines. Zipping and buttoning coats, we reached the parking lot before Callie spoke up again, leaning into me. "I'd hoped to stick with you. It's how we started this case."

Confirming my original suspicion from our first day together. "I read you and Wayne from day one, Callie." This wasn't the time for anger and frustration, but it crept up a tad, my emotional guard not without its bruises, especially after Connor. We reached her cruiser, and my lack of vehicle added another layer of frosting to my annoyance. "What did he say before he left? *Stick with Callie, please.*"

She unlocked our doors. "He cares. And we're not going to Mini-Hawk," she reiterated. "That's got nothing to do with babysitting and everything to do with common sense. We aren't prepared for that."

That I could believe. "Okay, then since I'm the only one who can reach Maggie, you sit with Connor in case he says anything."

"We have one car."

I shouldn't have caved to Wayne taking my truck . . . damn it. "Then we go to Maggie's. You sit in the car. Then we rush to Connor . . . and I sit in the waiting room."

She walked around to her side of the car. "Go ahead, get in. You go to Maggie's. I'll line you up a vehicle." She pulled out of the parking lot, and a few miles and ten minutes later, we eased into the Ford dealership.

Passing the new trucks, then the used ones, Callie nosed us into a slot outside the service center. By the time she walked to the garage bays, a bald-headed man in his thirties, the name Hoss embroidered on his coveralls, met her, grinning ear to ear in recognition. She spoke, he gave a lot of animated nods, and then he disappeared. He promptly returned with keys and aimed us off to the right side of a line of cars where I spotted Wayne's government car with two new tires.

I got out, wondering what took Callie so long to say thanks to the mechanic. Then I wondered how in the world they let her claim Wayne's car.

After a laugh over something, she shook the man's hand and returned. "Here," she said, shaking the keys in the air. "You owe me."

"That's federal property," I said. "How'd he let you . . ."

"I agreed to come to dinner with Raysor, at Hoss's mother's place. Don't ask."

I retrieved my purse. "You're awesome, Chief. Give me an hour with Maggie, then I'll come meet you at the hospital. Your phone will record, right? Right."

But when I rose back up from reaching in the car, Callie stood, hands on her utility belt. "If this guy wakes up, I can't talk finances. And I don't speak agriculture."

"Doubt he'll launch into an accounting dissertation. You can talk fraud, embezzlement, or whatever else this turns out to be. And you've grasped enough of Agriculture to wing it. Steer Connor toward discussing Jasmine, or Merrick."

She agreed, but looked at me with a hard focus in her eyes.

"Callie, worry about Connor, about Wayne and Raysor, but not about babysitting me." I swung my arms out wide. "Be happy. Nothing dangerous in my plan."

"Sounds like a decent plan."

"Damn right it sounds like a plan," I concluded.

A text ping sounded. Wayne had reached Merrick's.

It was three p.m. with no sign of when this day would end.

# Chapter 28

## *Slade*

THE DEALERSHIP had washed and vacuumed Wayne's G-car, but the swollen, drabness of the day detracted from the clean. Roiling gray clouds gave way to a flat, steely sky and a steady rain. Wipers flapping, I wasn't quite sure of Maggie's address, but GPS carried me most of the way until I regained my bearings on the turn to Sixth Street and its line of trailers on big, one-acre lots.

Not only was Maggie's car parked in the drive but so was Jasmine's yellow sedan, confirming to the world that the authorities had concluded with Jasmine.

The mother was most likely home; however, I drove past, heart punching my sternum. My interview tumbled around in my head like bingo numbers before they are drawn.

Parking at the dead end of the street, along the silted edge of a re-possessed home per the big sign with red lettering, I considered my delay to be a pondering of options rather than procrastination. Phone in hand, I debated notifying Maggie before knocking. Wayne didn't when I came last time with him, though, and I fully understood why. Training taught that interviews were best taken with the witness caught unawares, a tactic I long ago learned was usually best for all parties concerned. The easiest route to truth. But at this moment, on this dismal day, on a dismal street, about to talk to a mother about her dead daughter, following the rules and pouncing on this woman unawares felt too damned much like the actions of a bully.

Yeah, make the call . . . wait, no. My heart clashed with my head.

"Son of a bitch!" I about came out of my skin when the phone rang in my hand.

When the ID read Savvy, I bounced my head hard on the headrest, torn between being grateful for the delay and leery about how dramatic this conversation was about to be.

I'd utterly forgotten to ring her about Connor this morning and hadn't taken her ten calls.

"Hey, Savvy. I don't have much time—"

"Oh, so her majesty decides to answer. What the hell, Slade. Connor is circling the drain and you forget to inform me? I have to learn from Sue and Faye in the office after they've visited him? Goddammit, what were you thinking? Or were you not thinking? Sure tells me how high I rank with you."

She caught her breath. The silence would've been incredibly delicious if I could've heard it, but my blood pounded clear up into my ears. "Savvy—"

"No, there isn't a good enough reason, Slade. He's my responsibility. My staff was stunned that I didn't know, thank you very much. I had to request the day's reports to learn he's at death's door. I'm driving there as we speak, when I should've been there the moment—"

"Shut the hell up, will you? For Christ's sake, I was the one who shot him."

The rain abruptly stopped. So did Savvy's talking, the quiet so quiet I heard drips on the back window.

One hand over my face, the other cradling the phone in my lap, I told myself to exhale slow, inhale deep, because if I didn't, I'd bust out crying. I hadn't done so yet, hadn't wanted to until we'd reached some level of conclusion. Had intended to keep trudging until I was too exhausted to remain conscious so I wouldn't have to think about what I'd done.

But a direct hit from my angry, in-your-face friend was pushing me to my limit. I had to hold myself together for the task before me. I lifted the phone. "Can't talk about it now." I exhaled with the words like yoga therapy. "I'm sitting outside someone's house about to interview them about Jasmine. I need my head straight, and this isn't helping."

"Holy hell, Slade," she whispered. "Are you . . . all right?"

"Have no friggin' clue. Let me go, please, so I can get through this day."

A few drops hit here and there on the car's hood, bits of water forewarning of more to come. They increased, faster, fatter until they crescendoed and released as one huge chorus, driving my emotions into my throat.

Ordinarily, Savvy was support. Not here. "I'll talk to you when I can." I hung up before she could tell me how sorry she was in a voice that would make things about me instead of what I had to do with Maggie.

Throwing the transmission into neutral, missing drive before I got it right, I drove the one and a half blocks to that mailbox with faded yellow suns. Raindrops clicked irregularly on the car roof. In one fluid move I grabbed my purse with the envelope of pictures and strode to the door. Without hesitation, I rapped hard, wanting my knuckles to hurt from the effort.

I had to rap twice.

Maggie opened the door, eyes not as swollen as the last time, but a tightly controlled anger hid in the pinched lines around her mouth . . . her nose. Jasmine's geometric design necklace hung around her neck. Guess the coroner had returned all her effects, not just the car. "Get the hell off my porch," she said through tight teeth.

Fingers clenched around my badge, I flashed it as earnestly as I'd ever showed it. "You seriously need to speak to me about Jasmine. We've gathered new information that we need your take on. The coroner may have closed his case, but we haven't closed ours."

"I said leave."

She started to close the door. I did something I'd only seen in the movies, putting my foot across the threshold to block her shutting it completely.

The splash of panic in her eyes made me second-guess my action, but only for a second. Maggie had misled us about herself and St. Clair . . . been tight-lipped about her dead daughter. Wayne would never forgive himself if we didn't get to the bottom of this, which made this a meeting that wouldn't end until I'd uncovered some absolute answers.

"We've been busting our butts seeking justice for your daughter, Maggie. My partner, Wayne Largo, doesn't believe Jasmine died by accident. You've done nothing to help. Less than nothing, actually. You're holding Wayne accountable and acting the victim, and it stops now."

Though the rain was slight, enough time lapsed for it to start wetting my hair, and a couple drops ran through my scalp. So when she turned, lip pouted out twice its size, and returned to her living room like she'd done before, I let myself in.

I sidetracked through her kitchen, snared a couple paper towels, and dabbed my hair on my way back to meet her. My reflection in her entry mirror showed someone half-crazed and totally disheveled, but I didn't give a rat's ass as to my appearance. This meet would be about what I had to say, not how I looked delivering it.

"I'm burying my daughter tomorrow, and this is how you treat me." A statement, not a query. She spit it out before I reached the sofa.

"If you're so broken up, then help."

If the mother wasn't going to expose the truth, we could. I would. Wayne cared about this woman because he felt responsible. I wasn't proud of this moment, but I wouldn't retract or soften my blows.

And I sensed she saw my resolve.

Muscles crawled along her jaw as if trying to stop emotion from reaching the surface. Trying to outlast me.

Wasn't going to happen.

"Didn't know she was coming home," she finally said.

"Right. When she arrived oh-so-proud of having her first case in her hometown . . . targeting your boyfriend. How long have you been screwing St. Clair Simmons, Maggie?"

She eyed me with surprise, then interest, which quickly changed to loathing. "I won't answer that, and I much prefer your partner."

"Then you should've cooperated with him," I replied, hardly before she finished.

Maggie launched from her recliner, snatching herself up a foot short of a collision with me. "You cannot come into my home and treat me this way." A whiff of alcohol carried on her words. "I'll have your job. I'll have you arrested." Her nose sharply tilted up, her lips painfully tight. "And I hope you lose someone in your life like I've lost my baby."

She shook as mini, erratic grunts escaped her throat brought from deep down inside. I watched her hate me and let her hold that moment, a minimal sense of accomplishment that would soon crumble.

Horrible pain emanated from her, forcing her shoulders, arms, and head to shake. She wanted so badly to place the blame elsewhere, but it had so clearly taken residence in her bones. That guilt was going nowhere. I could help relocate some of the blame, but not before we covered some excruciating ground.

I opened the envelope from my purse, extracted its contents, and reaching past her, close enough to brush sleeves, I dropped the photographs on the coffee table. Her laser gaze on me peeled loose, her attention riveted on the pictures of herself.

I took a place on the sofa, leaving her standing alone. "Tell me you don't think St. Clair is responsible for your daughter's death? Happened on his land, during her investigation of him."

Hands nervous, she lifted the top two photos.

"Sit down, Maggie," I said.

She did, her hard-shell stare at me replaced by a despondent focus on the motel shots.

I didn't jump into her business right then. I'd taken the investigatory step of throwing ice-water on her, and she had to catch her breath.

She'd resisted, so I'd shamed her, then once she engaged, I'd shocked her. Basic interviewing, but following the lesson book wasn't making me proud. This business of getting someone to talk wasn't for the faint of heart. If Wayne were here, he'd do it, but he wasn't. He was part of the fallout of this stupid mess, and for a change this was all on me. I'd short-circuited Maggie. Time to reel her in.

"How long have you been seeing him?" I asked, only softer, empathetic. "Is your relationship serious or just fun?"

"It's real," she said almost in a whisper, turning the photos over on the table. "Three years real."

"How did it start?" Soothing. *Make them think you care.*

And I did care.

"We both attended a county council meeting. Him interested in some development toward the rivers, wanting to preserve the land. Me trying to understand about a proposed sales tax increase." Tissues already on a small side table from her mourning, she pulled one out, her rage having given way to weeping. "We were seated one row apart, him one up and one over from me. At the end we talked. He called the next day, like a regular guy seeking a date with a regular girl, only we were far from it. At least in these parts."

"He had a reputation?" I asked.

"We lived in opposite worlds, she said. He was beginning his hunting place with white men of the type who wouldn't understand, and none of my people my age would take a liking to me seeing him."

"Plus, he was married," I added.

She nodded into her lap. "He wasn't happy with Sally, but she had no place else to go. No way he could oust her and move me into that farmhouse. That was asking for trouble." She shrugged. "We had no option but the one we took."

"Did Jasmine know?"

Another nod. "She heard me take a call from him about a year into things, and you don't have to ask. She hated us. Not a racial hate, but an environment hate. I walked in one world and he walked in another. She felt if he cared he would've given up his *redneck pretense*, as she put it. By him hiding me, he labeled me a whore."

We'd not found anyone who connected St. Clair and Maggie. The concealment had been damn efficient. But as much as she hated the relationship, Jasmine couldn't expose St. Clair without making her mother an outcast. No wonder she'd been so thrilled at her first case. Taking St. Clair down was opportunity to liberate her mother from her impossible affair.

"Why not tell us before?" I asked.

Another shrug. I wasn't happy with shrugs. While not my place to judge Maggie's social life, this woman's daughter died. Jasmine was wrong in how she went at St. Clair, how she let a personal grudge override her training, but Maggie was wrong continuing to hide what could be important information in unraveling the details of the death.

"If St. Clair had your daughter murdered would that matter?"

Murder . . . the first time I'd used that word, though we'd all thought it.

"He wouldn't do that."

"He might to avoid exposure."

She shook her head in short, jerky movements. "He was with me." She shoved the pictures, then pushed them around with finger tips, selecting one, knocking another to the floor in her zeal to hold it up. "This was the night Jasmine died, Ms. Slade." She shook it. "St. Clair was with me. I know this man." The tears fell harder. "I loved this man."

"Loved?" I asked.

Instead of acknowledging the past tense, Maggie picked up her phone. The last thing we needed was more people in the room. "Maggie—"

"Read that," she ordered, and handed me her cell.

Texts from Jasmine. Only one out of twenty or more being from Maggie. The others started happy. *Momma, I'm coming home. May be there a couple nights.* Then when nobody responded, *Are you home?* With the time lag, I assumed Jasmine drove, on her way to Walterboro.

*I'm home. Where are you?* Various versions of that as a couple hours went by. A one-sided conversation that escalated until she got exasperated at being ignored and began with the accusations. *Are you with him? Seriously?*

One text from Maggie about eleven. *I will see you in the morning.*

Which sent Jasmine into a frenzy of texts, then nothing.

"Go to voicemail," Maggie said, not concerned as to who else I might see in her history.

There were eight voice mails from Jasmine. I put them on speaker.

How can my mother be so damn blind? she yelled, the memory of her voice prompting a hitch in my throat. You're not this stupid! If he'd do this to his wife, he'll one day do it to you. Hell, he's doing it to you now, Momma! He won't claim you. He hides you out of shame. You're worth more than that. It's the twenty-first century, for God's sake.

Seven versions of that message until the last. *I'm not waiting for you anymore.*

I copied and forwarded everything to my phone, then on to Wayne's and Callie's while Maggie tried to clean up the tears that had poured down her cheeks, her neck, and onto her sweater.

"I turned my phone off," she said, almost too faint to hear. "Didn't turn it back on until about five in the morning. Tried calling her and couldn't get an answer. That's when I talked to Agent Largo, asking if he'd heard from Jasmine. When he hadn't, that's when I told St. Clair to take me home."

The timeline fit. "What do you think happened?" I handed back the phone.

"After this," and she held up the phone, "I thought she went back to Columbia, or went to stay at my sister's house." She motioned at a framed picture on the bar. The slipper woman.

"Did you tell St. Clair about these messages that night?"

"No." She sighed heavily. "He would've sent me back to Walterboro earlier. We didn't get to meet but every week or two, and this one had been hard enough as it was. He was nervous about clients coming to town. I didn't want to add to that stress."

I'd angered her, stunned her, ultimately coaxed her into talking by meeting her on a personal level. I honestly felt we were being straight with each other. "What does St. Clair think about a federal agent, your daughter, being killed on his land?"

Her head fell into her hands. "He was devastated. After Mr. Largo came by and told me, I called him." Big sobs now. "I yelled at that fool. Told him his world, his make-believe soldiers, something out there killed my baby and I'd never forgive him for it." She ugly-cried now, fists tight and waving. "Told him how could I look at him and not relive my loss?"

My insides jittered at the spewed emotion. I became a mother feeling another mother's agony in that moment. Finally, I asked, "And that's the last time you spoke?"

She harshly shook her head, stare dark and fierce. "He called me back that night. Said there was nothing for Jasmine to find on his place. Nothing illegal. Made no sense for her to be out there." Her sentences were staccato, snapping. "He spoke to Merrick and one guy on duty at the gate. Nothing. Said they didn't have enough men to patrol the place. Merrick and another guy had gone out deer hunting that morning, and saw nothing." She bawled into a tissue. "He begged me. Asked what else could he do to make it up to me?"

She collapsed back in the chair, an absolute wreck of emotions.

"This may come out in the open, Maggie."

"Let it," she bit back through wet tissues at her nose.

My muted phone vibrated, the light hum indicating one, two, three messages in a row. Callie confirmed she was with Connor, and he'd said nothing, but she'd received the texts I'd sent and would take a look.

Texts received, from Wayne. Then, Told you to stay with Callie. I'd feel better if you two stuck together. Merrick is saying Connor killed Jasmine.

Almost mindless in my movements, I scooped up the photos.

"I've, um, I've got to go, Maggie," I said, reaching for my keys.

With my intensity so abruptly blunted, Maggie sat perplexed. "Did I . . . did I say something wrong?"

I held up my phone. "Emergency. I'll let myself out."

"Will you be in touch?" she asked, rising to follow, urgent in her need to recognize if spilling her guts had aided or hurt her . . . had gotten St. Clair in trouble or saved him. Would the conversation ruin both their lives in such a small county?

Studying her sobs, her red eyes, the pain in the creases around her mouth, I realized I'd stirred Maggie up royally, only to leave her torn up to cry alone when I left. I stroked her arm. "Yes, we will be in touch," I said.

I hated leaving her, but I was equally keen on getting to Callie . . . to Connor.

I finally turned and took the steps in a hurry. Trotting to Wayne's SUV, I realized I could be responsible for killing a killer before I'd known he *had* killed.

# Chapter 29

*Callie*

THE NOVEMBER temps and drizzle seemed to seep through glass into Connor's room, pimpling Callie's arms. After barely an hour, the monotonous beeps of telemetry by Connor's bed, by the beds up and down the unit, had her craving earbuds in the worst way.

The television was on but muted, the only voices on a different television down the hall, same channel. That patient probably wasn't dying.

For the umpteenth time, she approached his bed, studying his eyes up close for signs of consciousness. "Connor," she said, tapping lightly several times in the center of his forehead. "Connor?" she said, tapping on his hand, the one cuffed to the bed.

Stone still. Coma, asleep, unconscious . . . he didn't respond. Taking another sip of her two dollar Coke from the vending machine, she returned to the cheap, blue vinyl recliner, padding minimal. Hospitals didn't smell antiseptic anymore, not like old horror stories. Instead the scents were a mixture of soap, sometimes poop, and iodol, that sweet disinfectant odor made by that rusty brown liquid they slathered on everything. In another day or two, one could add the scents of sweat and blood to Connor's perfume list. ICU patients didn't bathe.

Callie hated these places. She hated stepping into their recirculated, germ-infested air. Once inside, her stomach always lurched with an unpleasant rhythm. Thus the reason for the Coke, now mostly gone.

She held barely a smidgen of confidence in both doctors and nurses. Whether overworked or under-motivated, in her experience they too often ignored the human being behind the patient in favor of logging orders and stats that nobody else seemed to read. They rotated these souls in and out of rooms like cattle pushed through feedlots.

She scoffed at the metaphor which she'd probably lifted from Slade at some point.

"Connor," she gently hollered from her seat. "Connor, Connor, Connor."

Nothing.

She didn't know the guy. Had only met him once with Slade. Had no opinion nor feelings for him, but she absolutely hoped he didn't die. However, better on her watch than Slade's.

Speaking of the devil. A text from Slade. *Forwarding texts from Maggie's phone number.* They soon came, one after the other. A lot of them. Messages mostly from Jasmine to her mother, if she understood right. Callie read them again, then again . . . and fairly well grasped the situation. Jasmine came home to an empty house. Of course, Maggie was with St. Clair, as they'd proven with the photos. The messages went silent about the time Jasmine might've taken it upon herself to go hunting for her mother. Or for St. Clair, under the guise of pursuing the case. Didn't matter which. Either way she'd probably planned to interrupt their evening.

The locked gate to the compound with its cams would've stopped her entrance, but she wouldn't have wanted to be seen. The acreage wasn't fully fenced, way too expensive, so she parked down the road. Her plan from there was anyone's guess.

The hot-headed daughter had probably done this to herself. A sad truth everyone would have to live with . . . the mother never getting over her part in all of this.

Then Wayne responded in a joint text to both her and Slade. Callie stared at Connor lying there pale, broken, riddled with Slade's bullets. He killed Jasmine?

Gut instinct said no, but her head told her not to draw fast conclusions. Too many remaining questions. Too few facts.

Either Merrick lied, was trying to take advantage by pinning something on a dying man, or there was way more to Connor than they knew.

She strode to the bedside. If he hadn't had holes in his chest, she'd have nudged knuckles against his breast bone, a last effort to make him open his eyes. She shook him at the shoulder instead. "Connor. Wake up. Connor . . . wake up."

A nurse technician stuck her head in the door. "Everything all right in here?" Then she came in, eying the telemetry, adjusting a sheet that didn't need adjusting. "Is there a problem?"

Only that this idiot might be a murderer.

"We've learned more about what happened," Callie said. "We want to help get to the bottom of how he got this way, and we need him awake to do so."

The nurse's concern eased off. "Well, he'll wake up when his body tells him to, Sergeant."

*Chief,* Callie wanted to say, but no matter. She only wanted the girl gone.

Finally she left.

Callie knew Wayne would ask the right questions of Merrick, but she wished she were there, reading the micro-expressions, the reactions, listening to the emphasis on certain words. Wayne had some experience, but Agriculture wasn't accustomed to homicide. She had fifteen years of it back in Boston. Sometimes she missed those days. Most days she didn't.

The interview questions rolled naturally through her brain, instantly forming the moment she pictured herself in the room with Merrick. How did Connor get control of Jasmine? Why bother in the first place? *Was* it an accident, which hornets sort of indicated? How did Merrick even know, and why hadn't he come forward sooner?

The deputy on the floor filled up the doorway, the same one who'd let almost anyone come in before. "They're holding someone downstairs who's demanding to be let up," he said. "Says her name is Slade?"

"Let her up," Callie said. "She's part of the agriculture team investigating this guy."

"Yes, ma'am."

Wasn't five minutes before Slade appeared, hesitating at the entry. Callie waved her in, fully understanding her friend's reservations to enter.

"How is he?" Slade asked, tentative, stopping a few feet from the foot of the bed.

"The same," Callie said. "Hasn't opened his eyes, though I haven't stopped trying to make him."

Slade's attention stuck on the still man. "Told Wayne I was hanging with you."

Callie nodded back. "Read the texts. Heard the voice mails. How're you doing after dredging that up? How's Maggie?"

"She's a wreck. She'll never get over this." Slade spoke as if Maggie were old news, other concerns taking her place.

"And St. Clair still has an alibi?"

"Yeah, like the photos confirmed." She uncrossed her arms, moving to the window to study the parking lot below.

Callie let her have her moment. They weren't in a rush anyway, just waiting on Wayne to proceed.

Slade snapped to. "I'm just not seeing it."

"Seeing what?" Callie waited for Slade to clarify what *it* she referred to.

Slade's phone rang, and she wrestled to grab it from her purse to stop the shatteringly rude noise in a room of soft, steady beeps. "Yes," she said gently, listened, then put the phone on speaker, closing the door while holding the phone up. "It's Wayne for both of us."

"How's Connor?" Wayne began.

Callie joined Slade, and the two of them slid further from Connor. "No change," Callie said. "Still unconscious."

"I see," he said.

Slade made a slight scowl, as though noting something off in his manner or answer. "Merrick still there?" she asked.

"Yes, absolutely."

Both women caught on.

"I'm having trouble believing Merrick's story," Callie said.

"Me as well," Slade added. "Just too damn convenient to blame the dead guy . . . figuratively, I mean. Connor can't defend himself. Might not ever. And Merrick says Connor confessed to him, only to keep it secret for several days after Jasmine died? Sorry, not buying it."

"I'll let him repeat it for you." Some shuffling. "Merrick, tell the sheriff what you told me about why you hadn't come forward earlier?"

*Sheriff?* Oh. Sharp cover. Merrick wouldn't give a damn about telling Slade and Callie, but he'd preen for the sheriff. Had maybe even had him out hunting a time or two.

"I said, Mini-Hawk has venture capitalists to accommodate." Merrick didn't act at all put out having to repeat himself, as though the extra telling only gave him more credence. "This kind of shit could kill our financial arrangement with a group out of Georgia. I'm only telling you people now because the group is on its way. Wouldn't even be coming over here if this shit hadn't made the news like it did. We're fucked if they pull out of their investment. We could lose the farm."

Wayne came back before Merrick could ask for the *sheriff's* feedback. "That was accurately close to what he already said."

"Wait," Merrick shouted from the background. "Keep in mind none of this involved us. Connor'd lost his wife, his home, and was hell bent on becoming an alpha. A pain in the ass to Mini-Hawk. But when he ran across Jasmine, he capitalized on what he saw as opportunity. Told me he accidentally killed her trying to make her leave. Didn't even tell me until two days later and said I was the only person he told. About bowled me over, and I wasn't sure who to tell because the stupid shit had hunted with me afterwards that morning. He was on his way to a deer stand when he killed her. We met at Waffle House afterwards about nine thirty and he didn't say a word then." Nothing for a few seconds. "Wished to God he'd never told me."

Wayne came back on the phone. "You hear all that, Sheriff?"

"Heard it," Callie replied. "Wonder if St. Clair knows?"

"Or Birds of Prey," Slade added, contemplating something awfully hard. Then she came to life, a mental decision made. "Wayne, tell Merrick that Connor just came around. Say he's talking. Doctor just said he's rallying, and they are cautiously optimistic." She accelerated, feeling confidence grow as she spun out her plan. "What can it hurt?"

"Wait," Wayne said. "You're kidding me. Connor . . ." He must've turned from the phone toward Raysor. "Don, they're saying our guy came around. Yeah, just now. He's trying to talk."

Wayne had accepted Slade's suggestion to bait Merrick.

"What'd he say?" Raysor replied, in the dark, enabling him to be all the more believable.

"Can't tell yet. Sheriff says they've got a deputy with him now, trying to make heads or tails out of his ramblings. Painkillers are sort of muddying things, but it's a start. Great news, Sheriff. Thanks for sharing that."

Still holding out the phone, Slade listened to the fantasy while staring at Connor.

"We're about to finish up here," Wayne said. "I'll be back within the half hour." He hung up.

Slade pocketed her phone. "Merrick's protecting his ass. If Birds of Prey is disturbed enough to appear in person, there's serious money at stake, and Merrick would say anything."

"Wonder who else he's told about Connor," Callie said. Couldn't be Maggie or that would've come out in Slade's interview. Why not St. Clair? The boss would need that intel to best cope with Birds of Prey . . . and the media.

"Nobody," Slade said. "Can't have. Or we'd have heard. The press would've splashed that news everywhere." She was cranked up. "Might not be Merrick's farm, but he's the right hand of St. Clair. Hemp, guns, whatever the deal is, still impacts his future. With the Birds of Prey coming, his future might be in jeopardy. He needs to take the heat off of Mini-Hawk, hell, all of them, but as quietly as possible. Without anyone looking any more closely at St. Clair's operation."

"So are you saying Connor didn't do it?"

"I don't know, but I am saying it's almost a cliché to blame the dead dude, don't you think?"

A weak voice mumbled from behind them.

Callie moved to the bedside. "Connor?"

The agriculture manager opened his eyes. "I said, I ain't dead yet."

# Chapter 30

## *Slade*

CONNOR SEARCHED the room until he laid a glare on me. "You shot me."

"Not until you shot at me," I countered, immediately sheepish about my response.

His voice was weak, broken, without enough energy to put emotion in it. I swear, despite him possessing answers we desperately needed, I didn't even want to talk to the man. *Go back to sleep.*

Callie backed off to let me move closer, and I balked, ashamed. I wasn't coming within arm's length of him.

"Did I *hit* you?" he asked with a harsh rasp.

"No."

"Then there you go." He closed his eyes again.

I took another step closer, unsure he was still aware. Another step more. I leaned over. "You in there?" I said, hoping he didn't respond.

"Yes."

"You're not exactly a sharp-shooter," I said.

Pain consumed him. "Apparently you are." A moan. "Am I dying or not?"

No way in hell I was answering that.

"Not yet," Callie said, moving in. "Why'd you shoot at her? That was an idiotic thing to do, Connor."

"Seems so," he said. "Just wanted to leave and her not follow me. She seemed so intent . . . never thought . . ."

"I'd carry a gun?" I asked.

He nodded.

Jesus, he was a moron. Shooting tires beside a federal agent. Shooting with an assault weapon thinking nobody would shoot back. All pretense and no . . . sense.

Before I registered it, my temper rose. "You stupid son of a bitch," I whispered back. "You risked your life and mine . . . and the lives of most the people out there last night. You nearly got killed . . . for what?

To show off? Act big and bad? Make St. Clair believe you belong? Guess Merrick's right."

The investigator in me returned with renewed vigor, and I welcomed the shift. I tired of feeling sorry for Connor, though I might regret the aggression later.

"You killed Jasmine, or so I heard," I said.

With stealth, Callie eased around the foot, closer to the other side, studying Connor's vitals on the machine.

"No," he said. "Not how it happened."

His chest rose and fell faster. Callie gave a tilted head motion toward the red and green numbers on the screen. His pulse had risen. His respiration higher. We had ourselves a homemade lie detector.

"Then how did it happen?" I asked.

His machine beeped louder, a heartbeat spike sending an alarm for help.

A different lady poked her head in. An RN this time. Worming her way in enough to push Callie aside, she messed with the machine, checking connections. She studied Connor, and when he opened his eyes, she jumped. "Welcome back, Mr. Boone. Do you know where you are?"

"The hospital," he croaked.

She pressed the call button. "Page Doctor Anderson. Mr. Boone's awake." She dropped the button and touched Connor's cheek. "Do you know what year it is? Who the president is?"

She tossed him several more questions he got right, then turned to us. "Y'all need to leave now. The doctor will require it."

We ignored her, and she went about her business checking and rechecking Connor and his assorted contraptions and lines, but when the doctor came in, she ratted on us. "These two refuse to leave."

The doctor stood a good six inches over me, a foot over Callie, and his white lab coat made him seem bigger still. "I have to assess this man," he said, reaching deep for his command voice. "Both of you . . . out."

"That man is my prisoner," Callie said, steering attention to the cuffs on Connor's right wrist. "I stay."

"Why am I cuffed?" Connor said, weary . . . as though unaware of why he was there.

The doctor and nurse bought his poor confused patient act. "I said leave," the doc said.

"Hey." Connor stared at me. "She's the one who shot me! Why is she in here?" And he cried.

The RN went to take my arm. I stiffened and gave her a heated stare that said she'd need the ER if she touched me.

"I've got this, Slade," Callie said, her uniform probably trumping the doc's white coat. "And Connor, you're cuffed because you're under arrest, whether you remember what you did or not."

"Deputy," started the doctor.

"It's Chief," Callie said. "Just like your title is doctor."

They exchanged no more words that I heard as I left the room.

But I didn't go far, settling against the opposite side of the hall, one room down, so I could keep an eye on the comings and goings . . . judge when to slip back in. To kill time, I looked up where Wayne was, my people finder app telling me he was almost to the Walterboro town limits. Done with Merrick. I could call.

"Hey," I said when he picked up his phone. "They kicked me out of Connor's room."

"For what?" he asked, meaning *what did you do, Slade.*

"Connor came to. Doc's in with him."

"How is he?"

"Talking, sort of," I said. "Can't predict his future, though."

The people I'd seen shot had died, and other people dealt with the aftermath. No bedside conversations or accusations. Just people hauled off in ambulances I never saw again. "Either he regressed or he put on a show when the doc came in. Said it was my fault, so they pushed me out." Then before Wayne could ask, I added, "Callie refused to leave. She's still there."

I tried to peer in the room. The nurse saw me and pulled a curtain.

"Still, he's really washed out, Wayne. Not really moving . . . he got excited when we questioned him, making his monitor's alarms go off."

"Gotta be careful with interviewing someone who's—"

"I've never dealt with this before," I blurted. "I couldn't tell whether he was conning us or telling the truth. I didn't meant to stress him."

"Slade, calm down," Wayne said. "He might die. He might not. But there's not a person in the world who believes you intentionally tried to put him down."

I stroked fingers up and down the middle of my chest, seeking calm. "I can think of one." An ex-wife named Rebecca.

"Go get a quick coffee," he said. "I'll text when I'm there, and we'll find each other. Don't want to leave Callie alone for long."

The nurse slung back the curtain around Connor's bed, and the doctor came out, stopping at the sight of me. "I told you to leave."

"You told me to leave the room," I reminded him.

He was ginger-haired, fair complected, and my oppositional stance had his cheeks flushed. "This is my ICU. I'm asking you to leave."

Shoulders back, I stood my ground. "Sorry, but no. You have your job, and I have mine."

Leaning, he about got in my space, but a nurse came up the stairway two yards from us and stutter-stepped at the scene. He straightened and motioned to the double doors. "We have very sick people on this unit, so would you please follow me outside?"

"Be happy to," I replied, leading the way. Outside the doors, I spoke first, in case I didn't get the chance later. We hadn't exactly hit it off. "How's Connor doing?"

"Who exactly are you?" he asked. "Are you family?"

For the second time in the same day, I showed my badge. "No, I'm not."

The doc barely looked at it. "Then I cannot tell you his status. Where's your uniform?"

"Don't wear one. I'm an investigator." Didn't have to tell him what kind.

"Was he right? Are you the one who shot him?"

"After he shot at me, but yes."

He gave a toss of his head. "Then you are banned from his room."

If I were in his shoes, I'd feel the same, but his attitude toward me only made me want to violate his rules and sneak back in. "Tell you what," I said. "I'll agree not to go in the room, if you—"

"Coming through," said a female voice. Rebecca had dolled herself up way better than the yoga pants outfit we'd seen on her doorstep, and she charged like she owned the path. Escorted by a deputy who seemed unhappy at his task, she took long strides with them always a pace behind, fighting to keep up as she aimed for the doors to see her husband . . . or rather the ex-husband whose rodeo move of shooting Wayne's tires had rekindled their romance.

Who let her out of jail?

"Excuse me," the doctor said, remaining in place, his tallness inter-rupting her momentum. "We can't have this commotion. These patients are unstable and quite ill."

"I'm Rebecca Boone, Connor Boone's wife. I have a right."

"Ex-wife," I said to the doc.

The doctor took it from there. "You can't go in then. He can't take this much disturbance."

Tucking her chin, perfectly insulted, she snapped, "Aren't you Ms. Slade?"

"Yes, ma'am. And Connor—"

She took a swing at me.

I managed to shift enough for her fist to glance off my shoulder. "You shot my husband!"

"He shot at me first, Rebecca." How many times would I have to say that for people to understand I wasn't the bad guy?

She attempted another punch, but I managed to move fast enough for her to only catch air . . . until she connected with the doc's chest.

Ultimately the deputy grabbed her. "That does it. We're locking you up again while you cool off." Then to me, "You can decide whether or not to file charges, ma'am."

Damn, I'd hate to have his reaction time backing me up against someone armed.

"Rebecca," I said. "He used an AR-15, which could've cut me to ribbons."

"Wish he had," she said, squirming.

"Officer, take this woman off my floor," the doctor said, massaging where she hit.

The uniform was a deputy not an officer, but I wasn't correcting the doc again.

"I'll shoot you before this is over," Rebecca yelled, struggling in the deputy's grip as they departed.

The doctor, however, turned to me, his skin red and riled, like Rebecca was my doing. Then instead of seeing me out, which I halfway expected, he stormed off in a huff. Maybe seeking another deputy for me, maybe just fed up with the dust storm that followed Connor Boone into Colleton Memorial . . . hopefully just to see other patients. I'd hate to be one of them.

Trying to decide if I would honor the promise I'd made to the doc, I peered through one of the rectangle windows in time to see the tail of a white coat going into Connor's room. How many doctors did Connor have? However, this one wouldn't know I'd been banned. I re-entered the ICU. The nurse who'd told on me must've been with another patient. Good.

The thump didn't register, making me believe the doctor just dropped something, or there was another nurse in the room who bumped into something, but when I reached the threshold, the new doc leaned over Connor. I mean, really leaned over him. As in, smell-what-you-had-for-lunch close to Connor. And all I could see was his back, and that his shoulders were hunched. Connor's uncuffed hand lethargically slapped the doctor's upper arm.

Then I registered the reason for the *thump*. Callie lay in a heap on the floor near the window.

"Callie," I yelled, causing the doctor to release the pillow and pivot. Connor's head remained hidden under the pillow.

I was one step in the room, in the doorway, in the fatal funnel for a shooter . . . where he shouldn't miss.

In a swift move, the doctor, masked and with his hair covered under a surgical cap, reached under his white coat and slipped out a Glock as neat and pretty as you please, and popped two shots in my direction.

But I'd already twisted, and in an almost exact repeat of Connor's shooting dove beneath a vacant hospital bed that hugged the wall outside. I hit the tiled floor in a fast, hard repetition of elbows, chin, then knees.

Scrambling for deeper cover, I hugged the mechanization under the bulky bed. Exposed, I debated at light-speed whether to wrap my body around that mechanism or stand and run.

He shot again, and I curled up tighter until it registered with me that he hadn't shot at me . . . he'd shot in the room.

Callie!

Pushing up to hunch on my knees, I heard him run away from me, and I peered out in time to see his white coat flapping as he hit the stairway entrance with his shoulder. The door banged against the concrete block stairwell.

Jumping up, I ran to Callie, hollering to whomever could hear, "Security! Security! Gun! Shooter!" Throwing out whatever buzz words would make them leap into DEFCON One.

Scanning her for signs of that last shot, I shouted, "Callie, Callie, are you okay?"

She peered at me, wincing, a hand inching up to her head. "What . . . are you . . ."

No holes in her I could see, and she sat herself up. She was only the *thump*, not the shot, thank God. "You were clubbed over the noggin. Are you okay? He's still out there, and I—"

"Go," she said with a meager wave. "Go."

In a sloppy rise, I reached for her weapon. Her instinct was to stop me.

"I'm not armed, honey."

She relinquished the weapon, then leaping to my feet, I shouted again. "Security! Where's security!"

I spun and froze at the image.

The pillow remained in place, but Connor lay still. Blood seeped into the mattress with blood and bits splatted against the white, plastic headboard. Parts of it oozed over the edge in long thick drips to the floor.

Two nurses ran in, one screaming at the sight of the bed, snatching me out of my own frantic thoughts. The other, the hard-nosed one from earlier, shouted orders to the other to straighten up and tend to Callie. The older RN lifted the pillow to assess Connor, quickly hitting a button to shout, "Code Silver ICU. Code Silver ICU."

Then she saw the weapon in my hand. "Gun!"

No time to explain ballistics would exonerate me and let the second doc escape. I bolted to the stairwell, yanking open the door. I waited a second, listening. A door slammed shut below, but I couldn't tell where. Phone to my ear, I ran the stairs like a track star, Callie's weapon in my other hand.

"Wayne," I gasped, already down one floor. "Connor's been shot. Callie hit over the head. Shooter escaped down the stairs." I sucked in more air, but not enough to make a difference.

"I'm turning onto the property," he said. "Find someplace safe and stay there, Slade."

On the landing above the ground floor outlet, I stopped, panting, and tucked the gun in my waistband. With a lone finger I lifted the white lab coat up off a riser. "Wayne, I found . . ." but he'd hung up.

Slipping the strings of the discarded mask over another digit, I collected it along with the cap that I found lying in a corner. My bruised elbow on the heavy lever handle, I managed to exit the stairwell to the first floor lobby . . . into the imposing presence of a twenty-something deputy resting a hand on his holster, his other hand palm up at me to remain still.

"Freeze."

"Whoa, wait a minute. I found this tossed on the stairs." I slightly lifted the garment. "The guy wearing them shot at me, shot a patient, and hurt the officer guarding the room. ICU," I added, in case the guy didn't know.

"How do I know that's not yours?" he asked, using his forceful voice taught in training.

"The shooter was a man?" I said, but then I remembered my weapon in my belt. "Also, just so you're aware, I'm armed."

Snatching the evidence from me, he slung it to the floor, his hand solid on his weapon now, the snap undone. "Show me some ID."

Slowly, I withdrew my creds for the third damn time of the day. Just took the sight of gold for him to back off. "Sorry."

"Mind protecting that evidence?" I said, sitting on the nearest bench to wait for Wayne as I'd been told, my heart pounding a snare drum solo in my chest.

I could see out into the main lobby if I leaned right to look around the elevators, and I stared at every person, demanding my memory try to picture which one of these men could be the shooter. Nobody was tall enough, or the right age. Maybe one, but he was almost full gray. God Almighty, had the man shed his disguise and simply stridden out of the hospital? Cameras, I thought. But were they on the stairs? Could they tell who went in dressed one way and out as someone else? Surely in this day and time . . .

Wayne came running in, and I shouted for him.

"Sir, please stand back," said the deputy, in the same pose as he'd addressed me, but Wayne flashed his badge and shoved past, not giving a damn about the younger man's reaction.

"Talk to me," he said.

I took a breath. "Saw a white coat go into the room. I followed. Saw him trying to smother Connor, and saw Callie on the floor. He stopped and shot at me. I dove. He shot Connor through the pillow then ran. He took the stairs. I ran down the stairs—"

"You what?"

Shifting my side around, I showed him. "I took Callie's gun."

Raysor had arrived, his speed took a drastic backseat to Wayne's, but he'd heard enough to roll his eyes. Which I didn't exactly appreciate.

The young deputy watched, his body language more obedient, the white clothing wadded in the crook of his arm.

"He took the disguise from me," I said.

Raysor took over. "Get a damn evidence bag for those whites, son. And it stays in your possession until you return to the station. I'll vouch for this woman. She's an investigator with us."

"Yes, sir. But she didn't show her badge at first."

I snatched it out again. "Care to look again?"

"No, ma'am," he said, stiffening so tight I expected a salute. "But sir?" he said, trying to please. "Who're we looking for exactly?"

Wayne and Raysor looked to me for the description.

"Male. Five-nine to six-foot. A hundred-seventy to a hundred-eighty pounds. Middle-aged, in his fifties. Moving fast to get gone," I said, standing.

"Hmmm," the deputy said, as if reaching into his data bank. "Haven't seen anyone who fits. At least anyone I didn't know."

Raysor exhaled sadly, before saying something he hoped he was wrong about. "Name those you recognized then . . . anyone that might've fit the description, son."

He shrugged. "Just Merrick Cox. When I waved he asked me when I'd be out to use the range. That what you mean?"

Wayne looked back around to me, stunned.

"Yeah, son," Raysor said, deflated. "That's exactly what we meant."

"Not sure I understand, sir. He wasn't running."

# Chapter 31

*Slade*

RAYSOR REQUESTED the APB on Merrick, able to describe the vehicle he and Wayne had seen at the brother's house.

It was a solid half hour before we broke free of the hospital, but by then units coated the grounds, city units scoured the city of Walterboro, and state troopers patrolled Interstate 95. Armed and dangerous, Merrick was now a wanted murderer.

Wayne and I got into his G-car, Raysor following in his cruiser in case he had to peel off in another direction, or Wayne and I got called back in. Raysor called for another unit to meet us at Mini-Hawk, just in case.

We'd sadly underestimated the effect our ruse about Conner would have on Merrick. He was nastier than given credit for. Maybe nastier than even he thought he could be. Most people took on a different personality when backed in a corner.

Every uniform in the region would want this collar, but Wayne was vested deep in this business and tore up road toward Mini-Hawk. He wasn't going to return to Columbia and wait for someone else to bring the man in. He wasn't waiting for the sheriff to orchestrate a team to descend upon the hunting club. And he wasn't letting some gun-happy officer put Merrick down so hard that we never learned the whole story about Jasmine.

I had no prattling conversation with Wayne. His jaw steeled, every muscle in him tensed from his thighs riding the gas to his neck. The tires whispered on the asphalt. I had no idea what the speed limit was, but I was sure we doubled it.

Having just hung up from Callie, though, I felt he needed the update.

"Possible concussion," I said. "He popped her hard. They want to admit her. She said no, but they're running a head scan."

Nothing.

"Stitches needed," I said.

Nothing.

From the reflection in the side mirror, Raysor hugged our tail. No sign of the other unit yet.

"Merrick's either running off or running home," I said. "And since Mini-Hawk is home, we're starting there I take it?"

"Yes."

"Then I'm calling St. Clair," I said.

He shot a glance over, then something in his head acknowledged my logic, and he returned his attention to the road.

I found St. Clair's number in my history and dialed.

When I reached voice mail, I hung up and dialed again. Then I dialed his house, only for his wife to say he had guests at Mini-Hawk. I went back to his cell number, leaving a message. "If you see or hear from Merrick Cox, you best be sharing with us. ASAP. We think he just murdered Connor in the hospital. You can assist us or be a part of Merrick's screwed-up plans. Your choice." I started to hang up, then tacked on, "We're on our way. Others will be following. Talk to us or the sheriff. You have my number."

Wasn't sure that was a good message or not. If I were St. Clair, I'd be on the phone to my attorney . . . unless Birds of Prey ordered otherwise. I didn't know how this militia thing worked. And how quickly would they turn their backs on St. Clair when we showed up asking about Merrick?

Or turn on us.

"What if there's a herd of people there, Wayne?"

I really didn't want to reach Mini-Hawk with none of them expecting us. This was not like interviewing Maggie where surprise could be fruitful. This was appearing unannounced to a bunch of guys who wore semi-automatic weapons like shoes and socks. My bet was they didn't like surprises. I also bet they weren't often surprised.

We weren't far. Under five minutes at this speed, and Wayne didn't seem to care what awaited us on the other end.

The longer St. Clair remained silent, the more nervous I became. The more aware I became of Callie's Glock I'd set in the glovebox for safekeeping until . . . until what? I wasn't putting another bullet in another human being . . . unless he tried to put one in me. But wasn't that how I'd shot Connor? And what the hell good was my firearm prowess if it was the three of us against . . . an army?

We turned onto Old Coon Road, apprehension building in my chest. The day had aged. There wasn't much light, but the autumn colors in the woods made it seem brighter in spite of the flat sky threatening more rain.

"St. Clair hasn't called back, Wayne. What's your plan?" When he didn't respond, I spoke harder, pushing through the anxiety. "We're only three, counting Raysor. If they want to hide him, they will. St. Clair has two hundred acres just in that one section."

We passed the place where Jasmine's car was found off the road, a misty drizzle began, and Wayne took a hard look in passing. He was so deep into his own head I feared he hadn't heard a word I'd said. This wasn't a side of Wayne I'd seen much of before, and I wasn't fond of it. "Damn it, Wayne, what's the plan?"

"Talk to St. Clair," he said, turning on his wipers. "Make him think we believe he's Merrick's partner in everything. Make him choose between jail and Merrick."

"We don't have enough to put him in jail," I said.

"I'll make the son of a bitch think we do. And he'll be my primary case to take to the US Attorney in terms of his Agriculture obligations, leaving him with nothing more than a dog house to live in." He slowed, the gate entrance to Mini-Hawk up ahead. "And if he had an inkling of knowledge about Merrick? His freedom is gone."

The gate was shut. We stopped.

"Call on the squawk box," I said.

He punched a button with overzealous force. No reply. Then again. Nothing again. A third time he mashed the call button and spoke anyway. "Senior Special Agent Wayne Largo to see Merrick Cox. Requesting immediate access."

No response.

"Can't we go around to the other access?" I asked.

"If Bird of Prey is expected, they'd have it guarded," Wayne replied, elbow on his window ledge, thumb stroking his beard, thinking.

Movement in the trees caught my attention with Wayne noting almost as quickly. We silently watched as Angus marched, dressed more crisp in what seemed like new camo fatigues and some sort of braid over one sleeve. A black beret cocked properly on a fresh haircut. His AR slung across his front, a sidearm in a holster. The kid cleaned up nice, but his feigned military-ness infused a wary alertness in me. Like he was willing to be more than a kid today.

He approached Wayne's side of the vehicle. "Can I help you, sir?"

"Senior Special Agent Wayne Largo here for Merrick Cox. Suspect is wanted for murder. We demand access."

"We'll also see St. Clair Simmons," I added.

Wayne acknowledged his agreement. "Open the gate, son."

Angus showed no reaction to the mention of murder, nor any intimidation at an order from a federal agent. He touched his ear, where I then noticed a wireless, Bluetooth earphone. Someone was on the other end. "Yes, sir," he said to the other party. Bending down, he asked, "Did you come with paper, sir?"

"No," Wayne said, tension clear at the challenge.

"Did you see your fugitive enter the property?"

"No, but we suspect he entered here a half hour ago."

Angus looked down at the ground, listening for instruction, then he stood straight, admittedly military in his movements. "Agent Largo, please wait."

"What the hell, son, open the damn gate."

"I'm holding for clearance, sir." He returned to his post at the gate and stared out, over us, into nothingness, awaiting instruction.

"They're allowing him to get away," I said. "Can't we just go in?"

"Not without having seen him enter and not without paper. Just like he said. Someone in there knows what they're doing." He picked up his radio. "Raysor, tell that other unit to check out the other entrance and immediately call back."

"Roger that," came the reply.

I called St. Clair again, getting voice mail again. "We're outside your damn gate, St. Clair, and we suspect you've let Merrick in. If you protect him, you're an accomplice. He killed Connor. Don't go down with him, you hear me? Don't let that lowlife make things more worse than they already are for you." I took a breath. "Open the damn gate."

I hung up and texted something similar to him.

We waited one minute, two. At five minutes, Wayne opened his door. "I'm getting in there if I have to . . ."

Angus left his post, walking toward us. Thin and lanky, he strode out and stood before the SUV, feet wide, his firearm in his grip but not in expectation of use. Or so I hoped.

Raysor phoned me, his cruiser still idling behind our SUV. "Not liking this," he said on speaker.

"We go in, Don, or we lose Merrick," Wayne said, remaining in his seat.

"Or get shot," Raysor replied.

I suspected Merrick had made his getaway during the stall for time. After all, wasn't that what this was? An effort to make us wait for business to be handled on the other end?

It felt like a standoff. Us staring at Mini-Hawk's man . . . Angus eying us for the guys on the other end.

"This is creepy," I whispered.

Then with a rigid snap of a motion, he turned sideways, and we were directed to enter.

Before I could ask if we dared, Wayne shut his door, shifted into drive, and drove toward the opening gates, wanting to get in quickly to allow Raysor to enter before it closed. Twisting back, I was relieved to see the cruiser get through. Angus disappeared into the darkness of the trees.

The familiar route took us to the parking area. Angus somehow beat us there, and like at a ballgame, he waved us where to stop. Then he returned to the trees again.

Lots of recent tire tracks in the moist ground of the parking lot, No trucks with Georgia plates, but we weren't sure they'd park here, not with more obscure accesses. Out came the dogs, but after last time, we weren't so quick to get out, uncertain which whistle had defined their mission. Friend or foe?

Repeating the elbow trick I'd shown Callie, I deemed them friendly, and peered back at Wayne. "We're here. We've been escorted in and," I nodded toward the dogs, "greeted."

Through the windshield, the rain no more than drips off the tree canopy, both of us scanned the rye acreage ahead.

"Hate that wide open field," Wayne muttered. "And if we hear another whistle, those dogs go down."

A sense of shakiness tried to swell through me, and I willed it back. Focus. I had to focus. Wayne needed to focus.

I leaned toward the glass, squinting. "There's someone on the porch of that trailer. God, I hope they aren't armed."

"Anyone could be armed anywhere in these woods, Slade. That guy on the porch is the least of our worries."

Just what I needed to hear.

"Then let's do this," I said, slipping Callie's gun into my waistband. I opened my door.

The dogs bounced, then stretched down with butts in the air, in their harmless mode. Just huge black muscled pets seeking love and hugs.

Wayne got out, then Raysor, then the three of us stood on the field's edge, judging, scanning, hoping we hadn't been baited . . . that nobody watched us through a scope, finger on a trigger.

"This is shit," Raysor uttered.

"It is what it is," Wayne said, and we struck out.

Felt like a slo-mo scene at the theatre right before the shoot-out.

The distance seemed to extend further, until the field felt a half-mile wide. The dogs disappeared, then suddenly they appeared at the trailer, having beaten us there, their attention on the person seated on the porch's edge.

He wasn't moving. His legs dangled, and he appeared to lean against one of the posts.

"It's Merrick," I whispered, slowing down. But when I looked over to the guys, my heart about came out of my chest at their hardness. They scouted everywhere but the porch.

This snail-crawling pace was about to make me puke, the coursing adrenaline threatening to stroke me out. *Let's get this crap the hell over with.*

I marched to Merrick, expecting him to rise as I approached, finding him bizarrely still until I saw why.

He was cuffed to the post.

"Wayne, get over here."

He trotted over, continuing to scan the area. Five feet from the porch, he paused to take in the situation. Merrick's cheeks freshly pummeled, swelling purple, the man sat slumped and resigned, peering up through the damaged slits of his eyes only a second, but long enough for me to watch him hate me. He was still breathing hard.

Weapon drawn, Wayne ran to one side of the trailer, motioning for Raysor to cover the other side. They returned together from Wayne's side, weapons holstered. "Don't see a single vehicle in that far lot."

"They can't be gone far," I said.

Raysor radioed the other cruiser, but the deputy hadn't known what he was looking for on the highway, and had just learned the other entrance was gated and locked up tight.

A paper was folded into thirds, jammed into the breast pocket of Merrick's flannel jacket, block letters stating READ ME appearing just above the material. Raysor put on gloves and extracted the notebook paper. Three pages.

"Read it," Wayne said, checking the cuffs once for assurance.

"*To Whom It May Concern,*" Raysor started. He read silent a bit before staring up at Merrick. "It's a confession."

Wayne spoke through his teeth. "To what?"

I moved to stand between Wayne and Merrick, reading the rise in Wayne's temper.

"To everything," Raysor said, and read on.

I, Merrick Landry Cox, confess to the following crimes. First, the murder of Jasmine Bright. The night she died, Connor Boone was to meet me to deer hunt. He saw a black woman park at one of the ATV entrances. I told him to stay put until I arrived."

Raysor read further and lowered the paper. "We can read this later."

"Maybe Raysor's right," I said.

Wayne glowered at Merrick. "No, we hear it now."

The deputy continued.

We dragged her from the car to the Jasper shack. I threw her in and latched the door after stirring the hornets. After a while we lifted the latch so she could leave. She was alive when we left. I told Connor Boone he was a silent accomplice or a dead man. We covered our tracks.

Raysor stopped again, wiped a hand over his mouth and tried to analyze Wayne. My lawman stood petrified, a harsh, dark, menacing threat of a snarl aimed at Merrick.

"There's two sentences where he admitted to killing Connor, but there's also a third confession."

My hand flew over my mouth in a gasp. "Oh, God." A third murder? Good heavens, how deep did this man go? And how connected were the bodies to Mini-Hawk's mission?

And who made him confess?

Third, Raysor began. I confess to misdirecting Birds of Prey by telling them about St. Clair Simmons's affair and his financial issues in an attempt to make them remove their funding from Mini-Hawk, so I could get the hunting club at a liquidation price when Agriculture foreclosed. I sabotaged the combine, delaying harvest such that Simmons could not pay his debt.

Now I wanted to pummel the man.

Raysor flipped pages. "There's a third page here."

"Thought that was the third page," I said.

He shook his head. "It says *Take him, he's yours. He'll talk.* Written in another handwriting."

Distant shots echoed far off. Repetitive. I ducked. The guys only stared in that direction.

"Firing range," Wayne said.

"Kind of late for target shooting," Raysor said.

"Not so sure that's what they're doing," Lawman replied.

I thought I caught on. "They're talking to us?"

Neither said no.

Light began to fade fast. With a cuff key he kept on his own key-chain, Wayne unlocked Merrick from the post then recuffed hands behind his back before lifting him to stand, torqueing his shoulders way high. Chilling me at his icy demeanor, Wayne spoke low and hard right at the man's cheekbone. "Why'd you kill the agent, tough guy?"

Merrick could barely see through bruised, bulged eyelids, but he licked his split lip to better answer. "She was a black on white land," he said. "Showing her badge only nailed her coffin, and being the daughter of St. Clair's whore . . . icing on the cake."

Raysor caught Wayne's fist before it would reach the side of Merrick's head, shaking it twice to get his attention. "Bastard's not worth your job, Largo."

"He wasn't worth Jasmine's either," Wayne replied, eyes so filled with disgust he couldn't unclench his shaking fist.

I wasn't touching Wayne, but I motioned to Raysor to get Merrick gone.

Raysor pushed him toward the cars. The dogs reappeared, trotting around our perimeter, catching sniffs of Merrick when they could, and especially when Raysor's boot somehow tangled in Merrick's, sending him nose-down into the rye field. "Clumsy. Get up, asshole."

The two lawmen snatched Merrick to his feet, shoving him until he stumbled again. Each time they grabbed him by the crook of each arm to steady him, then sent him forward again, off balance and tottering on the uneven ground. Over and over toward the parking area. I remained out of their way.

"Remember last time we were here?" Wayne said down to me. "When I said don't look back while walking away? I mean it a hundred times more this time, Slade. We don't want to see anyone." We continued across the field, each man on either side of Merrick, who'd had a lot of life kicked out of him in a very short time.

I dared let loose the apprehension clenched in my gut after Raysor put Merrick in the back of his patrol car, not ours. When he drove off, lights flashing, I let out the rest of my breath. Wayne, however, wasn't ready to let go of the pressure built inside him. Silently he watched Raysor until the lights were gone.

Absentmindedly, I petted the dogs, watching Wayne. When he got in the car, I did, too. Headlights on, he made his way to the open gate, tension radiating off him, his grip on the steering wheel white-knuckle hard.

We passed through the gate, and Angus gave us a salute then closed the entrance.

We rode back to Colleton Memorial Hospital to retrieve Callie, but we rode in silence. Angry, sad, somewhat sated we nailed the villain . . . we had all the emotions, yet we were anything but fulfilled.

Technically, we had our closure for Jasmine's death. Trouble was, thanks to greed, bigotry and a man with an insane irreverence for life, the facts were too ugly to close things properly.

As to our original case with St. Clair Simmons? That was easy. Either he paid or he didn't. Unofficially, we cared little who he partnered with as long as he paid. Birds of Prey would be his ally or they wouldn't. We'd take legal action against the farm or not have to. Textbook. We'd solved Jasmine's death and closed the circle on why Connor behaved like he did, but as far as I was concerned, Birds of Prey, or whomever partnered with St. Clair, wasn't Ag's problem. We were leaving anything militia up to ATF.

St. Clair's personal life wasn't our business, either, but I prayed the two women harmed in this melee, Maggie and St. Clair's wife, managed to reclaim their lives, on their terms.

I peered over at Wayne, had difficulty seeing him in the dark. But I saw enough. Stoic, jaw squared, and a weariness showed in his crows' feet when we passed the occasional street lamp. This was a new sort of wound for him.

# Chapter 32

## *Slade*

WAYNE AND I offered to stay the night with Callie after bringing her home to Edisto. We put her to bed and would have happily put ourselves to bed, but we had tasks to complete first. Call home. Update Monroe. Apologize again to Savvy. But one other chore in particular rose to the top.

"You've got to do this one," I said to Wayne.

He didn't say he'd rather not be the one to update Maggie, but his silence did.

"She needs closure, Wayne, as do you. Make the call." I rose and went out on Callie's side porch and shut the door behind me. The temperature had sunk to the low fifties and I'd forgotten a jacket, but I wasn't going back in.

Wasn't ten minutes before he came out. I worried whether the brevity of the conversation was a good or bad sign. Once he found me in the dark, and sat beside me on a worn rattan settee, I could see a few less wrinkles around his eyes.

"She took it okay, then?" I asked.

"She thanked me. Not *totally* my fault anymore. But she cried."

I patted his blue-jean leg. "She's supposed to cry. She has to cry. The only way she'll get through these days is by mourning. But it's good she heard it from you, don't you think?" My hand moved to his back when he leaned elbows to his knees, and I let the question go as rhetorical. I caressed gently in a big circle, then pretended I didn't see a couple of his tears wet the denim on one knee.

"She was just a baby, Slade."

"I know, Cowboy."

Moisture slid down my cheeks, silently, so my feelings didn't detract from Wayne's sadness. Just like Maggie, he had to get through this, too.

Yes, I cried for Jasmine but also for Connor . . . or was it for me? Though I hadn't killed the Agriculture manager, I'd started the wheels in motion by confining him in the hospital and making him an easy target.

And I'd suggested we tell Merrick that Connor was on the mend. I wasn't so illogical as to condemn myself solely for his death, but I surely owned a piece of the blame.

Connor had been ignorant, foolish, and in way over his head.

Rebecca would hate me to her dying day, but she owned a large piece of the blame, too. Much of what Connor had done was because he'd wanted her back, wanted to be some ridiculous silver cinema alpha.

A darkness had attached itself to my soul when I thought of my role in Connor's death, and I'd have to learn to live with, and hopefully learn from my actions over the last days, though I couldn't quite define the lesson.

WORD SHOT FAST around the beach the next day, and once Callie's world found out about her injury, she endured nonstop food deliveries and visitors until the evening. Every kind of seafood imaginable. Damn, she was loved on Edisto. Not sure I had this many people on my Christmas card list, much less expect this many to visit me if I was down. She embraced each one but had this innate talent of keeping her thoughts off her face. I bet she rarely let any of these people in her head . . . or near her feelings.

I'd spent most of the day answering the door and determining what had to be refrigerated, and now was tired and grateful that we were down to one visitor. One she apparently would let spend the night if he so chose. He was all but family.

We'd missed meeting Callie's old Boston boss Stan Waltham during our last visit. Not sure why. We could've probably used his advice.

Tall, gruff, buzz-cut hair and a voice to rival Raysor's, he had a rough coddling manner with Callie . . . his *Chicklet*, as he called her . . . along with correction and suggestions on how he would've handled Walterboro. He delivered an odd eye or two in my direction as he learned of my hand in events. Those looks prompted grins from Callie.

"You're a what?" he asked.

"Special Projects Representative," I said, delivering my spiel on where my job stopped and Wayne's began.

"Don't take this personal," he said, "but sounds like more trouble than it's worth. At least from the law enforcement side of things."

Callie gave a friendly scowl. "Stan, she's a friend."

"What are friends for if not to share honesty." Then he waved at Wayne. "You ever like a cigar?"

Wayne was better today, maybe from the distraction of meeting so many folks. "I do," he said. "Just not very often. They go stale before I remember them."

Lifting his jacket from the sofa's back, Stan pulled out two short, fat cigars and went to put on the coat. "Then let's share a couple." He pointed toward the entry hall. "Wind blows the smoke away from the house on the front porch." He gave Callie and me a half bow. "Ladies. The gentlemen are retiring for a smoke."

I waited until the door closed behind them. "I like him. And he's good for Wayne right now."

Callie reached for a throw pillow and hugged it to her. "Take my word, Stan's good therapy."

"Even if he is a Yankee," I said. "You need anything?"

"No, and you and Wayne can take half that food home with you. You have way more people to feed under your roof."

"You feel okay?" I asked.

"I've felt much worse. Don't worry about me."

Then for some reason, we ran out of conversation, So leaning back on my end of the sofa, I basked in what I realized was the first real silence of the day . . . of the week. We'd originally planned to head home today, but with dusk settling, Callie'd begged us to extend our stay for another night. Given all she'd done for a case that wasn't hers, I couldn't decline the offer.

That and part of me wasn't prepared to go home.

"You're messing with that ring again," Callie said. "You mess with it a lot."

Stretching my fingers, my thumb automatically went to feel the band underneath. Guess I *had* been fooling with it. "Feels weird putting something back on that finger."

She moved the pillow and scooted near me, beckoning with curled fingers to let her see my left hand. "It's lovely, Slade. Looks antique."

"Wayne's grandmother's, he said."

She cocked a brow and let my hand loose. "Says a lot about the man."

Clasping my hands as though to hide the focus of attention, my right hand instinctively went to twirl the stone around my finger. Then I caught myself.

"Are you having second thoughts?" Callie asked.

Everyone else who'd seen the diamond assumed my engagement the happiest day of my life, and the day Wayne proposed had been phe-nomenal . . . until Maggie called about Jasmine. From there things went to hell, and right now, on this sofa, was the first time I'd not been obligated to the investigation and had down time to give the fact I was engaged to be married full consideration. Like the time in between didn't count.

But that in between time had sucked much of the joy out of this ring. Or that's what it felt like.

Callie reached over and laid her hand over both of mine. "Slade. What's wrong?"

Eyes filling, I said what I'd thought a hundred times since they found Jasmine. Thoughts my mother would find immensely improper . . . thoughts that could badly hurt Wayne.

I started trying to describe my feelings, not sure my voice would follow through. "Part of me sees this engagement as almost rude in the aftermath of two murders, Callie. An even more selfish side of me worries if those deaths will forever scar our relationship, with this ring being the constant reminder." I wiped off tears with the butt of my palm. "There is no good memory here."

She took my ring hand again. "Law enforcement brought you two together, and I can honestly say it binds you. It bound me to my deceased husband. It bound me to Seabrook."

Mike Seabrook died on a case he shared with her. Her husband died at the hand of a mob family she'd bested. While she hadn't discussed the particulars with me, something she'd have to do at a time of her choosing, I understood enough to see that the deaths of two lovers made her an emotional recluse. Not that she hated her life, but I pitied her for putting her heart on pause, if not stop.

Yet here I was, with Wayne Largo alive and as close to perfection as I could ask for, doubting whether the very universe that introduced us, molded us, and drew us closer would keep us apart.

"That brain of yours is churning awful hard," Callie said.

I let out a long exhale. She reached around her to the skinny sofa table and grabbed a tissue from a box, handing it to me. "Think about it this way," she said. "Are you ever going to forget Jasmine and Connor?"

Kneading the tissue, I shook my head. "Never."

"If you postponed your engagement, would their memories not remain attached, regardless the date?"

She was spot on.

We may not have saved everyone, but we vindicated the ones we lost. That Wayne and I did together. "What you're saying is that the timing is never going to be perfect," I said. "The only thing that needs to feel right is the other person."

Her grin seemed to be a release, like I'd come around to what she hoped I would. "Go home tomorrow and pick up your life. Too many others' lives have stopped. Yours has miles yet to go, Slade. Embrace them with Wayne."

So much wisdom packed into that tiny body. "Damn, you're smart."

She chuckled once. "You're not so bad yourself."

"Mind if I step out a moment?"

She laughed. "I'd kick your ass if you didn't."

"You can't kick that high, *Chicklet*."

I left my spot on the couch and headed for the porch. Time to tell Wayne that I was ready for him to share my house on the lake, share my family, share my craziness, my half-assed cooking, and he could have all my heart. And while we were at it, I'd take a puff or two off that cigar.

*The End*

# About the Author

C. HOPE CLARK has a fascination with the mystery genre and is author of the Carolina Slade Mystery Series as well as the Edisto Island Series, both set in her home state of South Carolina. In her previous federal life, she performed administrative investigations and married the agent she met on a bribery investigation. She enjoys nothing more than editing her books on the back porch with him, overlooking the lake, with bourbons in hand. She can be found either on the banks of Lake Murray or Edisto Beach with one or two dachshunds in her lap. Hope is also editor of the award-winning FundsforWriters.com

### C. Hope Clark

Website: chopeclark.com

Twitter: twitter.com/hopeclark

Facebook: facebook.com/chopeclark

Goodreads: goodreads.com/hopeclark

Bookbub: bookbub.com/authors/c-hope-clark

Editor, FundsforWriters: fundsforwriters.com

CPSIA information can be obtained
at www.ICGtesting.com
Printed in the USA
FSHW022311210620
71391FS